SINGAPORE YELLOW

WILLIAM L. GIBSON

monsoon

monsoonbooks

Published in 2015
by Monsoon Books Pte Ltd
www.monsoonbooks.com.sg

Editorial / Sales:
No.1 Duke of Windsor Suite, Burrough Court,
Burrough on the Hill, Leics. LE14 2QS, UK

Registered office:
150 Orchard Road #07-02, Singapore 238841

First edition.

ISBN (paperback): 978-981-4423-65-6
ISBN (ebook): 978-981-4423-66-3

National Library Board, Singapore Cataloguing-in-Publication Data
Gibson, William, 1974- author.
Singapore yellow / William L. Gibson. – First edition. – Singapore : Mon-
soon Books Pte Ltd, 2015.
pages cm. – (Detective Hawksworth trilogy ; 2)
ISBN : 978-981-4423-65-6 (paperback)

1. Criminal investigation – Fiction. 2. Singapore – History – 1867-1942
– Fiction. I. Title. II. Series: Detective Hawksworth trilogy ; 2.
PS3607
813.6 -- dc23   OCN906888448

Printed in Singapore
18 17 16 15   1 2 3 4 5

And when they had decreed that Solomon should die, nothing discovered his death unto them, except the creeping thing of the earth, which gnawed his staff. And when his body fell down, the *djinn* plainly perceived that if they had known that which was hidden, they would not have continued in vile punishment.

Holy Qur'an 34:14

Contents

Prologue

In the year of our Lord fifteen hundred and eleven, The Great and Terrible Aphonso d'Albuquerque, a Portuguese nobleman who would eventually be known as the Lion of the Seas and the Caesar of the East, commanded a fleet of eighteen war galleons that carried nine-hundred Portuguese sailors and soldiers and three-hundred Malabari mercenaries. He sailed to lay siege to the port city of Malacca, on the Malayan Peninsula.

An ancient trading centre, Malacca was the portal between the hot brown lands of Arabia and India and the glittering treasures of the Far East. Situated across from the island of Sumatra on the narrow straits that bore its name, the city was a choke point for the vast riches that flowed from East to West and back again, along what would become known as the Maritime Silk Road. In the sixteenth century, he who controlled Malacca pressed his thumb on the jugular of world trade.

It took d'Albuquerque's fleet two months to sail from its stronghold at the Indian city of Goa, on the Arabian Sea, to anchorage within cannon range of the city. It took forty days more to defeat an army of more than twenty thousand men – Javanese, Persians, Turks, Arabs, Malays – under the command of the city's ruler, Sultan Mahmud Shah. The invaders commenced their attack on July 25, the holy day of Saint James the Apostle, son of Salome, and d'Albuquerque's patron saint. It is reported that Saint James requested to be at the right hand of Jesus when He came into His Kingdom. The Christ is said to have responded, 'For even the Son of Man did not come to be served, but to serve, and to give his life as a ransom for many.' What d'Albuquerque saw before him was a city worthy of a king's ransom.

The Portuguese bombarded the town for two weeks from the harbour. Their first land assault failed when it was repelled by the Sultan's war elephants, whose monstrous bodies knocked the panic-stricken men to the ground and trampled them to death, their deafening roars spreading terror in the trapped army shoving down the narrow streets. Eventually, however, with the connivance of local Chinese merchants, who tired of explosions disrupting their usual course of business, the Portuguese were able to defeat the Sultan's army. A shallow draft Chinese junk, ladened with men and ammunition and supplies, was sailed up the Malacca River and crashed into the town's main bridge. From its grounding point, the junk served as a forward firebase. Sensing the turning tide, the Sultan's Javanese mercenaries switched allegiances. The Sultan soon fled with his family and entourage to Muar, in the neighbouring sultanate of Johor.

D'Albuquerque's men burned the Sultan's wooden palace to ash, then set about demolishing the royal mosque with their bare hands, stone by stone by stone. Within days the construction of their walled fortress began, the famed *Fortaleza de Malaca*, and then using the same stones they tore from the royal mosque, the Portuguese erected the chapel of Saint Paul, in which, until they were transferred to Goa in 1553, would lay the mortal remains of Saint Francis Xavier, Apostle of the East and founder of the missionary order of the Society of Jesus, the Jesuits. The forces of Catholic Europe now controlled the fulcrum of the maritime hinge upon which global commerce rotated.

The Portuguese ruled Malacca for the next one hundred and thirty years. Then Protestant Europeans overran the place. The *Verenigde Oostindische Compagnie,* the Dutch East India Company, known simply by its solid acronym 'VOC', had tired of Portuguese interference in the spice trade of their far-flung colonies in the East Indies. The first Dutch siege occurred in 1606 – their fleet was repulsed, but the battle impressed the locals, who also had grown weary of Portuguese rule – and over the ensuing decades the Dutch were able to forge alliances with the Sultan of Johor, and on the island of Sumatra, with fierce Acehnese fighters. In 1641, a combined Dutch-Aceh-Johor force routed the Portuguese, and Malacca fell to the blonde-haired, blue-eyed men of the VOC.

Except for a brief period during the Napoleonic Wars, the Dutch ruled Malacca for the next one hundred and eighty years. They dismantled Catholic iconography, transforming the popish altars to the Virgin into cleanly houses of worship. The VOC ran Malacca as a way station for its spice ships and an unsinkable gun platform in the middle of the long water road that led to the Indian Ocean and back home to Europe, but their prized possession and the capital of their Eastern Empire was the city of Batavia, far to the south, on the island of Java. And so Malacca under the Dutch began a long slow decline.

By the time the British assumed possession under the Anglo-Dutch Treaty of 1824, the town was a desolate museum of its own history. The streets where the Sultan's war elephants had trampled mercilessly, the empty grave that once held the bones of Francis Xavier, the ornate *Porta de Santiago* set into the grey stone walls of the *A Famosa,* as the old Portuguese fortress was known in Malay, the red-washed stolidity of the Dutch Stadthuys, all were cloaked in a twilight haze of languid degeneration.

The British included Malacca as one of the Straits Settlements mostly as a means of ensuring that it would never compete with their more ambitious port cities of Penang and Singapore. In 1867 the Straits Settlements became a Crown Colony, independent from government administration in British India, answerable only to the Colonial Office in far off London, and thus largely autonomous in the East. But by that time, Malacca had lain so long in its humid somnolence that only the sickly sweet smell of rotting organic matter on the mudflats at low tide welcomed those who landed on her shores.

CHAPTER I

Saint Xavier's Curse

THE TALL MAN FELT CLAUSTROPHOBIC in the cramped cabin aboard the SS *Trunnion*. The dull throb of the engines, the inescapable acrid odour of burning coal that pervaded every enclosed space, the dryness in his throat from the gin and water he drank instead of taking his evening meal, and the slow roll of the vessel as it pushed through the swells, all contrived to induce a slight nausea that seemed as elusive as it was consistent.

In his rapid departure from Singapore, he had packed hastily and forgotten to bring his pyjamas, so he consequently had to make do with sleeping in his undergarments in the narrow bunk that was too short. His feet painfully hung over the end when he stretched his legs. Now he lay atop the bedding, staring at the ceiling, feeling queasy, the edge of the bunk cutting into his Achilles tendon.

He could not recall exactly the last time he had slept alone, and though it was a condition in which he had spent most of his life, for the past few years he had grown accustomed to the warm snugness and gentle respiration of his common-law-wife, half his height even prostrate, lying beside him.

Finally he could take it no more. He leapt from the bunk, flung on his clothes, then doused the lamp and made his way through the sleeping ship toward the stairs to the upper foredeck. Outside, the fresh air and open space almost immediately dissipated the current of nausea running through him. He breathed deeply of the humid night, watching the prow of the ship as it rose and fell in the dark swell. On the starboard side, the coastline of Malaya lay in a dark blue mass under a late moon haloed in mist.

He was just beginning to feel comfortable again, the familiar pangs of hunger and heaviness of sleep returning, when he spotted an ember burning low red on the far side of the deck, arcing through the darkness like a will-o'-wisp. He realised it was the glow of a cigar.

'Hello, who is there?' he called, his voice more gruff than he intended. Since boarding more than six hours before, he had only spoken to the cabin boy, and then only to order more tonic water for his gin.

'Hello, good evening, sir,' returned a voice in an accent half between Malay and British. 'Or should I say "goodnight", as it is rather late.'

'Nice night for a stroll,' he said. As he moved toward the point of red, he watched it trace a curve in space as it was lowered to hang at the man's side.

'It is indeed, though I confess that I did not expect to find company on deck this late,' the stranger replied. From the darkness of the softly rolling deck emerged a short, compact man in a smart linen suit of Western cut, albeit with a black velvet *songkok* planted firmly on his head. A short manila cigar was smoking in his hand; his other was tucked into the fold of his jacket, as though to keep it warm. He had the hooknose and sharp chin of an Arab but the dark skin and jet hair of a Malay.

The tall man introduced himself first. 'I am Chief Detective Inspector David Hawksworth of the Singapore Police.'

'How nice to meet you, Chief Detective Inspector. I am Suliman Amjad bin Ahmed Alsagoff,' the stranger said with a self-possessed gravity that indicated he believed his name should bear recognition.

'Splendid.' The stranger's face betrayed his irritation that his name did not make an immediate impression on Hawksworth. They remained quiet for a long moment, the engine reverberating in the background, the sound of the prow cutting the waves, the slap of the water on the hull filling the silence. He was familiar with the name Alsagoff as it belonged to an established family, though they were of a station high above his own and he knew little about their businesses. 'Are you of the Singapore Alsagoffs?'

'I am indeed, sir,' the man spoke proudly, puffing on his cigar. 'However, I have made my home in Malacca for many years. I dare ask, is this your first trip to Malacca, Chief Detective Inspector?'

'Yes, how did you guess? Despite a lifetime in Malaya, I have not yet had the opportunity to visit the town.'

'Ah, I see.' The cigar glowed again at Alsagoff's mouth. Another moment of extended quiet followed, as though he were inhaling not only the smoke but Hawksworth's words as well. The question went unanswered. Then he gazed at the moon and exhaled before asking enigmatically, 'You know of Francis Xavier?'

Hawksworth was taken aback by the man's strange question. 'The saint? Yes, of course. In fact, I was raised by Jesuit brothers in an orphanage in Georgetown … in Penang.' He immediately regretted giving out so much information.

'Then you will know that Francis Xavier, too, visited Malacca. And that what he found there so appalled him, the aberrant activities of the residents so horrified him, that he cursed the place forever and anon.'

15

'Saint Xavier's curse?' Hawksworth guffawed. 'I had not heard of that.'

Ignoring him, Alsagoff continued in a steady voice, 'They say he stood at the door of the same church that one day would hold his very bones, and he took off his sandals and knocked the dust and gravel from the tread, claiming that the town was so wicked that he would not even take from it its dirt. He said the place would be cursed until the citizens ceased their filthy ways. And they say the curse lingers on, hovering over the town, making it all wretched.'

Hawksworth remained silent, examining the dark face as best he could. It was like gazing at a stone idol. Then the idol moved and spoke: 'You will find the place interesting, no doubt, on your holiday. Or is it, I wonder, official business that brings you to my home?'

Hawksworth merely smiled superciliously in the darkness.

Alsagoff leaned in almost close enough to touch and Hawksworth caught an unpleasant whiff of heavy tobacco on the man's breath. 'And where is *your* home, Chief Detective Inspector Hawksworth of the Singapore Police who was raised by Jesuit brothers in Georgetown, Penang?' There was a smirk in his voice.

Before Hawksworth could answer the impertinence, the dark face cracked into an obsequious grin. 'But forgive me, sir, you look tired and I should not pry into your personal affairs.' Then Alsagoff bowed slightly, so that Hawksworth glimpsed the top of the *songkok*, and bid him goodnight before merging into the moist darkness, the burning ember of his cigar diminishing as he moved away, as if he were dematerialising.

Alone again on the deck, the only sound the thrumming of the engine, Hawksworth leaned against a damp rail and watched

16

the murky line of the shore of Malaya slide past under the blue moonlight.

* * *

The *Trunnion* anchored off Malacca in the wee hours. At first light, they began to load the passengers onto a launch that would take them to the jetty that extended above the river mudflats, past the palm trees on the beach, into the sandy shallows of the green sea. Hawksworth was one of the last to depart the ship. He did not see Alsagoff's face and *songkok* amongst the passengers who disembarked.

As he limped along the uneven boards of the jetty, his throbbing foot told him that the fair weather would soon change. It had been broken and not set correctly months before, and now acted as an accurate predictor of the weather.

He surveyed the shoreline of the unfamiliar town. There were wooden huts on stilts with *attap* roofs built over the mudflats – the home of the *orang laut*, the sea gypsies. Farther inland where the mud turned to soil, on the left side of the narrow river, were the red-tiled roofs of the native quarter. The buildings looked short and squat, the sort of shophouses he knew from Singapore and Penang, jumbled together on narrow streets. He spotted the high sharp roof of a Chinese temple jutting above the residences. Colourful ceramic-tile dragons gambolled toward a ruby red sphere, which represented the light of knowledge, glistening jewel-like in the morning sunshine.

On the right bank was visible the roof of the Dutch Stadthuys and the white cross of the church erected nearby. Above, on the crown of a steep hill with slopes of bright green grass, were the ruins of Saint Paul's chapel, supposedly the oldest Christian edifice in the Orient, now in the year 1892 merely a roofless façade, and beside that, a square lighthouse that looked to be erected in the past century. Farther inland, half hidden in foliage on the crowns of other small hills, he could see the rooflines of bungalows where the wealthy Europeans lived. And behind it all, farther back in the lavender haze of early morning, the distant top of Mount Ophir, jutted above the rolling hills.

There seemed to be no one about. Other than a fat white man in a dark suit, with whom he had shared the launch and was now shuffling on the jetty behind him, and the baggage boys wheeling the luggage cart noisily over the wooden boards, he was alone. Only the cool sea breeze of morning – he was aware it would turn devilish hot later – rustling the palm trees created some movement on the landing. Otherwise the place looked like a stage set, or an engraving from an illustrated newspaper, the sort of image created by a designer in London who had never set foot in any place more exotic than Brighton.

Slithering movement on the mudflats below the jetty caught his attention, and he paused to peer over the side. In the dark mud he spotted little goby fish, slimy things with bulbous heads that looked like miniature prehistoric monsters, crawling on flattened fins in great herds across the moist ground.

'Blighted and blasted!' a voice yelled from behind him. 'Cursed Malacca!'

He turned to see the red-faced sweating bulk of the other white man rolling its way up the narrow jetty. The man paused to catch his breath, mumbling to himself angrily while moping his sopping brow with a handkerchief.

Turning back to the shore, which was quite near now, Hawksworth noticed for the first time the cannon set upon the embankment, resting in the shade of a thick casuarina tree. Under this tree was a white man dressed in a linen suit and solar topee helmet, and beside him was what appeared to be a palanquin sedan chair. Two pigtailed Chinese coolies were leaning against the trunk of the tree. As he stepped on the jetty, the man shouted out, 'Chief Detective Inspector Hawksworth?'

'I am he.'

The man waved, then shouted past him to the heavy, panting figure stepping off the jetty, 'Good morning, Mr. Bosworth, we have not seen you in a while!'

'Not long enough, if you ask me! And of course my bloody carriage is not here! Bloody, blasted Malacca!'

Hawksworth came under the shade of the casuarina. The suited man moved aside, to stand next to the wheel of the cannon, which the Chief Detective Inspector now saw was an antique that had not been serviced in decades. The weapons at the foot of the jetty were merely ornamental. The palanquin was not much better. Such conveyances had gone out of use decades before in the East – even as a boy he had only seen such things in picture books. The one before him looked worse for wear, too, its sides splitting in the humid atmosphere. He could make out the outline of some sort of crest on the door, long since painted over, and could discern the letters 'VOC' beneath the black paint. So the chair had belonged to the Dutch and was indeed a curio.

'Good morning, Chief Detective Inspector. My name is James Shaw.' He was a young man with fair skin and a slight Irish lilt to his voice. He could not have been more than thirty-five years old. 'I am the Resident Councillor of Malacca. Well, really, I am the Acting Resident Councillor but since I have held that position for nearly three years, people here simply call me "Resident Councillor". We have been expecting you – your telegram was most helpful. Though we had to guess the ship on which you would be arriving.' Hawksworth was aware that Shaw was studying him, looking up at his face. Remarkably tall, and despite now in his middle years growing a slight paunch, the Chief Detective Inspector remained of lean build, his face still sharp, with more than a passing resemblance to his namesake animal. After speaking downward to people for most of his life, he had come to habitually think of himself as 'the tall man'.

'I apologise for not being able to inform you of the ship's name in advance, but I departed Singapore in a great hurry. In fact, I only have one small bag, and I did not have the time to arrange for a place to stay.'

Shaw leaned against the cannon as he spoke, arms crossed causally over his chest. The wind lightly ruffled his linen suit, and he pushed his topee back on his head, face to the sea breeze. The coolies barely stirred; one had his eyes closed. 'We have plenty of room in Government House, Chief Detective Inspector. That is the official name, but we all call it the Stadthuys, after the Dutch.' He pronounced the foreign word as *stud-hoeys*. 'And you must be hungry. I imagine it was too early for breakfast on the ship. Come, we will have a repast for you at the Stadthuys in no time.' He gestured to the chair but Hawksworth demurred.

'I need to stretch my legs, Mr. Shaw, after my long voyage. The Stadthuys is not far: I saw it from the jetty.'

'We were not sure ... Well, you see, we trot out the chair for all our visiting ...'

'I am more than capable of walking under my own power, thank you.'

'Ah! Good to hear!' He motioned for the coolies to carry the chair away. They laboriously positioned themselves on either end then grasped the poles and walked at a sluggish pace, the chair slung between them. Shaw had already started to saunter through the dirt road that ran along the bottom of the hill toward the Stadthuys, the clock tower rising three stories before him. Beyond lay the quiet town and brown river.

* * *

The thick walls captured the night air and kept the interior rooms coolly refreshing despite the oppressive heat outdoors. After a brief rest, during which he nearly fell asleep, Hawksworth was roused by a knock at the door that opened to reveal a boy of no more than twenty. He wore no livery or uniform but possessed the distinct air of obsequiousness that indicated he was there to serve.

'Breakfast, sir, if you will follow me.'

The boy was as dark as any Tamil, with the curly hair of a Bugis trader, yet there was an angularity in his features, a straightness to his nose, that suggested the presence of European blood. Hawksworth guessed that he was a Kristang, a Malaccan creole, a descendant of mixed Portuguese and Malay ancestry. They were rare in Singapore, though he had come across one or two in the past.

'What is your name?' he asked as they walked on the large flat stones of the hall.

'Aloysius Santa Maria, sir.'

'You were born in Malacca?'

The boy nodded gravely, and then said in Malay, 'I am Portuguese … and a Christian.'

'You are Kristang?'

'I am of noble Portuguese blood,' he said proudly. 'In Europe, I would be a prince,' he added with a note of defiance just as they reached the threshold of the main dining hall. Aloysius stopped at the door and pointed to a long wooden table with worn wooden benches arranged dormitory style. 'Do enjoy your breakfast, sir,' the boy said before slipping away.

Seeing him enter, Shaw, who was already seated at the table, called out, 'Good morning again, Chief Detective Inspector, I do hope you are hungry! Our chef has prepared a special meal. He used to serve in a Peranakan house and serves mostly that sort of food – I do hope you are not put off by it. He also makes superlative coffee.'

Seating himself, Hawksworth said, 'Excellent on all counts, Mr. Shaw. Peranakan food is fine for breakfast, and I am devoted to *kopi*, as our Malay friends call the dark brew.' Before the detective was an earthenware pot full of robust black coffee. Beside it steamed a bowl of noodles flavoured in a red-curry-oil-and-coconut concoction with small clams and shrimps and mushrooms he knew to be *laksa*, a Straits delicacy. Besides this there was hard European bread and Chinese steamed buns heaped on a plate. Cut dragon fruit and small sweet bananas were piled in a carved wooden bowl. Before he left the table, Hawksworth knew he would consume it all.

He tucked into the noodles first, slurping the spicy broth. As he looked up, a hand-drawn map framed on the wall caught his attention. It depicted the Malayan Peninsula from Siam to Singapore along with Sumatra and the Riau Islands. His gaze travelled from the portolan compass along the rhumb lines past fanciful sea monsters spouting in the Andaman Sea. 'Dutch, is it?' he asked around his mouthful of noodles.

'It is. We have many of these old charts and maps. It seems sometimes as if we are still living in Dutch times. This one was framed quite a long time ago, to judge by the worm damage.'

Finishing his *laksa* and guzzling down one full cup of *kopi*, Hawksworth nodded at Shaw, then poured himself another cup and shifted the steamed buns closer. The first one he bit into contained deliciously greasy *char siew*, sweet and savoury pork meat. The next filled his mouth with a sweet red paste: mashed lotus root. He drained the coffee pot, smacked his lips then focused his attention on Shaw.

'I am here because Sergeant Major Hardie Walker sent me a letter expressing that my presence was required with some urgency.'

'We suspected that you were coming here because of the Sergeant Major.'

'Something puzzles me. If the matter was so urgent, why would he send a letter and not a telegram?'

'Ah, well, you see we have only one telegraph operator and he was down with dysentery when the Sergeant Major was here.'

'I see,' Hawksworth said then popped a slice of white dragon-fruit into his mouth. 'In his letter, the Sergeant Major specifically mentions a local woman named Lim Suan Imm whom I am to meet.'

Shaw looked baffled. 'Why would you need to meet with Mrs. Lim?'

'It is a matter of personal importance. Indeed, it is why the Sergeant Major sent the letter.'

'I do know her. We all do. She is a widow from a very prominent family in Malacca. They are Chinese Peranakans that go back to the Portuguese days, perhaps even before. But she is the last of her line, so to speak. Her children have all long gone under the ground.'

'How old is she?'

'Lord knows! And she is not the sort of woman that I would think it polite to ask. But if I had to guess, somewhere near seventy years of age. She seldom ventures from her home, a rather regal affair on Heeren Street, although she does come here to dine about once a month. But I am perplexed.'

'What about?'

'What she would have to do with the disappearance of the Sergeant Major – and his entire party.'

'What? What are you saying?' Hawksworth sat bolt upright on the wooden bench, unable to conceal his shock. Sergeant Major Walker was known for many things, including an unaccountable hatred for all things Oriental, but disappearing acts were not known to be part of his repertoire.

'Well, sir,' Shaw continued languidly, 'that was rather why we thought you were coming here. To locate the Sergeant Major. To go about the business of, well, *detecting* his whereabouts.'

'When did the Sergeant Major and his party go missing? I understood that he came here to lead a force to look into the death of the British Resident of Negeri Sembilan,' he spoke quickly. 'You had better start from the beginning.'

'We were ... Ah, the next course of breakfast has arrived!'

Hawksworth nearly snapped at the man to continue his explanation of the Sergeant Major's disappearance, but when he saw Aloysius returning with more food, he realised that he was working against local custom, which moved at a decidedly slower pace than the rapid-fire efficiency of Singapore. Settling himself to the circumstances, the Chief Detective Inspector was gladdened to spy another large pot of coffee being placed amongst the plates of curry rice and freshly poached fish with spicy *sambal* sauce, and slices of fresh jackfruit.

Shaw continued, 'The Sergeant Major led a force to look into the disturbances that led to the death of the Resident, Mr. Rosswell. He was killed, or so it was reported, during a coolie riot at the government bungalow at Ayer Panas, a hot springs near

Mount Ophir.'

'Why was the Resident at Ayer Panas? Negeri Sembilan and Ophir are quite a distance apart.'

'He was on holiday, I believe. We were told that he was a veteran of several campaigns against Chinese clans in Negeri Sembilan, so his violent death was something of a surprise.'

'In Singapore, Mr. Rosswell was respected as a man filled with initiative and zeal. He perhaps saw trouble and unwisely decided to step in on his own accord. When did Sergeant Major Walker depart Malacca?'

'He first came to Malacca to arrange for supplies and men – and he met Mrs. Lim at that time, yes, I now remember, at a dinner hosted here. The Magistrate was present as well. We later remarked that the Sergeant Major is a taciturn man, something of a martinet really. When describing his work he mentioned your name, and Mrs. Lim said she had heard of you, which we all found rather odd.'

'As I gathered from his letter.'

Aloysius poured more steaming coffee into Hawksworth's earthenware mug.

'He left Malacca with a force of five men, including our Superintendent of Police, and sailed to the town of Muar, about twenty-five miles down the coast south of here, then took a native boat upriver. From there he planned to march to Ayer Panas. He was supposed to support the police investigation then return here within a fortnight. This was a little more than five weeks ago.'

'And you have not heard from him, or anyone in his party, since that time?'

'A band of bird hunters reported seeing white men and Malay guides near Mount Ophir – that was about a fortnight ago.'

'Sounds like he is pursuing someone.'

Shaw plucked a piece of jackfruit from the plate and popped it into his mouth. 'Possibly, but that is rough country. The territory around Ayer Panas is mostly primitive forest. To lead a group of men through that terrain for more than a fortnight would require not only fortitude but knowledge and training.'

Hawksworth pictured Hardie Walker marching through the jungle, a grim smile on his face, his Martini-Henry rifle slung on his back. He would be in his element. 'The Sergeant Major is a veteran of Gordon's war in China and has led numerous actions in Malaya. That was why he was sent from Singapore to lead this expedition. If anyone would be able to lead a pursuit through unexplored terrain, it would be he.' Hawksworth sipped his coffee, feeling the energy flowing into him. 'Tell me more about the riot that led to the death of Mr. Rosswell.'

'There is not much to relate. Coolies from a nearby mining camp rioted – we are not sure why, though they do riot frequently. We believe that he was not alone at the government bungalow. Two Chinese surveyors were also killed.'

'Chinese surveyors?'

'Yes, we originally thought they were there to lay out a tin mine, or perhaps gold, but now we have heard that they might have been there looking for suitable land for rubber plantations.'

'And the riot? What more do you know about that?'

'From our reports, it started in a place called Labis, which is a camp of freebooter Chinese migrants. The Sultan of Johor does not like their presence – nor frankly do we – but short of sending in the Army, we cannot evict the blighters.'

'Who were the murdered Chinese surveyors working for?'

'A company called Straits Mining owned by a man named Loke Yew. He already operates a very profitable mining operation in the nearby town of Gading.'

'Were the freebooters perhaps more interested in Loke's surveyors than in the Resident? They might have been concerned that their land was to be taken.'

'We really have no idea why they rioted. In fact, we have no eyewitnesses to the death of the surveyors or the Resident. Their bodies were terribly mutilated, that is all we know. We do know that Mr. Loke is trying to create a joint venture with a Singapore outfit to explore growing rubber in this region. This is why we are not certain if the surveyors were looking for tin mines or rubber plantation land.'

'Or gold, you said.'

'Or gold, yes. But not likely. There have always been rumours of gold in the hills around Mount Ophir. I mean,' Shaw laughed, 'that is how the mountain got its name!'

Hawksworth leaned back in his chair to study the old Dutch map on the wall. After a thoughtful silence, he said, 'This matter of the Sergeant Major – who I assure you has not disappeared so much as engaged in an enthusiastic pursuit – is something that you would like me to look into?'

'Yes, if for no other reason that our Superintendent of Police is with him as well.'

'Ah,' he finished his coffee and set the cup on the table. 'I also have my own business to look into. You will let Mrs. Lim know that I am in town and hope to see her?'

'Of course. I will send a boy over immediately.' Shaw paused, then added hesitantly, 'There is one further thing that may be related to the Sergeant Major's expedition. This might be silly, but the natives in the districts around Mount Ophir have been complaining of,' he cleared his throat in embarrassment, 'a sort of ghost that has been haunting them. They claim it steals their children.'

'What type of ghost?'

'A *pontianak*, I believe it is called.'

'There is nothing silly about a *pontianak*,' Hawksworth retorted sharply, before continuing calmly 'The local beliefs usually hold a grain of truth. If children are disappearing, it may be a tiger. In fact, it may well be a man-eater the Sergeant Major is pursuing. You said the bodies at Ayer Panas were mutilated but that you had no witness to the killing.'

Shaw silently mulled the implications as the table was cleared of empty plates.

'If I do travel up country,' Hawksworth continued, 'I will inquire about this *pontianak*. I am also curious about what the Resident was doing so far from his home base. His office staff in Negeri Sembilan can offer no assistance?'

'We sent a cable but received only a vague reply. Apparently the Resident left in rather a hurry and put off making a proper report until he returned ... Which, of course, he never did.'

Hawksworth stretched his arms and cracked his back. The men stood, then paused at the doorway. 'That was a lovely breakfast, Mr. Shaw. My sincere thanks to you and your chef.'

'Our pleasure, of course. Please do join us at dinner tonight. We usually invite some local businessmen and other luminaries to dine. We are a bit old fashioned in that way.'

'I look forward to it. I would also like to meet the Assistant Superintendent of Police, if I may.'

'I am afraid he is down with fever.'

'And the Superintendent is with the Sergeant Major's expedition. So who is currently in charge of the police force?'

After thinking for a moment, the younger man replied happily, 'Well, until the Assistant Superintendent mends, I suppose that I am.'

'I see,' Hawksworth said, hiding his dismay.

'Would you like to rest? Aloysius will show you to your room.'

'I think after being on that cramped boat, I would rather like to stretch my legs.'

'The hill behind has spectacular views. Tomorrow I will take you on a tour of the town. This is your first time in Malacca?'

'It is,' Hawksworth responded, already feeling weary.

* * *

He strode alone up the narrow path winding up the hill behind the Stadthuys, toward the ruined chapel and the neat whitewashed lighthouse. The heat of the day had risen, and the dusty path, barely shaded, was deserted.

He stopped at the top of the hill, the view sweeping toward the sea. The *Trunnion* lay still at anchor. The only other ship in the harbour was a native craft, a river-going sampan with a single mast from which was rigged a simple sail of woven mat. Otherwise the sea was empty and calm – he could hear the small rollers breaking off the beach far below. The mudflats were now covered with a thin skein of water: the tide was coming in. Past the flats, the stone houses of the native town stretched for a short distance up the coast before giving way to wooden houses on stilts, then wild shoreline far beyond.

Turning toward the deserted chapel, he paused and shouted a loud 'hello'. No answer came. There was a round window toward the top of the front wall, and large glassless windows that let in the sun, but the light was not quite high enough to shine through the top of the roofless structure. He stepped over the threshold. Crates of supplies for the lighthouse were stacked inside the open doorway. The thick dark brick walls were covered in green creepers and weeds. He walked further in, his footfalls muffled by the debris in the nave, where massive tombstones lay on the ground. There were more stacked haphazardly at the back of the chapel, for successive generations had pulled up the stones over the centuries to make room for their own dead in the sanctified ground.

At the foot of the chancel was an open grave – supposedly that of Francis Xavier – covered with a heavy metal grille. Beyond this were more scattered stones. Most had skull and cross bones, others finely detailed ships, engraved in the granite. He read aloud from one: 'Hier Lecht Bregraven Anganeta Robberts.' On another were words that he sensed translated to 'Venerated Wife' and the name Verdonck, and the date February 6, 1652.

Farther in the chancel, in the dark portion where the roof remained partly intact, he saw another stone marked in Portuguese: *Aquijaz DOM GAS FRÃ, Filha de Luiz Frñ e de Ant. de Faria, falleceoaos de Avril de 1581 Ano.* Later he would learn that the Portuguese words meant 'Here lays Domingas Franco, Daughter of Luiz Franco and Antonia de Faria, who died April, 1581'. The exact day of her death had been engraved, but was now impossible to decipher on the weathered rock.

In the chapel there were more. One stone was prominently featured with a very fine engraving of a seventeenth-century Dutch sailing ship called a *boyer*, flat-bottomed with a gaff-rigged sail, which remained vivid despite the passage of time. There was a short text accompanying the engraving that Hawksworth would later learn translated to 'The gaffel-boyer is our grandfather's first discovery. Our father's first house now closes our mouths'. That grave held three occupants. It did not reveal their names, only their ages: triplets aged thirteen who died one after another between December and March in the years 1659 and 1660.

Hawksworth turned from the graves to climb through a breach in the ruined wall. He sought sunshine and fresh sea air, and to get away from these spectres of death, but found himself in a yard with graves set into the steep hillside. Most of the headstones were askew as the slope subsided, as though ready to tumble down the hill, and were marked in English with the familiar locutions. He read one aloud, 'Sacred to the Memory of J. T. Leicester, Late of Bencoolen, Sumatra, who departed this life on May 26, 1846, aged forty-nine years and five months.' There were many more.

At the base of the hill, he could see the sole remaining gate of the centuries' old Portuguese fort. It was ornate and functionless; its yawning portal led now only to the quiet sloping green of the graveyard.

He turned back to the steep narrow path to the Stadthuys. It was exceptionally hot now, the bright sun bearing down relentlessly as he made his way toward the coolness of the thick-walled building. Spending so much time among the ancient dead left him feeling vacant.

After being shown to his room, he found himself longing suddenly for human company, noise and animation. It was not a sensation with which the Chief Detective Inspector was on familiar terms, and it left him uneasy once he lay on the cool sheets under the mosquito netting in the dim and echoing old Stadthuys.

CHAPTER II

A Princess and a Nonya

HAWKSWORTH AWOKE FROM A DEEP AND DREAMLESS SLEEP, to the shuttered darkness of the unfamiliar room. It had rained while he slept – he could smell it in the air, the crisp dampness soon giving way to the odour of tropical rot – and he could feel it in the coolness of the air.

He was washing the sleep from his face in the porcelain basin of water brought in fresh that afternoon when the knock came at the door, which he already recognised as belonging to Aloysius. It must be dinnertime. Slipping from the borrowed pyjamas, he quickly dressed for dinner; it meant pulling on the cotton trousers that had been pressed while he slept, pinning a frayed collar to his dress shirt and shrugging into a linen suit jacket that had also been pressed but did not match the trousers. All told, he looked less like a respected visitor and more like a beachcomber washed in with the tide.

The noble prince Aloysius led him quickly and quietly with a paraffin lantern through the dark hallway, padding on bare feet. In the cool of night, the interior of the Stadthuys felt particularly damp. They moved in silence to the main dining room, which after the journey through the dark halls seemed especially bright and inviting. This was not the room where he had breakfasted but another more grand space, with a mahogany sideboard and a polished dining table with high-backed chairs and china flatware laid at each place. There was precious little Dutch about this room – it looked like a replica of a dining room in an English country house.

Mr. Shaw was already seated, as were two other men, one of whom Hawksworth recognised as 'Bosworth', the fat man on the jetty who had not seemed too keen on disembarking at Malacca. The other man could have been Bosworth's Malay double. Both of them fat and dressed in identical cotton summer suits, one black, one white, the two resembled each other like a photograph and its plate. One clear difference was that the Malay had a prayer scar, what the Arabs called *zabiba* or raisin: a dark mark on the forehead, caused from touching the forehead to the ground repeatedly while praying. It was a mark of piety and matched the man's serious mien, contrasting with Bosworth's louche demeanour.

'Ah, there you are, Chief Detective Inspector! Just in time for dinner. Had a comfortable sleep, I assume?' Shaw asked.

'Yes, thank you.'

He was surprised to find that the chandelier above the table was lit with wax candles. Noticing the look on his face, Shaw apologised, 'There is no gas in the Stadthuys, and it is not yet wired for electricity. All a bit primitive compared to modern Singapore, I suppose, but it keeps the town close. Allow me to introduce Mr. George Bosworth and Mr. Muhammad Hasrat.'

'A pleasure to meet you both.'

'Thank you, Chief Detective Inspector,' Hasrat replied in impeccable English. 'I am honoured to sit at table with a representative of the constabulary of Singapore.'

'Mr. Hasrat is a surveyor with my team,' Bosworth offered bluntly, without any greeting, to Hawksworth. 'He was trained in

London. His father has money. Tin mining, you know.'

Hasrat smiled at Hawksworth, explaining, 'My family is related to the Sultan of Selangor. My full name is Muhammed Abdul Samad Hasrat Abdullah.'

'You are a business partner of Mr. Bosworth?'

'Indeed he is,' Bosworth interjected. 'We are competing with another consortium for the lands around Mount Ophir, though I believe that with the recent killings in Ayer Panas – of which I was only just made aware – our plans will have to be speeded up.'

A side cart was wheeled out, and a bottle, corked, with remnants of a label painted on the side, was placed on the table next to heavy crystal glasses. There were several more bottles in similar condition on the cart.

'Real Dutch *genever*!' Shaw said proudly. 'An oddity exclusive to Malacca.'

As the slightly yellowish gin was being poured into the glasses, Shaw explained, 'It seems the Dutch were somewhat suspicious, Chief Detective Inspector. The old place is honeycombed with hidden passages and false walls. We are always knocking them down and finding caches of ruined ammunition and crates of old bottles. The beer and wine have long gone off, but the *genever* still seems good. What do you think, Mr. Bosworth?'

Bosworth pulled from his waistcoat a small bottle of Siegert's Angostura. 'I think gin, new or old, always tastes better with some bitters in the glass.' He tossed a few drops into the bottom of his crystal then poured in the *genever*, which turned amber when it came into contact with the dark bitters. He took a glug and sloshed it around his mouth while holding the glass to the light of the candelabra on the table. Loudly smacking his lips, he proclaimed, 'It is as good as the day it was made by a Dutchman.' He took another triumphant gulp, his face flushing. The man's left eye was especially proptosic; it bulged so badly that he appeared to be looking in two directions at once. Hawksworth recognised it as Grave's disease.

'I am glad to hear it, because this time we found a dozen bottles hidden behind a false door at the foot of the stairs that led to the old latrine ... and we wondered about the contents,' Shaw said mischievously. Bosworth laughed as loudly as the rest of them at the joke.

Aloysius led several more servants into the room; a dinner of grilled freshwater fish and garden vegetables, prepared in the plain British fashion, was placed before the men. The food was consumed quickly, replenished by a second course of red curried mutton and coconut rice with fiery, pungent *sambal* to one side. He noted that Bosworth did not touch the spice. By the end of this course, Hawksworth was full, and not anxious for dessert.

While they ate, the talk turned to the infrastructure works being carried out at the outpour of the Klang River, up the coast, and the railway that was being built to ferry goods from the port to the boomtown of Kuala Lumpur, which was growing from the mud of the upper Klang Valley.

'The talk in Singapore is that Kuala Lumpur will soon be chosen as the new capital of Malaya,' Hawksworth said nonchalantly, smacking his lips at the deliciousness of the old Dutch gin.

Hasrat sighed heavily. 'Once the railway and new port are completed, I fear that will be the end of Malacca. History will have bypassed us for the last time.'

'Not a moment too soon,' Bosworth opined loudly. 'Damnable place. The buggery capital of the East, that is what Francis Xavier thought. Pederasty. It was the Arabs who introduced the foul practice.'

Muhammad Hasrat shifted uncomfortably in the seat beside him while Shaw cleared his throat and even blushed a little at the implications, but Bosworth pressed on. 'As it says in the book of Isaiah, "I will cause the arrogancy of the proud to cease, and will lay low the haughtiness of the terrible. I will make a man more precious than fine gold; even a man than the golden wedge of Ophir." That was what Xavier was thinking as he shook his sandal and cursed this town.'

'Mr. Bosworth knows that the mountain the English call Mount Ophir is known to us as Gunung Ledang,' Hasrat spoke quickly, cutting off the gin-soaked man. 'He knows this because we are interested in surveying the land for our rubber tree enterprise. But Mr. Bosworth does not know the story of *Puteri Gunung Ledang*. Do you know it, Chief Detective Inspector? No? What about you, Mr. Shaw? No again. Then I shall tell you.'

'Before you do, Mr. Hasrat, perhaps we should open another bottle of gin?' Shaw said eagerly, his face already pink and shiny from the first bottle.

'I second that opinion!' Bosworth boomed. Hawksworth merely nodded his head in approval. Despite the lovely flavour of the gin, he was not as prodigious a drinker as the fat man and did not relish the thought of a hangover the next morning.

The servants' slippered feet whispered on the flat stones, and presently a second bottle was uncorked. Bosworth splashed his bitters into his crystal glass, tested this second bottle, and proclaimed it sound. The three Europeans poured themselves another round then turned their attention to Hasrat, who began in a rumbling voice, 'The Sultan of Malacca during d'Albuquerque's siege was named Mahmud Shah. It is said that before that unfortunate time, he attempted to woo a princess who lived on Gunung Ledang.'

'A princess?'

'As you might say, Mr. Shaw, a fairy princess. We say she was *orang bunian* …'

'The whistling people?' Hawksworth asked. 'I have heard of them.'

'They are a race possessed of exceptional beauty and elegance, but they are hidden, or shall we say that they are invisible except to those who have …' Hasrat struggled for the word. Hawksworth offered 'second sight', to which Hasrat shrugged assent.

'While he was hunting on Gunung Ledang, the princess appeared before the Sultan. The man was immediately smitten and decided that he must possess her, no matter the cost. He sent an emissary to enquire of the—'

Bosworth cut him off, speaking loudly, 'I thought you said she was invisible. How did the emissary find her?'

'On that point the story is silent,' Hasrat said, causing Bosworth to chortle.

Undeterred, Hasrat continued, 'The princess said that she would allow the Sultan to take her as bride, but to prove his love, she required him to fulfil seven tasks. She asked that he build a bridge of gold for her to walk to Malacca from the mountain and a bridge of silver for her to return. She wanted laid at her feet seven large clay jars of virgins' tears, seven large clay jars of betel nut juice, seven trays filled with hearts of fleas, and seven trays filled with hearts of mosquitoes …'

'With all those fleas and mosquitoes, no wonder the virgins were crying,' Bosworth joked, but the others ignored him.

'The Sultan asked what the seventh requirement was, but the princess would only reveal that to him once he had fulfilled the first six. So at great expense, the Sultan set about building the bridges and sending his soldiers to tear out the hearts from insects. All the while the princess would appear to him in dreams, floating above him, her elegant perfection just beyond his reach. They say that after many months and the near bankruptcy of his treasury, his workers finished the first six tasks. He then sent his emissary to ask the princess what she last required of him. She replied "a bowl filled with the blood of the Sultan's youngest son". This was especially cruel as his youngest son was his favourite. The man spent night and day agonising over the decision, riven by his desire.'

'What did he finally do?' Shaw asked in a dazed voice, seemingly spellbound by the gin-enhanced images in his mind.

'Some say that he was unable to fulfil the final wish, and the princess forsook him. Others say that the Portuguese invasion occurred during that time, and he fled before he could make up his mind.'

'Ha!' Bosworth barked, gripping his glass. 'If he built the gold and silver bridges, where are they now, eh? I trust that your skills at surveying are more scientific than your fairy tales, Mr. Hasrat.'

The pious man was about to respond in anger when Hawksworth said coolly, 'I am intrigued by this connection between gold and the mountain. It appears in both the Bible and in this Malay tale you have narrated.'

Hasrat spoke with calm restraint, 'As I was about to explain to Mr. Bosworth, it has long been said that the gold and silver on the mountain came from the Sultan's bridges.'

'Wait one moment,' Shaw cried. 'The Bible was written long before the Portuguese invasion, so how could the Sultan's gold account for the legend of Ophir?'

'I rather think that the story itself predates Sultan Mahmud Shah. Most likely, his name was attached to a very old legend,' Hawksworth said. 'What do you think, Mr. Hasrat?'

The heavy man shifted his weight toward the table, regarding the three men. He spoke in an admonishing tone, 'Time is an illusion made for man, but truth is eternal. As the holy Qur'an teaches us, "Verily a day in the sight of our Lord is like a thousand years of your reckoning".'

They were quiet for a time, then Shaw innocently asked, 'Has anyone actually ever found gold in quantity on Mount Ophir? Is there a viable business concern in gold mining?'

Bosworth carefully set his empty gin glass on the dark wood of the table. 'There will be gold there soon. We are going to grow it. Rubber trees. Gold will grow on trees!' he laughed, then rose. 'Mr. Shaw, Mr. Hasrat, Chief Detective Inspector, I am drunk. It is time for me to retire.'

Hasrat rose as well, 'And it is time for me to take my leave as well. Thank you, Mr. Shaw, for a most delightful evening. Chief Detective Inspector Hawksworth, I wish you the best of your stay in Malacca.'

Shaw rose, calling to Aloysius to see the men out, then thanked them both in turn for attending. When they were gone, he regained his seat across the table from Hawksworth. The lamps were burning dimly now.

Shaw finished another glass of gin then set the heavy crystal down clumsily. Running his fingertip over the rim, he eyed Hawksworth ruminatively. 'Our Mrs. Lim has sent word that you are to see her tomorrow for tea,' Shaw said, then added, 'I did not want to mention this before the others.'

'This is good. Thank you.'

'One strange thing, though.'

'What is that?'

'I sent word that Chief Detective Inspector Hawksworth has arrived from Singapore and would like to see her. She replied in her note, "Please tell Chief Detective Inspector Lightheart that it would be my delight to meet him." I sometimes think the old dear is a bit dotty. Who in the blazes is "Lightheart"?'

Hawksworth gazed at one of the low burning flames, watching the shadows flickering on the wall. 'I have no idea,' he said, 'though in my experience, dotty old women are rarely as dotty as they seem.'

* * *

The next morning much ado was made about arranging a carriage to take the Chief Detective Inspector to meet Lim Suan Imm. Aloysius fussed around like a chambermaid; Shaw was on hand to ensure that the carriage rolled up before the Stadthuys; at least three separate Chinese servants helped him into it. After the fanfare he expected a long journey – no one told him that the roofline of his destination was visible from the second floor of the Stadthuys.

The carriage crossed over the river. The bridge was close to the mouth, and it being low tide, the river was little more than dark mud. Three monitor lizards, the biggest he had ever seen, were sprawled lazily in the muck, basking in the sun like pariah dogs.

They passed along largely empty streets. In Singapore, the early morning hours before the sun's heat became intolerable were the busiest of the day, the streets bustling with pedestrians, rickshaws, buffalo carts, and steam trams. Here in Malacca, he spotted only a few Chinese with bamboo stretched over their shoulders, wicker baskets of steamed buns or fruit dangling from either end – they were breakfast deliveries. Breakfast at 10 o'clock; half the day was already gone.

The first street they rolled down was lined with shophouses. Tradesmen's stores, Chinese chemists and tailors and sweet sellers were all announced by signboards, but none appeared to be open.

The street was abandoned and eerily quiet in the late morning sun. It was as though the residents were in hiding from a coming plague.

The carriage rounded a corner onto Heeren Street. Much like Singapore and Penang, the narrow street had a five-foot-way, a recessed arcade that covered the sidewalk and provided shelter from relentless sun and torrential rain, for in Malaya it was always one or the other. He noticed that this five-foot-way was broken up by walls with portholes in them, so that each house had its own front area and neighbours could communicate – and spy – on each other, even if pedestrians had to walk unsheltered in the dirty street. Most of the houses were nondescript two- and three-story affairs, little different in appearance from the shophouses around the corner. Each seemed to be boarded up against calamity.

They came to a stop before a house that was far more ornate than the others. He stood alone on the hot street, watching as the carriage rolled away, echoing down the deserted street. Before Hawksworth could knock, the red front door swung open, and he stepped from the bright heat and dust into the cool inviting air of the house.

He found himself in a courtyard that was open to the sky two stories above so that the afternoon rain would fall directly into the house, onto the brick floor, circulating and cooling the interior. Now in the morning, the shaft formed a light well that brightened what would otherwise have been a gloomy room. A luxuriance of potted palms and ferns on the floor of the courtyard created a moist interior garden. The green curls of the plants seamlessly merged with the decor. Every surface glistened with patterns, from the rosettes on the risers of the stairs to the vegetative patterns on the floor tiles to the miniature vignettes inlaid in mother of pearl in the dark rosewood furniture, and to the gilt that flowed along the edges of the folding screens.

Yet all the wild profusion of patterns and colours created a sense of solidity. What should have been a riot for the senses became instead an intricate and delicate structure that radiated an ambience of stillness and calm, as though the interior of the house were a sylvan glade.

In the quiet, he could hear the servants bustling about in the kitchen in the back of the house, cooking sweets. The odour of sugar being caramelised mingled with the perfume of joss sticks, rendering the air delicious.

A demure female servant ushered him into a parlour lit by windows of red glass. The room was dark despite the brightness of the day, and it took a while for the Chief Detective Inspector's eyes to adjust to his surroundings. Once his eyes were accustomed to the light, he discerned the dour faces of life-sized ancestor portraits hung high up on the wall, glaring down at him.

Another servant brought in a pitcher of water and a tea service and placed them on an elaborate sideboard before silently slipping out of the room without so much as a nod in his direction. Then he was alone in the dim space, listening to the sound of a clock marking the passing minutes. He found the ticking sound ominous, as though whatever the enigmatic Mrs. Lim was about to reveal would be less a comfort than a discovery of further tribulation.

Shortly the first girl returned with a tray of sweet smelling glutinous rice cakes cut into bite-sized rectangles, known as *kueh wajek*, and his dark foreboding was duly relieved. She placed them on a low table next to Hawksworth before pouring him a cup of tea. She did not speak but made motions for him to eat and drink. He had not had the treats in many years and found them especially delectable. As soon as the tray was empty the girl returned with a dish of *getuk-getuk*, tapioca palm-sugar cakes coated with shredded coconut. He was eating one of these when a woman entered the parlour.

She was petite, dressed in a florid purple *baju panjang*, a silk one-piece dress worn over a long batik sarong. Slippers decorated with tightly packed brightly coloured beads were on her feet, and three yellow gold *kerosang* brooches in a peacock motif were pinned to her chest. Her hair was pulled into a bun so that her face was completely revealed. It was a sylph-like face, fair and smooth, except when she smiled: then it creased with mirthfulness that bordered on insouciance. She was smiling now.

He rose and offered his hand, 'Thank you for seeing me, Mrs. Lim. Pardon my intruding on you like this.'

'It is no intrusion, Chief Detective Inspector Lightheart. I am happy to see you,' her voice, he noticed, was delicate without being dainty, and she spoke with the accent of an English lady. 'Please address me as Suan Imm. I am none too fond of formality.' Despite her saying this, the first servant never left them alone in the room; such isolation would not be proper between a man and woman who were not married to each other, no matter their age difference.

'Thank you, madam. You have a lovely name.'

'In Hokkien it means "the sound of diamonds tinkling"', she smiled impishly, shaking her head slightly as if to make invisible earrings tinkle. It was a practiced move, he noted, but charming nonetheless.

As she spoke, the serving girl returned with a platter of yet more sweets. Hawksworth recognised banana fritters and *kueh khoo*, red and lavender steamed sweet potato and glutinous rice cakes served in dome shapes, pressed with the Chinese symbol for happiness. There was a heap of *onde-onde*, glutinous rice balls made with bright green *pandan* and dusted with shredded white coconut, which had been his favourite as a child. Around the rim of the platter were arranged *kueh bolu*, small sponge cakes shaped like star-anise seeds.

Hawksworth spoke first, 'I came because I received word from … Well, look … I … Why do you call me "Lightheart?"'

She smiled then motioned to sweets. 'Do help yourself. Lightheart was your mother's maiden name. And that was the name she used when I knew her.'

It felt as though the floor had suddenly tilted beneath him. Hovering between fascination and mortification, he gazed into the woman's irenic face. 'You knew my mother? How?'

'You have her eyes, you know. This name you use, Hawksworth, I suspect was your father's name.'

His heart racing, he maintained his outward composure, following the woman's hints. 'I have to confess to being very confused, Mrs. Lim. You knew my mother but not my father?'

'I met your mother when she came to Malacca. She stayed here a short time before moving upcountry with a missionary man named Nathaniel Cooper.'

Hawksworth exhaled sharply, his eyes roaming the room. They stopped on a cut glass decanter, tinted burgundy. 'I am afraid I do not understand. You see, I was raised in an orphanage in Georgetown. I was a ward of the government. They told me that my parents had died of a fever during the crossing from England.'

'And did they tell you where the ship was headed when they died?'

'I was told that they were en route to Singapore. The ship was held in harbour at Penang until the fever broke. I was taken ashore once it was deemed safe. When I was older, they told me that my parents' bodies were buried at sea, in the Bay of Bengal. They were the first on the ship to perish.'

'Your mother survived. She knew that you had survived, too. She told me that she kept away from you for your own safety.'

'She knew that I was alive all these years and yet she did nothing about it. She made no attempt to … But why? And what of my father?' as he spoke his voice cracked, as if he were suddenly thirty years younger.

'It was your father she was protecting you from.'

'I beg your pardon, but this is all hard for me to believe. You mean that my father also survived?'

'I do not know what became of your father. I know that the fever disfigured your mother – but her beauty still shone. She told me that she gave you up to the orphanage and later kept her distance from you, although it stabbed her heart. She had to keep you from your father's business associates.'

'My mother is still alive? Do you have any proof of what you say? Forgive my rudeness, but it is all rather incredible.'

'Your mother is named Isabella. But understand that I have not seen my dear Isabella Lightheart in many years. But, as I told the Sergeant Major, I believe that Gading town, in which her orphanage is located, is under threat, and knowing your mother's headstrong ways, she will not back away from a fight.'

'She is in danger? The letter the Sergeant Major sent indicated—'

'We all are in danger, though in Malacca our safety will last longer than for those in the hills.' Her voice had grown distant, as if she were commenting on the world from very far away.

Hearing her abstraction, Hawksworth briefly thought that perhaps Mr. Shaw was correct, that the old woman was indeed dotty. His thoughts drifted to the story of the fairy princess and her golden bridges and buckets full of fleas' hearts. What worth were any of these farfetched stories? The only way he could be sure, he knew, was by venturing into the ancient, wild hills to see for himself.

She offered him a *kueh khoo* on a small doily, which he accepted with a smile to mask his doubts.

'You see, Chief Detective Inspector,' she said before popping a *kueh bolu* into her mouth, 'though the intelligence I have for you is bitter, the food I serve is sweet.' She wiped her fingers then reached for a fritter.

'What is this danger that you speak of?' he asked, expecting another abstract answer. He was surprised when she swiftly answered, 'A tin mining consortium wants to take the orphanage land.'

'I have also heard that the land is wanted for rubber plantations.'

'Yes, that too. There are several consortiums vying for the same land for the same purposes. The last I knew, your mother was fighting to save her orphanage. However I have had no news from Gading for the last year or two. My letters have gone unanswered. Unfortunately I am too old to travel over such remote territory, which I fear grows more treacherous by the day.'

'Yet you believe that she is still in danger?'

'The consortiums fight battles in the court and with more physical means, especially in the hills. I fear that the villagers – and often the coolies themselves, once the clans get involved – are caught in the action and suffer. I would suppose that your Resident of Negeri Sembilan found himself in the same hot soup. And as perhaps your mother will, also.'

'What is the name of the consortium in Gading?'

She scratched her head and screwed up her face, then shrugged her shoulders and went slack. 'It is Chinese, that is all I can recall. I am sure Shaw can tell you.'

'Mr. Shaw mentioned that a *pontianak* is mixed up in this business as well. A scare tactic, I suppose, to frighten villagers off their land?'

She was quiet, gently sipping tea, then she looked at him, her eyes narrowing. 'I saw one when I was a little girl. She came floating toward me out of a banana tree. I remember it was dusk and the sky was the colour of blood. I heard a baby crying and went to see. Then it flew down at me and I screamed and screamed. That face ... like a rotted corpse, with red eyes like coals and teeth like a tiger. I get goose skin merely remembering her.'

In the silence that followed, the ticking of the clock became almost unbearable.

'But that was a long time ago and I have not seen one since.' She leaned over, plucked a *kueh khoo* from the platter, then asked breezily, 'Let me ask, how did you come to Malacca?'

Hawksworth smiled inwardly at her abrupt change of expression. The woman could have been an actress. The fluidity of her character was exquisitely charming. 'On a ship called The *Trunnion*,' he said, reaching for another treat.

'Ah, an Alsagoff ship. Most of them that sail here are.'

'I met a man named Suliman Alsagoff on the ship.'

'The same family. They own several shipping lines. Suliman Alsagoff is a powerful man in this town. I knew his grandmother Hajji Fatimah, rest her soul, when she was a girl here in Malacca. She married the Sultan of Gowa Karaeng Chanda Pulih, a Bugis, and moved to Singapore to live the life of a queen.'

He smiled in understanding. 'The mosque she built in Singapore still stands.'

'So they tell me. I have never seen it. She was a good woman, but these Alsagoffs ... I always thought would be trouble. It was her daughter, the Princess Raja Siti, who married into the family.

Now one of their children runs their companies in Singapore and the other, the one you met, Suliman, runs the businesses here in Malacca.'

'I knew of the Alsagoffs in Singapore, but this Malaccan brother was unknown to me until we met on the ship. He seemed a very shifty character.'

She nodded as if in agreement. 'They are secretive by nature. Have you heard the rumours of the French family?'

'No.'

She bit into an *onde-onde*, chewed slowly then swallowed, 'Yes, it would seem that Syed Ahmed Alsagoff, Raja Siti's betrothed, kept a second family in secret. All I know is that they were said to be from Marseille.'

'This brother in Malacca, what is it that he does here?'

'Ah! Well, if the Chinese *kongsi* do not own it, he does, which is another way of saying that the *kongsi* run the Chinese town and Alsagoff runs everything else, including most of the European interests. The family owns much land outside of town, too, including several of the tin mines.'

'Any nefarious enterprises?'

She leaned in close. 'Have you ever known a businessman who did not keep at least one toe in the chamber pot?' Her voice was an exaggerated conspiratorial whisper.

Hawksworth laughed, then sipped what he knew would be his final cup of tea. The empty snack tray had not been replenished, which meant that the tête-à-tête was coming to a close. 'Thank you for speaking with me today, Mrs. Lim.'

'It was my pleasure, Chief Detective Inspector Lightheart. I do wish you the best of luck in your ventures, both personal and professional. Do tell me what you discover of Isabella.'

He thanked her again for the delicious treats, then as he rose to leave, Hawksworth had a sudden inspiration. 'Forgive me,' he said, 'one question further. Have you heard any rumours of large quantities of gold being found on Mount Ophir?'

She smiled indulgently. 'The legends are very old. The Hokkien traders who first came to Malaya in the fourteenth century called the place *Kim Sua*, or Golden Mountain. You ask me if I have heard rumours of gold on Mount Ophir? My answer is yes, all of my life.'

'I see.'

'Be careful while you are searching in those hills, Chief Detective Inspector. As the unfortunate Sultan learned, gold and lust are often found together, and both lead to sin and damnation.'

He glanced past her at the sombre faces of her ancestors high on the wall staring down at him, the descendants of the fourteenth-century traders who had helped d'Albuquerque defeat the Sultan. At times it seemed like everyone had dead ancestors hung on their walls. There were cemeteries in every town filled with the bodies of their offspring. It was in this swirling muddle of pictures and stones, he knew, that people traced their history, proved to themselves that they were of a lineage, found their place in the continuum. Everyone except himself, who had been born, for all intents and purposes, into a Jesuit orphanage in a land far from any ancestors' graves.

Until now. If this old woman was to be believed, his lineage waited for him, dead or alive, in the hills above this very town. With the aftertaste of the sweets cloying in his mouth and the sour faces of the dead Chinese elders glaring at him as though judging his vaporous past, he bid Suan Imm goodbye. Then the tall man smacked his solar topee onto his head and strode out of the cool domestic sanctum into the steely daytime heat and vampiric humidity of the desolate flat narrow streets of Malacca.

CHAPTER III

Solomon the King

ALOYSIUS POURED HOT WEAK TEA into a porcelain cup stained lemon-yellow with use. As with most of the domestic items in the Stadthuys, it was impossible to place an age on the thing. A chinoiserie motif of a pagoda and bridge offered no clues, and other than the discolouration and a hairline crack that ran jaggedly beside the little bridge, the signs of wear were indistinguishable from those of age. It may have been brought over by previous British administrations, or left behind by the Dutch, or perhaps it had been brought to Malaya even before that, when the Portuguese ruled the land, in a shipment of Chinese goods bound for India or beyond.

The liquid in the Chief Detective Inspector's cup was a locally concocted version of Earl Grey. Black tea leaves from Assam, dried and pressed into bricks for coastal trade, were mixed with desiccated pomelo rinds as substitutes for the Bergamot orange oil. The result was a bitter brew that stained teeth as rapidly as it did porcelain and often caused the stomach to churn unless accompanied with heavy butter biscuits; yet the tea was a commonplace drink in the smaller towns and outposts in Malaya. 'We make it ourselves with pomelo from the garden,' Shaw explained with pride as he sipped from his cup.

'It is lovely,' Hawksworth said in a strained voice, his lips puckering. They were in the library, the walls of which were largely free of bookshelves and plastered instead with maps, many of which looked as ancient and mysterious as Hawksworth's teacup.

He had finished explaining to Shaw the story he had heard on Heeren Street, leaving out the more improbable information about his father and mother. 'You mentioned before about a tin consortium near Gading. What was the name of that company?'

'Straits Mining Company, owned by a man named Loke Yew.'

'You mentioned a joint venture with a Singapore company as well.'

'Currently they are only mining, but they are building facilities to process the ore as well. The next step is to add manufacturing, to make the tin containers, which will be sent to Klang or Muar or Johor to be shipped to points beyond.'

'Do you know the name of the Singapore company?'

'I do not, but I know the family involved. It is the Low family. Rather prominent, I believe.'

'The Lows!' Hawksworth could not hide his surprise. 'Yes, very prominent indeed.' A Singapore Teochew family that operated a vast empire of licit and illicit trade spanning from Siam to Borneo, their tentacles reached far and wide. Hawksworth had crossed the Lows – and experienced the tentacles' squeeze – more than once. Seeing his look of dismay, Shaw continued, 'Yes, I gather that Loke Yew is small beer and is about to be absorbed by the Low family operation. The problem is that there are other consortiums who want that land as well, and sometimes the disputes turn bloody.'

'So I have been told. I do not wonder if the deceased Resident somehow got himself mixed up with such a business.' Hawksworth swished about the last of the tea in his cup and immediately wished a heavy butter biscuit were at hand. His stomach was already registering the effects of the strange brew. He stood and stretched, then walked over to a large map of the southern portion of the Malayan Peninsula. It looked relatively new compared to most others in the room. 'I have a proposal. I would like to follow in the Sergeant Major's footsteps, as far as his trail is known.'

'He travelled along the coast to Muar, then up river to Ayer Panas, where the Resident was found dead, near Mouth Ophir.'

'I shall follow that trail,' he ran his finger along the imaginary line on the map, 'then from Ayer Panas, I will make my way toward the other side of Ophir to Gading to get a closer look at the dispute between the tin consortiums,' Hawksworth contemplatively tapped his finger on the spot on the map marked *Gading*. 'Then I will return to Malacca before heading back to Singapore by ship.'

'How fortuitous!' Shaw exclaimed. 'You see, I was already assembling an overland expedition. Mr. Bosworth was planning to rendezvous with his surveying party at Ayer Panas. Given the perilous state of the territory, we are offering escort to business parties who enter the wilderness. They are scheduled to depart early tomorrow morning. Perhaps your parties can travel together?'

Hawksworth sighed grimly – he had been hoping to travel lightly and quickly with few men – but nodded his assent. 'If I am to search for the Sergeant Major and offer protection to Bosworth's party, then I will need men who know the terrain. I will need at least two weeks of supplies, including food and medicines.'

'Of course. Anything you need. I can offer two of our constables who are from the area, plus an additional three to four men, and rifles and ammunition as well.'

'Are rifles necessary?'

'It can be rough terrain. Even the Malays keep out as much as they can. It is the *orang asli* you will find there,' Shaw responded direly.

Hawksworth had seen depictions of the *orang asli* – their name translated to 'original people' – in illustrated magazines and he knew that they had been living on the peninsula when the first Malay settlers arrived centuries before, but like most people in Malaya he had never see one in person, for the *orang asli* lived elusively in remote forests. With dark skin and frizzy hair, they resembled the Aboriginal people of Australia. Little was known about them, although the locals believed they practiced a primitive magic that was especially powerful. The Malays tended to avoid contact with the forest folk, whom they regarded with a mixture of fear, reverence and repugnance.

'A further point,' Hawksworth said. 'I met a man on the ship named Suliman Alsagoff. Mrs. Lim told me he is mixed up in many businesses in town. Perhaps he knows something about these operations in Gading as well. I would like to speak with him again before I depart.'

Shaw's eyes widened then he guffawed loudly. 'Ha! I forgot to tell you. Alsagoff will be at dinner tonight. I was not aware you both have already met!'

*   *   *

Alsagoff arrived at the Stadthuys punctually. Stepping from his carriage, he puffed the last of his manila cigar then briefly studied the glowing ember at the tip before dropping it at his feet and squashing it with his heel. He tugged down the bottom of his velvet dinner jacket, smoothing the material. The deep burgundy plush contrasted nicely with the midnight black velvet of the *songkok* he wore on his head, and which he now touched, making sure the angle was appropriately rakish. The white silk shirt was fastened at the throat with a silver hoop and gold pin of a Chinese dragon chasing a pearl.

Approaching the front of the solid Dutch edifice, he nodded and smiled at the guards, uttering a clear and friendly *selamat malam*, 'good evening', as he sauntered past the massive front door of the house and into the foyer adjacent to the sitting room where Shaw, Hawksworth, Bosworth and Hatras were lounging with aperitifs.

'Mr. Alsagoff! Welcome!' Shaw sprung from his chair, hand forward.

Alsagoff pressed both his hands together before his chest in the traditional Malay greeting, then took Shaw's hand. 'My dear Resident Councillor, it is a pleasure to have been asked to dine with you, as always.'

'I believe you are already acquainted with Chief Detective Inspector Hawksworth.'

Alsagoff bowed slightly. 'Our esteemed visitor from Singapore. It is my pleasure to see you again.'

Hawksworth smiled slightly in acknowledgment, but remained seated, as did the others. 'The pleasure is mine. I was not aware when we met previously that I was speaking to the owner of the ship.'

Alsagoff cocked his head arrogantly. 'Indeed, The *Trunnion* is an older ship in our fleet ... or, more correctly, my brother's fleet.'

'I have heard of the Alsagoff Company in Singapore, but not of the operations in Malacca,' Hawksworth said as Suliman took a seat opposite him.

'Allow me to introduce Mr. George Bosworth, just up from Singapore,' Shaw continued with the introductions.

'Good evening, Mr. Bosworth,' Alsagoff nodded politely from his chair.

'And his partner, Mr. Muhammed Hatras, whom perhaps you know?'

'I know the family, of course, but am yet to have the pleasure of meeting Mr. Hatras in person.' Turning to the man, he smiled warmly and said, '*A'salamaleikum*'.

'*Wa'aliekum a'salam*,' Hatras replied.

Gesturing to the man's green scarf, Alsagoff said, 'I that see you have made the *hadj*.'

'Indeed, I have. I was fortunate enough to visit while en route to university in London, where I learned not only English but engineering as well.'

'And you have returned to Malacca?'

Hatras nodded, 'It is my privilege to have studied abroad. It is a greater privilege to return that knowledge to my home and people.'

'And what of yourself, Mr. Alsagoff?' Bosworth asked with a slight sneer. 'What is your privileged background?'

'I am the son of Syed Ahmed Alsagoff, grandson of Syed Abdul Rahman Alsagoff, from the Hadhramaut.'

'Then you are part of the Alsagoff family of Singapore?'

'Very much so. My grandfather first arrived in 1824, not long after the Dutch ceded Malacca to the British East India Company. Twenty-four years later, my father established the Alsagoff Company in Singapore.'

'Which is where the family fortune comes from,' Hatras said to the company.

'Has shipping always been the family business?' Bosworth

asked.

'We started with spices and sago, coffee and cocoa, pineapples. The Hadhramaut is the home of many spices, so it is "in our blood", as you say.' Puffed up, he continued in a rising voice, 'When the three *magi* visited the infant Christ in Bethlehem, the frankincense and myrrh they carried came from the Hadhramaut.'

'But in the modern age it is shipping that makes your fortune,' Hawksworth noted, while Bosworth frowned at Alsagoff's pomposity.

'That is true. Because of the complicated cross trade between Singapore, Malacca and Java, my grandfather purchased several ships to carry our goods. Over time, the fleet grew and we found ourselves in the shipping business.'

'That would include the lucrative trade in pilgrims bound for Mecca,' Hatras interjected. 'The Alsagoff Company acts as both booking agent and as one of the main transporters between Singapore and Jeddah.'

'Do not forget our operations out of Malacca and Penang as well.'

'I thought Alfred Holt and Company, the Blue Funnel Line, plied that route,' Bosworth said.

'So they do,' Alsagoff replied, 'and their fleet is our greatest competition. However, we are in discussions with Holt and Company to pool our resources and create a dedicated fleet for *hadj* pilgrims with ports of call in Batavia, Singapore, Bombay, Cairo and Casablanca. We also run shipping services in European ports and have an office in Marseille.'

'You are also interested in land around Malacca, are you not?' Bosworth asked sharply.

'My own company, The Solomon Company, is interested, yes ...'

'The consortium the Alsagoff brothers have put together is our fiercest competition,' Bosworth said curtly. 'They want the same land for the same reasons that we do. And with a fleet of ships at their disposal, they believe they can undercut us on price, as well.'

Attempting to lighten the mood, Shaw said brightly, 'Mr. Alsagoff is also our local historian. There is nothing about Malacca that he does not know.'

'Yesterday evening we were discussing the old myths of there being vast quantities of gold hidden around Mount Ophir,' Hawksworth stared intently at Alsagoff.

'This is the land of The Golden Chersonese,' the man replied with a curving smile that showed no teeth.

'My understanding is that it was Ptolemy who first identified Malaya as the seat of The Golden Chersonese. Correct, Mr. Alsagoff?' asked Shaw.

Alsagoff nodded sagely, raising his voice. 'In his *Geography*, Ptolemy describes a land he called The Golden Chersonese, and rather usefully he provided exact latitudes and longitudes for the rivers and towns. Unfortunately, his measurements were often incorrect. For example, he misplaced his prime meridian to such an extent that his longitudes reckoned eastward were about seven degrees less true. But nevertheless, Ptolemy was accurate enough in his inconsistency that later scholars were able to deduce the true location of The Golden Chersonese.'

'Did he mention any gold near Mount Ophir?' Hawksworth asked.

'His description of the terrain is unfortunately bland,' Alsagoff continued condescendingly, 'though he does mention a race of shaggy-haired dwarves with white faces that he calls *Saesadai* who dwell near a Mount Bepyron. Pure fantasy.'

Shaw piped in, 'So how did it come to be called Ophir? Besides the gold, I mean.'

'Besides the gold? What else is there?' Bosworth spoke loudly but no one seemed to take notice.

Alsagoff continued speaking directly to Shaw. 'It was the Portuguese who first called it Ophir. Perhaps they believed Ptolemy and thought they were sailing into a golden land – and with that they thought they would find King Solomon's mines.'

'The ground is known to be auriferous, though most mining operations produce little and frequently fail after a short time,' Hatras pointed out.

Alsagoff focused his attention intensely on Hawksworth. 'You will recall that in the Hebrew Bible it is related that Solomon receives his gold from Ophir by the navy of Hiram, the King of Tyre.' The man's supercilious tone was beginning to annoy the Chief Detective Inspector immensely.

'You named your own enterprise "Solomon and Company".' Bosworth observed.

'My name, Suliman, is the Arabic form of "Solomon". He also appears in the most holy Qur'an.'

Hatras interjected, 'The *djinn* taught Solomon the speech of the birds.'

'*Djinn*?' Shaw asked.

'Supernatural beings that served in Solomon's conquest of Sheba. Demon spirits, they dwell in the deepest desert and are not to be trusted by mortal men,' Alsagoff said.

'But no mention of Ophirian gold in your holy book, Mr. Hatras?' Bosworth asked, his gin-reddened eyes glittering in the candlelight.

'None.'

'It would not be likely, as the name is Greek, not Arabic,'

Alsagoff said placidly. 'From the word *ofis*, which means "snake". Perhaps a reference to an army of guardian snakes.'

'Which is precisely the kind of monster people would invent to frighten others away, for instance, from a secret ore mine,' Hawksworth said. 'So we come back to my original question. Is there gold in that mountain?'

The men fell silent. 'There is vast wealth everywhere,' Alsagoff finally said with a smirk, 'if one only knows where to look.'

* * *

The dinner played out predictably, with Alsagoff frequently lecturing on history while Bosworth became increasingly drunk and Hatras fell into a pious disapproving silence. Shaw did his best to referee the conversation, but in the end the task proved fruitless. By the time Hawksworth retired for the night, he was exhausted. He felt like he had passed the night with a quarrelsome family.

He was up before the sun the next day. He could hear the *fajr*, the dawn call to prayer, in the distance as he sipped his coffee. One of the pillars of Islam, five daily prayers were required of the devout, and each time the muezzin called *Allahu Akbar*, 'God is great', to the cardinal directions. Four times he called and then the men assembled in the mosque or in their homes to kneel on mats, their heads pointing in the direction of Mecca. Then began the discordant rhythmic chanting, of text being recited from the Qur'an.

Many years before, one of Hawksworth's Malay detectives had pointed out that while a Nazarene would have to master Hebrew, Greek and Aramaic in order to read the Bible – three languages not used by contemporary Christians – the Arabic of the Qur'an, though antique and difficult, was accessible to any speaker of the language. For believers, the detective had claimed, the Qur'an was a living connection to the words of the Prophet, whereas the Bible was merely a translation of collected stories.

The object of veneration in distant Arabia, the recitation of Arabic verses, the adoption of Arabic script and Arabic names: at times it seemed to Hawksworth less a religion than a ritualised language. It was a code of conduct, of requirements and prohibitions, which the locals followed closely before returning to the ancient superstitions of the village, the *kampong*, the ghouls and phantoms that had always ruled the land. Hawksworth knew that if he asked, they would tell him that there was one god and one prophet, but the *pontianaks* were real, too. In the smaller villages, the *imam* and the *bomoh*, the modern holy man and the practitioner of the old black magic, were often one and the same person.

The chanting stopped before the first light of day was streaking the sky. The men soon gathered in the foreyard of the Stadthuys where Shaw had assembled the expedition. He introduced Hawksworth to two fit, fierce-eyed constables, Razin Mustafa Kamal and Razif Ariff, who would act as the lead scouts on the expedition. They had just come from the mosque.

'Constable Ariff speaks the *orang asli* language,' Shaw offered.

Razif said, 'I also speak English, but Razin does not.'

Speaking to Razin in Malay, Hawksworth said with a smile, 'I speak your language, but my English is not very good.'

Both constables laughed at the joke. Shaw, who understood little of the local language, looked puzzled. Hawksworth explained with a straight face, 'I told him that I am afraid of the jungle at night.'

'Oh, I doubt that,' Shaw grinned. 'I know the word for "night" and I did not hear it!'

In addition to the constables, there were four other men who would act as guides and porters. Bosworth had an attendant as well, a Chinese youth with buckteeth and thin limbs. 'Does not speak a word of bloody English!' the portly man complained.

'I hope he can endure. I think once we are in the jungle, the journey will become rather arduous.'

'He will do, I am sure,' Bosworth said. 'He is no match for my boy in Singapore, but he knows his place, which is all I ask.' Tapping the side of his head, he continued, 'This is where all the knowledge is stored, you can be sure, Chief Detective Inspector. All the boy needs to do is ensure that it arrives safely at Ayer Panas.'

'This is your first trip to the place?'

'Ha! More than that, it is my first trip to the interior. On previous trips Mr. Hatras made the trek, but I wanted to see with my own eyes the land that we are yoking to our investors' cash.'

'Time to go, I think,' Shaw said. He pointed out the crate with the rifles, then handed a wrapped bundle and several paper boxes to Hawksworth. It was a Webley pistol and ammunition.

'You may wish to load it now, before you take the launch to the steamer,' Shaw said.

'Why?'

'The tidal shallows can be dangerous this time of day. The salt-water crocodiles gather at the mouth of the river to feed on the effluent that washes out from the town with the morning tide. If you fall into the water, you risk being eaten alive.'

Hawksworth was surprised. 'Does this happen often?'

'Twice a month at least. It is a terrible thing to see,' Shaw said, looking dour. Then brightly he added, unaware of the non-sequitur, 'Do have a safe journey. They are expecting to receive you at Muar.'

Hawksworth thanked the Acting Resident Councillor, then he and Bosworth made their way on the foot of the jetty where they watched the crates and bags being loaded onto the launch. The steamer that would take them to Muar was anchored in the calm water beyond the shallows. He scanned the tidal flats, looking for crocodiles, but knew that they would remain nearly invisible, mingled with the slime and mud just below the surface.

The heat of the day was already creeping up Hawksworth's back and across his chest. At heart he was an urban creature, most comfortable in a brick-and-mortar jungle of narrow alleys, and did not relish the thought of trekking through terrain he knew would be inhospitable, with the slow and large target of Mr. Bosworth huffing and puffing behind him. But he kept his jaw set as he wiped the sweat from his brow, pushing the negative anticipations aside. The disclosure of the unexpected, the hunt for the missing Sergeant Major, the bizarre enigma of the woman in Gading, the rumours of the *pontianak*, shifted uppermost in his thoughts, and his excitement grew.

Bosworth spoke, breaking the silence. 'What do you think of Alsagoff's talk of Solomon's mines and all that, Chief Detective Inspector? Do you think all the riches of the world will be found up on Ophir?'

'One moment, Mr. Bosworth,' Hawksworth replied. He unwrapped the Webley. It was holstered and belted. He fasted the belt around his waist then slipped the pistol slipped from the leather, broke the breach and began to feed rounds into the chambers. After snapping it shut, he held it close to his eye and looked down the barrel; then, satisfied with the sights, he holstered the heavy revolver. 'I think, Mr. Bosworth, that we are both men who know chronic rot when we hear it,' he said.

Bosworth merely grunted in reply.

They made their way along the narrow jetty, walking down the same path they had taken only two days prior. He paused to gaze back toward the ruined chapel on the hill, grey in the morning dimness. The memory of Domingas Franco's tombstone, her bones mouldering beneath the broken stone, the day of her death forever illegible, flashed in his mind. Then he helped the portly man into the launch, took one last look at the roofs of the sleepy town emerging in the fast light of an equatorial dawn, and stepped aboard.

CHAPTER IV

The Hot Springs

As THEY STEAMED SOUTH, Ophir loomed inland. The tide was low when they reached Muar, causing them to wait for the smaller launch to come and take them over the sandbar that girded the wide bay of the river. Once over the bar, the launch brought them to the town of Bandar Maharani, which sat on the bend of the bay. Several of the crocodiles for which the place was famous could be seen sunning themselves in the mud along the river; the biggest Hawksworth could see must have been over sixteen feet in length.

The palace of Prince Mat, the nephew of the Sultan of Johor, dominated the riverfront town, which until a decade previously had been little more than a fishing village. Houses of rough wooden slats on stilts ran along the edge of the shallow embankment, while unpaved streets lined with Chinese-style shophouses radiated outward from the royal estate.

They stayed the remainder of that day and night in a guesthouse on the estate. The Maharaja himself was not in residence, so they were restricted to the guest compound for the night while their supplies were loaded and the boat – a narrow flat-bottomed one that would take them upriver, moored at the end of a slip – was prepared for their journey next evening.

That night, the guesthouse was quiet and peaceful, the sound of palm fronds ruffling in the gentle breeze audible through its open windows. Hawksworth lay spread-eagled in his drawers under a soft linen sheet, on a thick and comfortable mattress, beneath a mosquito netting. He wrapped his knees around the starched white bolster. A feature of all tropical beds, the cushion was colloquially known as a 'Dutch wife', the bed companion of the lonely planter. He lay still hugging the faux woman, his thoughts centred on Ni, his Siamese common-law-wife, picturing her sleeping alone in their bedroom in far off Singapore. He imagined his fingertips running along the smooth skin of her dark shoulders, the soft flesh of her inner thighs, her moisture. The vision became vivid, and suddenly they were making love, he on top, panting with the thrusting effort in the tropical warmth. They had been this way right before he left for Malacca, and now in the intensity of his dream, her presence was as real as if she had been there in the room with him. He dreamed that he had already woken up in that room, and she was missing. Certain he was awake, he grew frantic searching for her in the strange estate, endlessly thwarted by shifting walls and self-locking doors.

He awoke suddenly, sweating and cramped, to the sound of industrious activity, yells of instruction as crates were being loaded onto the launch. It was morning. The tide was running against them, but in the evening it would reverse, and they would get an extra push upriver. Once clear of the bay, they would be propelled by a small steam engine – and strong boys with poles – up the spiralling curves of Muar River.

The bright day passed in the sort of tropical turpitude that travellers to the region found so beguiling. A late breakfast of *nasi goreng*, fried rice and egg, with coconut milk and fresh pineapple juice followed by a ramble around the estate gave way to an early lunch of roasted chicken, curried sweet potatoes, grilled prawns, pale ale, and a dessert of chilled mangosteens. An hour spent lounging in a sarong on the veranda in the warm salt air and watching the sunlight dappling the waves dissolved into a late afternoon nap in the rattan chair, which ended abruptly when he was roused for tea by the sound of a chick-chack, a chirping gecko, above his head. By suppertime, the launch was ready and they shoved off in the last light of the day.

They rounded the first wide oxbow in the river, the convex shore home to a *kampong* nestled amongst an areca palm plantation. The glow of yellow lamplights silhouetted the huts through the narrow palm trunks so that the village appeared like a miniature diorama, the jagged black crowns of the trees fine and distinct against the violet sky. Once past this village, they entered the jungle, and the vegetation closed in around them along with the darkness. They were in the wilderness now.

Hawksworth sat under a tarp awning spread over the aft deck, in the dim light of a lamp swinging from the crossbeam. Bosworth was there, too, a bottle of gin beside him. He had not shaved, so a field of grey stubble now offset his thinning hair. The detective had not seen the man all day, and now he knew why: Bosworth had been boozing. His face was more florid than ever, the eyes bulging as if about to burst. Yet incredibly the man remained upright and coherent, and spoke to Hawksworth heartily over the steady stroking of the little steam engine.

'Tell me, Chief Detective Inspector, what do you really think has become of your Sergeant Major?'

'Based on the information that Mr. Shaw provided, it is my belief that a tiger mauled the Negeri Sembilan Resident along with two Chinese surveyors. The Sergeant Major is now pursuing the man-eater. But this is conjecture based on a poverty of fact. I will not learn more until we arrive at Ayer Panas.'

Bosworth drank down a mouthful of gin. There was no glass; the man was swigging directly from the bottle. 'And why do you believe it was a tiger?'

'According to Shaw, children have recently been disappearing from local villages. The natives blame a *pontianak*, but the more reasonable explanation is a tiger.'

'A *pontianak*?'

'The ghost of a woman who died while pregnant. *Pontianaks* appear in flowing white robes, and have pale skin and long black hair. They can fly, like witches, and are undead, like vampires. They are said to roam the land at night, seeking out victims. Adult men are usually their first choice, but I have heard that children are also taken. During the day they dwell in banana trees, suspended upside down like bats.'

The fat man laughed into the still night. 'Supernatural twaddle.'

Hawksworth cast a steady eye on the corpulent face already steamed pink with heat and gin. 'It is of course easy to dismiss such tales in the snug comfort of your home, perhaps less so out here in the wild dark with the trees hanging overhead and the jungle nearly too dense for passage,' he said, gesturing to the blackness around them, to the branches and creepers scraping along the sides of the boat, to the lianas drooping overhead thick as telegraph cable. 'If you are alone in the jungle at night and hear a baby crying, be wary, for that means that the *pontianak* is near.'

'Bosh! You are only trying to unnerve me,' Bosworth guffawed loudly, though he was watching Hawksworth closely, as though he doubted his own confidence. Overhearing them, Razif stepped into the dim light, 'What the Chief Detective Inspector says is true. When I was a boy, our *kampong* not far from here was infested by a *pontianak* who killed my uncle. She sucked out his eyeballs and tore off his ... his manhood, so that we found him with holes in his head and with his private parts missing.'

'Perhaps that was the work of a tiger?' Bosworth offered, shifting in his seat uncomfortably and gulping more gin.

'Actually tigers tend to bite the neck in a leaping attack, and given the power of their jaws, often behead the victim as they struggle. No, missing eyes and genitals would indicate that the victim was dead a few days. Soft tissue is usually the first to be devoured by ants and maggots,' Hawksworth explained patiently, enjoying the look of abject terror on the man's face.

'Every night for a month we heard the unnatural cries of babies all around our *kampong*,' stated Razif matter-of-factly. 'Wives begged their men not to venture outside at night.'

'How does one kill one of these things?' Bosworth asked in a slightly quavering voice.

'You must plunge a nail into its neck.'

'Then she will become a beautiful woman and an obedient wife,' Razif added earnestly.

'What?' Bosworth bellowed, his expression relaxing. 'The wicked witch becomes a docile helpmate? Ha! The Brothers Grimm could not do better.'

A nightjar swooped in chasing a moth, a grey wing briefly fanning the lamp as it passed within inches of their faces, and Bosworth leapt from his seat, dropping his bottle and screaming out, then flailed about like an overgrown child before collapsing to the floor of the boat, covering his face with his hands.

Razif began to laugh uncontrollably while the others scrambled over the narrow craft to see what was causing the ruckus. Grinning despite himself, for it was funny to see the big man sprawled there like a helpless turtle, Hawksworth sent the laughing constables and porters away.

Bosworth sat upright, shaking, and reached – Hawksworth assumed – for his unbroken bottled rolling on the deck. Instead he pulled a small calibre revolver from his bush jacket and brandished it drunkenly at Hawksworth.

'Put the weapon away, Mr. Bosworth. There was no insult intended,' Hawksworth instructed in an even voice.

The man examined the pistol a moment, then tucked it back into his jacket pocket before scooping up the gin bottle, which was about to roll out of his reach. 'A nail in the neck to kill one of those things, you say? A bullet in the neck is all the same.' He tilted the bottle against his mouth, drinking deeply, then picked himself off the floor.

After sitting with Hawksworth in silence a while longer, Bosworth said goodnight and ducked down the hatch into the narrow berth below decks. 'It takes so little to make a man a believer,' Hawksworth whispered to himself after the man's bulk had disappeared from view.

He sat a while longer, feeling the rock of the boat every time one of the boys poled it forward. Further upriver the thick lianas hung so low he could no longer stand, as though they were arms reaching toward him, grasping at him in the dark. He recalled when he had first heard stories of *pontianaks* in his Penang childhood. A tough youth, he had dismissed them then as mere ghost stories to scare children, but as an adolescent, and even later on as an adult, every once in a while, he would dream of being lost and alone in the jungle, his clothes torn, running through the darkness away from something terrible. In his dream, the jungle was thick and dark like the one he was in now, with only the sound of a crying baby filling the air, as though a throat was hovering around him, and he was pursued not by a figure in white but by a woman whose body was red flames, burning and shrieking and running in the shadows just beyond the nearest trees. She drew nearer with each echoing cry until she was close enough to burn him, her face a hideous mask of fire. Then he would awaken with a scream, just as she threw herself at him.

*　*　*

The next morning they reached the headwaters of the river – or more accurately, they reached the point at which it had shallowed so that their boat could travel forward no further. The vessel was pulled several yards and deliberately beached and tied to a tree trunk, the vegetation enclosing it like the maw of a giant octopus.

After hacking about for more than an hour, Razin discovered the overgrown trail leading to Ayer Panas – it would later join the main overland route from Muar, though they were assured that the travelling conditions would not improve greatly thereon. The road had been cut into the wilderness when the government bungalow was built, but had since been allowed to degrade into rutted tracks in a rough parallel. It ran through several *kampongs*, and the Chief Detective Inspector intended to gather information as they moved. There was no need to announce their arrival: not only would the boat have been spotted on the river long before, but even a small column of men moving through the rugged terrain would draw attention to itself like a circus train.

*　*　*

The European men had tucked damp handkerchiefs into their cork-helmet topees so that the cloth dangled in the back, cooling their necks. Mango leaves were stuffed inside the helmets for padding and sweat absorption, otherwise the perspiration would pour down into their eyes, and the skin on their faces would chafe from the constant wiping. Bosworth, whom the Chief Detective Inspector had expected to whinge and whine, proved to be surprisingly resilient. His size made him slow, but he was steady, and seemed to be enjoying himself despite the gin that was sweating through his pores, giving him an acrid odour akin to rotting citrus.

Two peregrine falcons spun wide gyres high overhead. The men were making their way through an abandoned tapioca plantation, the fibrous green stalks having grown wild, forcing them to move disconcertedly through a crowded field of plants as tall as themselves. Interspersed with the tapioca were coffee shrubs and pepper vines; the porter who doubled as cook exclaimed what fine specimens they were and excitedly plucked a handful of fresh green pepper corn for later use.

Once past the overgrown rows they entered a field of tall *lallang* grass rippling in the breeze. In the distance was a line of gutta-percha trees, also gone wild. Heavily wooded foothills lined the horizon, quiet and dark: their destination lay there. The falcons wheeled overhead. The land was quiet except for the hypnotising drone of cicadas. It was as though they had entered a pastoral world where civilisation had come then gone, leaving the land to revert to nature.

The peaceful illusion did not last long. Once they pushed passed the trees the jungle closed in around them and the trail sloped gently upward. They passed a small fishing hamlet, little more than two or three *attap* huts perched over the stream that would widen into the Muar River, and saw the first people they had come across outside of Bandar Maharani. Two Malay men were sitting on the porch of a raised hut, fitting an axe head onto a rough-hewn handle. They looked up with unfriendly faces: many strangers went down the uneven road, not all of them polite. Razif greeted them, asking for information, and after a brief exchange, the men waved him off and returned to their task.

Ayer Panas lay not far ahead, Razif explained, but at the rate they were going it would be another day until they reached the outpost. He had also learned that the road between the Chinese camp at Labis and Ayer Panas had been washed out a week ago. They would have to hack their way through the path they were currently following, which it turned out was an older disused road and not the government road as they had originally thought. The Sergeant Major had not passed this way, Razif informed them, and the fishermen had heard nothing about a *pontianak* hereabouts. The men did tell him that there was a *lallang* field further up where they could camp for the night. All they had to do was follow the stream.

The road became worse as they progressed until it was barely more than a rough track fit for bullock carts. Gigantic palm fronds lay across the road, forcing the men into a single file line, the vegetation creeping in on either side. The day's light was fading fast.

'Are you sure this is the direction the fishermen gave us? Perhaps they are having a bit of sport,' Hawksworth said.

'This is the only trail, so it must be this way. Hopefully we will reach before dark,' Razif replied. 'Before the *pontianak* comes,' he said under his breath, eyeing Bosworth, trying to hide his grin.

Bosworth caught the dreaded word and was about to retort when the jungle around them suddenly shifted. Something big was moving in the foliage, staying just behind the scrim of dark green. It crashed against the trunk of a tall tree, causing leaves to cascade down on the men; then all was menacingly still. The sensation of being watched was unmistakable.

Hawksworth slipped the Webley from its holster. 'Crouch down, Mr. Bosworth. We might be seeing some action.'

'What is it?' the big man whispered fearfully, 'A tiger?' Too corpulent to crouch, he simply sat down heavily on the muddy trail, slipping the revolver from his pocket to his hand. His Chinese servant sat beside him, his face fearful. Not speaking any English or Malay, he had no clue why his boss was sitting in the dirt and looking about nervously at the bushes while fumbling with the small pistol.

'Razif, Razin, your rifles,' Hawksworth hissed, though he had no need as both constables had already slung their weapons off their shoulders.

Razin crept forward warily, his eyes steadily searching the dim jungle, the barrel of his carbine preceding him. Razif raised his carbine to his shoulder, covering the other. Hawksworth kept the Webley tight in his fist. It was now almost completely dark, but no one dared move to strike a match.

There was a snort from beyond the foliage. Razin paused with his carbine cocked, then used his left hand to push aside a branch, his finger on the trigger.

A mass burst through darkness and vegetation, snapping the branch back and flinging Razin through the air. His rifle fired as he flew, then all hell broke loose.

The thing towered above them, huge curved horns glowing above a massive head, its white cloven hooves pawing at the earth. It snorted loudly, looking as though it were going to charge into them. Hawksworth fired twice at the creature, and it bellowed loudly – one of his shots must have hit – then the air was filled with incoherent shouts and explosions. He was on the verge of firing again when he became aware that the porter behind him was yelling '*Seladang! Seladang!*'

73

The beast groaned grievously then shoved its mass into the undergrowth, which parted before it like land before a plough. How many shots it had absorbed was anyone's guess, but it moved slowly as if mortally wounded.

Hawksworth realised that Bosworth, seated in the mud at his feet, was still pulling the trigger of the empty gun, breathlessly moaning over and over, '*pontianak, pontianak, pontianak*'.

The tall man leaned down and plucked the weapon from the man's pudgy hand. 'Steady, Mr. Bosworth, the danger has passed.' He held out his arm and with a great deal of effort hoisted the fat man up. The Chinese boy scrambled to his feet, tears streaming down his face.

'It was only a gaur, a type of wild ox,' Hawksworth explained. 'A small one, too. Probably an adolescent. There is nothing to fear. They are incredibly large but eat only plants.' The big man stood trembling, nodding as though he comprehended.

Razin stumbled up. He had taken a bad knock from the gaur and was shaken but otherwise unharmed. Razif helped to brush the dirt and leaves off his mate. Luckily he had landed on a soft patch of ground, for only inches away from his head the sharp point of a rock protruded and would have smashed his skull if he had fallen on it. Seeing this, he muttered a quick prayer of gratitude.

'We had better camp near here tonight,' Hawksworth announced, 'I think we have had enough for one day. Ayer Panas cannot be more than half a day further on.' He returned the empty gun to Bosworth, whose hand shook as he took it. 'You had better have a gin before dinner, Mr. Bosworth,' he said, and gave the man a wry smile.

* * *

The government bungalow at Ayer Panas was part of a system of purpose-built structures scattered across Malaya. When not used by touring officials and circuit judges they were rented to holidaymakers and hunting parties. Shaw had told him that the rates were $1 per day or $12.50 per month for Ayer Panas, slightly less than the commodious government bungalow at Changi Beach in Singapore Hawksworth had once visited.

The bungalow at Ayer Panas was not especially luxurious, and the location was remote even when the roads were in top condition, and no provisions were provided, but after the long journey it looked like paradise to the men.

The hot springs from which the location took its name bubbled into a bathing pool a short walk away. Durian and jackfruit trees shaded a small garden patch, while red-trunked McArthur palms lined the perimeter. The front veranda offered a view from the foothills across a panoramic patchwork of green and gold paddy fields, the River Muar meandering through like a silver thread. Mount Ophir was visible only thirty miles distant, over what deceptively appeared to be gentle terrain. It hardly seemed the type of place to witness a gruesome murder, but Hawksworth had been familiar with violent death long enough to know that it came to all places eventually.

The bungalow was empty when they arrived except for two Malay constables, lounging in sarongs by the front door so only their police *kepi* hats identified them. An Indian groundskeeper, originally from Kerala, white-haired and bent double, lived in an adjoining hut. To judge by the state of the place, he mostly spent his waking hours tending the garden and chewing betel nuts.

After taking the refreshment they had carried through the jungle, Bosworth went to rest while Hawksworth spoke to the constables stationed there. They were young, only in their early twenties, and told him that they were lifelong friends from a village near Malacca. At times they seemed to function as one person, with one completing the sentence of the other; or they would lapse into silence simultaneously, as though they could communicate their thoughts without speaking. They knew about the murder, of course, but could offer no information because they were replacements for the previous constables, the ones who had been on duty when the Resident was killed.

'And where are those constables now?' Hawksworth asked.

They had no idea, they said. The previous constables had not been seen in the district since the attack. All they really knew, which they only explained after further prodding, was that the previous constables had not been at the bungalow when the attack took place. That night the Resident had been left alone with the elderly groundskeeper. They themselves had arrived with the Sergeant Major's expedition and had not left since. There had been no other visitors, they said.

Sensing that they were holding something back, Hawksworth pressed further. There was a rumour, they reluctantly admitted, that the previous men were either threatened or paid to leave, maybe both. They then asked to be excused for *salat*, time for prayer. He watched them perform the ritual, amazed at their synchronicity: it looked like one man beside a mirror.

The groundskeeper, by contrast, seemed eager to talk, for he must have been lonely, but Hawksworth quickly recognised that the man suffered from slight dementia ... Or perhaps he had always been somewhat slow. He could not remember exact times and days, or even years. How long had he been at Ayer Panas? Since Ferrier was Resident Councillor in Malacca, he said, but how long ago that was, the groundskeeper could not say.

He did remember the murder of the Resident very clearly,

however. It was no tiger, he said. He had not seen a tiger hereabouts for years. The Resident was hacked to pieces by *parangs*, traditional machetes. He saw the attack? No, he said, rocking slightly from side to side, muttering that he had neither heard nor seen anything. But he was the one who found the body, and he was the one who walked to the neighbouring village to alert the residents to send a boy to Muar with the message. The constables had disappeared the night of the attack. But the Resident was not attacked by a tiger, he was killed by men, of this the groundskeeper was adamant.

As they spoke, Hawksworth watched a mason wasp construct its mud nest. It flew in straight lines and sharp angles, working with its mandibles and front legs to manipulate the construction, suspended upside down. Slowly a tiny wattle and daub dome the size of a grape became visible, stuck to the roof beam. Inside the dome, the wasp would place paralyzed grubs it had plucked from the ground. When the wasp larvae hatched, the wriggling grubs would provide nourishment until the larvae pupated and broke free of the nest; then the cycle could continue.

He asked about the riot and the death of the Chinese surveyors.

The groundskeeper simply shrugged. That was in the camp at Labis, he said with disdain. He knew nothing about what the Chinese got up to there, except that it surely was disreputable.

* * *

He and Razif walked alone to Labis. The road had been washed out by a mudslide but subsequent rains had beaten down the debris, so that the two men could walk over it, though no wheeled conveyance could pass.

Much as Hawksworth suspected, Labis was little more than a makeshift village constructed by itinerant miners. However, it was much larger than he had anticipated. Based on descriptions, he had expected several hundred men, but there were more than a thousand in the camp. He could see that it was a self-organising municipality, for there were no water or sewerage systems but improvised latrines and ditches that nonetheless appeared to fulfil the necessary function of separating fresh from waste water.

Three main roads, little more than stamped mud, radiated from a central hub, and from those roads spread a branching network of footpaths that lead into the housing, the tarps and tents and shacks made of scavenged material. Closer to the centre junction were more solidly built structures, including a stable for Sumatra ponies and a wagon repair shop. The most permanent structures overlooked the junction, including a hectic carrefour, an open-air market for vegetables and meat and spices, pungent of rotten foodstuffs tramped into the dirt underfoot and infested with countless flies and daylight rats. Encircling the market were opium sheds and gambling dens. The only brick structure housed a two-story brothel that offered a handful of what must have been severely overworked Chinese women, for the females were outnumbered more than a hundred to one. Off to the side of the brothel was a little temple, erected crookedly. The heavy smell of joss was a relief from the stench of the carrefour.

He heard mostly Cantonese and Hokkien. The men looked especially low rate: drifters and dead enders breaking their backs in the tin mining operations that were slowly displacing the paddy fields in the neighbouring valleys.

There were no constables or other evidence of government, either British or native, in sight. *Kongsi* were evidently running the vice operations and taking protection money from the provision and food stalls. Hawksworth realised that, for all intents and purposes, he might as well be standing in a miners' shantytown in Fujian province in the motherland.

There was no one in charge to ask about the deaths of the surveyors, though to judge by the anarchistic camp, it seemed very likely that the same thing could happen again and swiftly, only this time to the Chief Detective Inspector and the constable. From the moment they stepped into the camp, a thousand eyes had peered at them from stony faces, watching in wary silence. Beside him a man was sharpening a long-bladed knife on a wet-stone; nearby, another was cutting a bamboo pole for a fence; yet another was hammering a wooden peg into a wagon wheel. He knew that in a heartbeat all of these rudimentary tools could become deadly weapons; despite their badges and guns, one false step and the police would quickly be overcome by a mob. Hawksworth realised that any reports of a riot happening were incorrect: in a lawless place like Labis, riot was the norm. The surveyors had probably wandered in and quickly made themselves unwelcome, and were then just as quickly dispatched. In any case, except as a place to recruit brigands and murderers, he could see no connection between this pit of iniquity and the death of the Resident. It was coincidence, he realised, that the three killings, the two surveyors and the Resident, had occurred at roughly the same time.

'There is no point in asking questions,' he said abstractly to Razif. 'Any provocations, and we will wind up like the surveyors. And then the government will send the Army to clear the place, resulting only in more pointless slaughter.'

After the brief inspection, he and Razif made a hasty retreat from the camp, glad to be going on their own legs and not in wooden boxes.

* * *

It was late afternoon when they made it back to Ayer Panas.
Bosworth was nowhere to be seen. Before Hawksworth could
inquire what had become of him, he heard shouts from higher up
the hill and thought the worst. A mad dash up an overgrown path
led him to the pool where the hot springs bubbled. Bosworth,
dressed only in a long night shirt, was immersed in the steaming
water, waving his arms and sloshing about like a child, while his
Chinese servant stood by, quietly watching with a bewildered
look on his face that suggested he found the antics of the white
man incomprehensible.

'Chief Detective Inspector!' Bosworth yelled, waving from
the pool. 'Come and join me. The water is invigorating!'

'Mr. Bosworth, what in the world are you doing?'

'I am washing my sins away,' he said gleefully, then waddled
to the edge of the pool where Hawksworth stood. 'Truth be told,
I have finished my supply of gin and the hot mineral water is
helping to keep the fits away. If it were not for this spring, I would
be in dire straits.' He fell back into the pool, then floating and
flapping like a turtle, propelled himself back into the water. 'Do
change and join me.'

'No, thank you. It looks refreshing, but I am going to see
about having our evening meal prepared.' He cast a glance at
the thick vegetation that surrounded the pool, ferns and mosses
backed by thick foliage. It was the type of undergrowth that
attracted pythons. 'Do not stay here past dark, Mr. Bosworth. I
will send someone for you when the meal is ready.'

Bosworth simply smiled then ducked so he was completely
submerged in the water.

Hawksworth sighed then turned to leave. 'Do watch him. I

do not need any more dead Englishmen in remote outposts,' he spoke in Malay to the Chinese boy, who, not comprehending the language, merely stared at him in utter confusion.

* * *

The surveying team was expected to arrive shortly from the direction of Johor, and given the grisly fate of the Resident of Negeri Sembilan, Hawksworth did not want to leave the fat man alone at the bungalow with only the two boyish Malay constables, a senile Indian groundskeeper, and a befuddled Chinese servant. They waited three more days for the surveying team, then another two to be sure that everything was sorted: that the provisions would last, that the ammunition was dry, that the team knew the route. Meanwhile, the Chief Detective Inspector thought grimly, Sergeant Major Walker was slipping further and further into the jungle.

The morning Hawksworth's party departed Ayer Panas, Bosworth was already splashing around in the mineral water. The detective left specific instructions with the young constables to care for him – mostly to get him out of the pool before either a snake found him or he parboiled himself.

'In which direction had the Sergeant Major's party headed?' the Chief Detective Inspector asked the groundskeeper, while he shouldered his heavy pack and strapped the Webley to his thigh. He believed that he already knew the answer, but wanted to be sure.

With a finger crooked painfully from arthritis, the groundskeeper pointed solemnly toward Mount Ophir, towering in the distance.

CHAPTER V

Ophir

THEY PUSHED THROUGH THE JUNGLE following a network of trails, some of which were no bigger than the shoulder width of a single man, while others were practically roads, wind bands of dirt cut through the vegetation. One was frequently used by pack elephants, or had been until recently, and proved particularly rough going. An elephant tends to place its massive feet in the tread of the elephant that goes before it, with the result that holes more than a foot in diameter are pounded into the roadway in an unevenly spaced quincunx pattern. The holes inevitably fill with rainwater, which quickly becomes fetid, turning the trail into a swamp of pitfalls. After several miles of trudging through knee-deep green muck as thick as milk, the expedition rested – and began removing the leeches, plucking them off and flicking them into the foliage. They were small creatures, with iridescent yellow skins that swelled quickly with the intake of fresh blood. Hawksworth found that it did not hurt when they bit, and after they had their fill they dropped off, so that often the only way to know about the encounter was to discover that his clothes were saturated with blood. The wounds itched fiercely, reopening easily if the men scratched, which seemed unavoidable. In future, he declared, they would avoid elephant trails.

They were skirting around Ophir, marching through a

forest of rhododendron bushes, when they came across a Malay *kampong* where they could stop for refreshment. It was a very poor village, for there was no industry halfway up the mountain – no plantations or rivers or mines. Nonetheless, it was far from squalid. The central area was neatly swept, hard packed dirt. The *attap* thatch huts, each one raised on *nebong* wood posts about the height of a man, had sturdy ladders to ascend into them. Inside of several, Hawksworth could hear the clack of a handloom being worked: they made their own sarongs.

A group of children, all very young and almost nude, were playing a game called *ragga,* in which a wicker ball was passed around without the use of one's hands. Knees, feet, elbows, shoulders, heads, and any other body part could be used, which meant that the fast-paced game resulted in wild jerky movements; if it were not for the laughter of the children it would look like an outbreak of Saint Vitus' dance. That several of the otherwise sweet faces were badly scarred from smallpox only contributed to this vision of calamity.

Young mothers wearing sarongs woven in simple patterns, only in their late teens but already aged into full-grown women from multiple childbirths, formed a protective circle around the gyrating children. When they saw the column of men headed by an *orang putih*, a white man, entering the village, they quickly snatched up the children, who started shrieking because their game was interrupted, and scrambled into their huts. In seconds, the central area was empty, and the *kampong* looked deserted.

'Not a typical Malay welcome,' Hawksworth said, recognising that something was amiss. It was then that he noticed the images daubed in blood-coloured mud on the sides of the huts. The doorways were marked with ornate patterns of curving lines resembling crossed scimitars. He had never seen anything like it before. Razif noticed them too and shuddered.

'What are they?' Hawksworth asked.

'Spells,' the darker man replied, eyeing the images carefully, 'to protect the villagers from evil spirits. Some are verses from the Qur'an, some are incantations in the local dialect, while others are just pictures. Look at that one,' he pointed to the nearest hut. There was a crude image of figure in a long flowing gown, arms outspread. The painter had taken the time to illustrate long sharp teeth in the face, whereas the eyes were only thumbprint circles. Human hair was smeared and stuck in the mud along the top of the skull, and a real arrow had been jammed into the wall where the creature's heart would be.

'A warning,' Hawksworth said.

'They must be terrified of the thing,' Razif said, his voice low. 'The *pontianak* must visit here often.'

The men walked further, then stopped at the centre of the village. Razin called out for the *penghulu*, or chief. Hawksworth spotted movement by a little thatched hut with a rusty metal crescent stuck atop it – the only metal visible in the *kampong* – that served as a *musholla*, a prayer hall. From behind this structure emerged a young man; he approached them cautiously. Wiry and strong, with only a sarong around his waist, he looked no more than thirteen or fourteen years old – already a man in the *kampong*, though with the smooth face of a boy.

The young man did not make eye contact with Hawksworth, though his curiosity that bordered on awe was obvious. Hawksworth guessed that he was probably the first white man the lad had ever seen. He turned out to be the *penghulu*'s son. The chief was in the bush with a hunting party – they were going for boar, he explained, *hambat babi*, literally a pig drive. Being devout they would not eat what they captured: they sold the meat to a Chinese who in turn sold it in a market, such as the carrefour Hawksworth had seen in Labis. Such was the economy of the hinterlands.

Razin spoke with him gently, demonstrating respect for the son of the village leader. First they needed refreshment, he explained, and second, any information the villagers had about Sergeant Walker and his missing expedition. The boy knew nothing about a troop of men, nor had he heard anything from nearby villages, but perhaps his father would know more. He should return before nightfall. In the meantime, he said, they could rest in the shade near the *keramat,* and gestured to a mound with short standing stones planted on either end beneath a large Flame of the Forest tree.

'Who is buried in the *keramat*?' Hawksworth asked in Malay. The boy nearly jumped out of his skin at hearing the white man speak his language, albeit strangely. Grinning nervously, he explained that the venerated man was the founder of the village. His name, the boy said, was known as Mohammed Aziz. He was born in Mecca and knew the Prophet, peace be upon him, the boy said breathlessly in mangled Arabic, and he was a powerful *bomoh* who first brought the word of God to the region. The *keramat* had been there for two thousand years or more, since the time when the first Malay people came from Sumatra. What is more, Aziz had fought the Portuguese, and the Dutch, to keep them away from the village. The boy spoke proudly, then his face darkened and he muttered that now Aziz was fighting to protect them from a spirit of the forest who was causing much trouble. When pressed, however, the boy merely trembled and stared at the ground. To even speak aloud of such evil was bad luck, he said in a whisper, for it could invoke the angry spirit.

After thanking the boy and assuring him that they were there to help protect the village, too, they lounged in the shade of the Flame of the Forest tree, a respectable distance from the mounded *keramat*. While they waited, several women, no longer fearful though still timid, demurely brought fresh fruit and ragged strips of chicken meat grilled on bamboo skewers for the men. The meat was a great sacrifice for such a poverty-stricken *kampong*, and a mark of high respect for the visitors. Hawksworth saw that some of the women had filed and blackened teeth, something he had not seen since his younger days, a practice usually reserved for the more affluent girls of a village, wherein their teeth were filed flat then rendered black with lime acid before their wedding night. It was considered a mark of beauty – and it hid the inevitable decay brought on from chewing betel nut from their early teenage years. The wealthy Malay girls in Singapore had stopped this practice, he knew; perhaps they felt that it did not accord with the modernity around them.

He was about to doze in the afternoon heat when a cry went up: the hunting party had returned, and they were successful. Half a dozen men marched through the village square with a medium-sized boar trussed and swinging upside-down from a pole. Though there was a wide and raw gash in his side, the poor beast was still alive, his thick bristles matted with blood, drool dribbling from around his tusks, snot pouring from his nostrils. His thick neck muscles were still strong, his eyes bright as if filled with anger and fear; had he escaped, he might well have survived the wound that brought him down.

As is the way of such things, the hunting party was aware of the presence of the visitors long before they returned to the village. Someone must have slipped into the forest to tell them. The chief saluted the troop of strangers who was now standing to watch the parade of the pig, then, once the animal was secure, he approached Razin, speaking in the local dialect. Although perhaps only fifteen years older than the son who had greeted them, the father looked like an old man, with wrinkled skin on his face, grey streaks in his hair. One arm was bent wrong – a broken bone that had mended poorly. Nonetheless, his hunting sarong was new and he held himself before the strangers with all the dignity of his office. They treated him with the deferential respect he commanded.

They were welcome to stay the night, he said. The expedition of white men they were asking about had not come into the village, but did pass not far from them, further up the side of the mountain. That was only several days, perhaps a week, before. They were moving in dense jungle, evidently tracking something.

'Is it a tiger?'

Like his son, the chief's surprise when the white man spoke his language was evident in his shocked expression. No, he said, he had not seen a tiger in a long while. But these were strange times, with many strangers roaming the hills.

'Strangers?' Hawksworth asked, thinking of the surveying teams who must frequently pass through the territory.

'And spirits. There is an especially evil *pontianak* who has been haunting the village. She takes our children. We think she might be the spirit of a witch,' he said in a low voice, so the evil presence would not hear him.

'How many children? And how old?' Hawksworth asked.

'Four children have gone missing so far from our village,' the chief spoke distantly to hide his fear, 'all between the ages of nine and twelve.'

'Both boys and girls?'

The chief nodded affirmatively. 'Now we keep our children inside after sunset, and do not allow them out no matter how urgently they need to go.'

'How long has this been going on?'

'The first child disappeared about one year ago.'

'Does the *pontianak* steal children from other *kampongs*?'

'It does,' he said, then listed the names of the villages, none of which the Chief Detective Inspector of Singapore had ever heard of. Hawksworth turned to Razif for explanation: 'That is most of the villages in the area of Mount Ophir, both in Johor and Malacca and also in Tampin district.'

'Tampin is now part of the Negeri Sembilan confederacy, where the dead Resident was based,' Hawksworth spoke aloud. 'That might explain why he was in Ayer Panas. Perhaps he was investigating the disappearance of village children.' Everyone was listening to him, but no one said anything in return. They were simply awaiting instructions. He suddenly realised how much he had grown used to having his adjutant in Singapore, Detective Inspector Rizby, with his fox-like face and agile mind, at his side. Here, he had no one with whom to share his suspicions and ideas.

He thanked the chief and assured him they would help keep the villages safe from the *pontianak,* then asked where they could make camp out of the way of the *kampong*. The chief in turn thanked him and took them to a clearing nearby. All through the evening before the sun set, the women from the village came with cooked and steaming delicacies presented on platters of woven rattan. He chewed silently, watching his men eating and flirting with the village girls, knowing that tomorrow they would trek through some of the worst terrain in southern Malaya.

* * *

They were moving again by dawn. Not far beyond the *kampong*, through a wall of bamboo, was the darkest, densest jungle he had ever seen. The chief had warned them that the ground was thick with snakes – they villagers avoided the area completely – but had also said that it was the shortest route to the direction the Sergeant Major's team had gone. Otherwise they would have to trek for two days around an impassable ravine to get on his track.

There was no trail in the jungle. Instead they followed a tunnel created by overhanging creepers and lianas that had become interwoven above them, like the fan-vaulted ceiling of a cathedral. It was slow going in the murky light, the men stepping carefully. The footing was treacherous, with vines as thick as a man's arm twisting around rocks and fin-like roots of trees. Twice Hawksworth nearly stepped on a python that lay still, indistinguishable from the roots and vines. There were insects, too. A black beetle as big as an open palm, with long sharp horns, buzzed past his ear on giant yellow wings and landed on Razif's pack right before him. His sangfroid fled: he yelped loudly, much to the amusement of the others. One of the porters carefully caught the vile looking thing, making it clear that he intended to roast and eat it.

All around them, inch-long iridescent leeches stood erect on the ends of the moist leaves, their heads waving back and forth as they searched for food, and it was impossible not to experience several attacks at once from these the stalk-like worms while moving through the dense foliage.

They pressed on, the sweat pouring down their backs, the blood pooling in their boots. Mercifully they were shaded from the full light of the tropical sun by the nearly impenetrable canopy, but that same overhead vegetation also trapped the heat, so that they were marching through a hothouse. The fresh water ran out by mid-day, the morale flagging soon after. Hawksworth's boots were chafing his ankles until they bled, and just as he was beginning to despair the canopy above them began to open.

Ahead of them they could see blue sky, open space. Never before had he been so happy to see the steely sunshine. Exhausted, they made camp not far beyond the edge of the dark jungle. There would be no more evidence of human hands on the land, he knew, no more roads, no abandoned plantations, no cheerful *kampong* women with skewers of grilled chicken. They had broken through the swamp into a land primeval. They were in far Ophir.

* * *

The next morning, they were on the march again, only in more hospitable terrain. Large forests of hardwood trees widely spaced on even ground made travelling easier. A brilliantly plumaged kingfisher flitted from branch to branch overhead, following the troop like a mascot: a good omen. Still, they were becoming exhausted in what was increasingly looking like a pointless journey. He could hear his men muttering under their breath. Himself, he was looking forward to a new pair of boots: that was the kernel of optimism that propelled him forward.

All at once they became aware that the insect noises had ceased. The deep forest had fallen silent. At the head of the line, Razin stopped abruptly, bringing them all to a standstill. They were in a natural declivity, a shallow basin fringed above by the high hardwood trees and towering Matonia ferns. Thick bushes completely obstructed their view beyond a few feet. It was the perfect place to ambush a troop of men from the higher ground.

Without taking their eyes off the wall of green, Razin and Razif were silently slipping their rifles from their shoulders; Hawksworth already had the Webley in his hand, thumb on the hammer.

From the foliage a bronze face emerged, glaring at them. Then appeared the head and the nearly nude body of a small dark-skinned man; he held an arrow strung to a bow, pulled and aimed ready at Razif's face. Soon there followed half a dozen more men, all of them dark and with wildly curled hair sprouting from their heads, some armed with spears, some with rusted cutlasses, and at least one with a flintlock rifle. Two had blowguns. They were all nearly naked except for loincloths, and one man, who held no weapon, was wearing a necklace made from monkey bones strung together and spaced by sharp teeth, the top of a monkey skull dangling over his heart.

'*Orang asli*!' Razin rasped.

Hawksworth could sense that the porters were scared stiff. Even his usually courageous Malay constables looked as if they had stumbled into a waking nightmare. He found himself detached from his own fear – aware of his pounding heart and shallow breathing – while he gazed in fascination at the menacing apparitions all around them.

The man with the monkey-skull necklace spoke rapidly, pointing at Hawksworth. It was a fricative language that sounded like a series of clucks and clicks that in no way resembled Malay, or any other language Hawksworth had ever heard.

'Razif, translate,' Hawksworth said, his pistol held steady in his hand, though he had not cocked, or aimed it.

'He says that foreign devils are forbidden entry to this land. He wants to know why so many foreign men keep coming here to do evil.'

'Keep coming? Who else has been here?'

The man spoke further, cutting him off. Again Razif translated, 'He says that the foreign devil is to come with him to their village, and the rest of us must go back the way we came.'

Hawksworth kept an eye on the headman wearing the monkey skull while also watching the hands of his men, who kept the arrows strung in the bows. Already their wrists were weakening, the pulled bowstrings beginning to quiver: an accidental shot and they would have a battle on their hands.

'Tell them that we are not here to cause harm but are merely passing through. Ask them their kind permission to trespass.'

As the words were translated, the porters remained tensed, as though about to drop their loads and make a run for it through the undergrowth.

'He says that no foreign men will ever again be allowed into their forest, sir.'

'Why?'

A quick exchange followed, then the translation, 'He says that foreign men come and steal their children.'

'What kind of "foreign" men? Ask him to describe them.'

He described not white men but Chinese. 'He says they come at night and make sounds like a *pontianak* but they have seen them, and they are men, not spirits.'

Hawksworth's mind raced. So the *pontianak* was merely a ruse. Flesh and blood men were using it like supernatural camouflage in order to steal children. 'Tell him that we are here to stop these men. We are here to help him.'

The headman stared into his eyes, searching there for a measure to judge his true worth. Hawksworth shifted uncomfortably, assessing the outcome if things went wrong, but he held his gaze firmly, while quickly calculating how many of the attackers he could aim and fire at before half-a-dozen arrows pierced his throat. Finally the headman uttered something that sounded like an oath, then turned his gaze to Razif and spoke. Hawksworth could sense the tension relaxing in the *orang asli*.

After an exchange, Razif breathed a sigh of relief then translated, 'He says that he sees that you are a truthful man and agrees to allow us to continue. He also said that they have seen a troop of men who are now camped not more than a half day's march away. They have a white man as leader.' Razif then added, 'It might be the Sergeant Major.'

'Will he take us to these men?'

'He agrees to lead us to the camp, but they will not leave the forest. Once we know the way, they will return to their home.'

Hawksworth thanked the *orang asli* headman, gesturing that they were ready to follow him. He issued brief commands to his men, who seemed to melt back into the foliage. Hawksworth had no doubt that these men would shadow them, unseen and unheard, as they moved through the jungle.

The headman and two of his men led them further through the primitive vegetation. Hawksworth's men hacked with their machetes but the *orang asli* seemed merely to glide through without recourse to tools or blades.

After a long day of straining to keep up with their guides, they emerged on a rocky point overlooking a granite field strewn with boulders. '*Padang-batu*, the stone field,' Razin said. 'A legendary place. Few people ever see it.' The field extended more or less level along the side of the mountain as far the eye could travel. There was an expanse of granite rock, in places covered with long stemmed canary grass and mounds of rhododendrons and mimosa, while the ground was split by gigantic fissures through which slippery tropical vegetation, ferns and mosses and carnivorous pitcher plants the size of a man's head, grew in abundance. It was an ideal place to set up camp: the open ground was easy to defend while the moist fissures made natural mantraps.

In the distance he could see a campsite, a thin wisp of smoke from a cooking fire rising towards the pale sky. Through the distorted glass of a small brass telescope, Hawksworth could discern the strong shape of the Sergeant Major, who appeared seated on a rock, cleaning his rifle. Lowering his glass, the tall man turned to thank the *orang asli*, but they were already gone. 'Did anyone see them go?' The Malay crew were just as surprised as Hawksworth. The headman and guides had noiselessly vanished, though no doubt they still kept watch.

He made no attempt to hide the troop as they crossed the stone field: he wanted the Sergeant Major to see them coming – to surprise him could prove fatal. They walked in a zigzag line to avoid falling into the fissures, pushing away the masses of purple and orange rhododendron flowers that occasionally blocked their way. Hawksworth pushed through a particularly heavy mass of rhododendron into a clearing only to find himself looking down the dark snout of Walker's Martini-Henry rifle.

'Good afternoon, Sergeant Major. We have been looking for you,' Hawksworth said calmly.

'Chief Detective Inspector,' Walker lowered the rifle. 'I was rather expecting someone, but I did not think it would be you.'

'Nonetheless, here I stand. You are discovered.'

The rest of Hawksworth's troop pushed through the bushes behind him while Walker led the way. Once they arrived at the campsite, without so much as a handshake, the two men sat opposite one another. Only a wry smile betrayed the satisfaction that Hawksworth felt at finding his old friend and colleague safe. Walker merely nodded vigorously, as though reading the detective's thoughts and agreeing that, yes, it was good to see a familiar face.

'Now tell me,' Hawksworth said, 'where is the Superintendent of the Malacca Police?'

'Dead. Dysentery. I have sent the body with a three-man guard to Gading. We lost a porter to a poisonous spider bite, too, but him we buried on the trail.'

Quiet a moment to absorb the news, Hawksworth continued unfazed, 'Is Gading far? I have personal business to attend to as we pass through it.'

Walker cocked an eyebrow quizzically at Hawksworth, but knew better than to ask for information that had not been offered. 'Only ten or fifteen miles distant. Once off the mountain, the terrain should be fairly easy. However, I had intended to turn back to the bush, continue the pursuit.'

'Tell me, who are you pursuing? And what did you learn at Ayer Panas of the death of the Resident?'

Walker stretched his legs, rubbing his knees. He was strong and experienced, but he was not young. The arduous expedition was beginning to take its toll on the old soldier. Nonetheless, where Hawksworth sported three days' growth of beard and clothes splattered with mud and blood, and stank to high heaven, Walker was shaved, his clothes wrinkled but clean, and he had obviously found a way to wash regularly. Hawksworth would later learn that he used the fresh water accumulated in the pitcher plants to bathe and shave.

'What I learned,' Walker said matter-of-factly, 'is that the Resident was supposed to be there on holiday. While there he made tentative and clumsy inquiries into reports of kidnapping in his district. After only four days, he was found dead. There were no witnesses to the deed.'

'The caretaker told me much the same. He insisted he was murdered.'

Walker nodded affirmatively. 'The Resident was hacked into

six pieces. From what the caretaker told me, I gather that the limbs and head were removed from the torso.'

'You did not see the body?'

'No, it was sent back to Negeri Sembilan before I arrived.'

'The constables were not there the night the attack occurred. Apparently they were either intimidated or bought off, or both.'

'Yes, I heard the same. It sounds to me that the Resident was purposefully targeted and killed. Something to do with his making noise about these supposed kidnappings, perhaps.'

'I ask again – who are you pursuing?'

'That is a good question. Our first night in camp outside of Ayer Panas we were attacked. They used pistols and a bird gun.'

'Any hurt?'

'None seriously. We could not see the attackers in the dark, though we were able to track them by morning light. I decided to give chase immediately and we have been pursuing ever since. Twice again we were ambushed, albeit clumsily. These are not professional soldiers. In one encounter I injured one of them for we found the blood, but both times they managed to slip away into the back country.' Walker's frustration was evident in the flexing of his jaw muscles.

'Perhaps they were trying to lure you away from Ayer Panas.'

The old soldier was silent, rubbing his bald pate before muttering quietly, 'The thought had not occurred to me.'

'As you travelled, did you hear reports of a *pontianak*?'

'Yes, at several villages they mentioned that a ghost was in the area. I rather believed that if children were missing it was most likely a tiger, though the death of the Resident indicates otherwise,' the Sergeant Major stared absently into the enamel blue of the hot sky.

'We encountered a band of *orang asli* who may have shed

some light on the situation.'

Walker looked genuinely surprised by this news.

Hawksworth continued, 'In point of fact, they led us to you. They told us that foreign men – Chinese – were taking children while perpetuating sounds and sights to make the villagers believe that a *pontianak* was responsible. However, unlike the Malays, the *orang asli* were not fooled.'

'Go on,' Walker said, leaning forward.

'So it appears that the Resident had heard something similar about a kidnapping gang, which as you say, brought him to Ayer Panas under cover of a holiday. He then began asking questions obtusely and was targeted as a result. But by whom?' After a moment's pause, Hawksworth asked, 'Did you recover any of his personal belongings?' Walker led the Chief Detective Inspector to his tent and produced a tin chest. 'This is all there was by the time we arrived. I have been through it, but did not find anything of interest. The chest was open when it was given to me. I assume it had been pilfered.'

Inside the chest Hawksworth found only soiled clothes. There were no valuables, no papers or pocket watch or cash, not even boots or a topee helmet. He believed the Sergeant Major to be correct: the chest had been thoroughly looted. Whether this was merely a crime of convenience or a means of removing evidence, there was no way to say.

Their evening meal consisted of meagre rations but the convivial sodality of the camp made up for the light bellies. After the meal, two of the Sergeant Major's men produced a small flute and a *rebab* strung for finger plucking, and along with the constables, improvised a singing group, one of the men keeping time with the flat of his hand on an empty box. From what the Chief Detective Inspector could understand, it was a song about innocence lost in the passion of a prohibited love. Yet the melody was upbeat, the tempo brisk. The song lifted their spirits after all the long hard slog and depressing news from the villages. By the time they had retired to their separate tents, everyone was cheerful.

Hawksworth and Walker were sitting before the flames of the cooking fire, and for the first time since leaving Singapore, Hawksworth found himself if not relaxed then contented. His mind wandered to Gading and the mysterious Isabella Lightheart, and he found himself speaking aloud, 'You sent me a letter about a woman in Malacca, Lim Suan Imm. I meet her. She told me a miraculous tale about my mother – not only that she placed me in the orphanage but that she may indeed still be alive. That she has been living in Gading with a missionary, running ... of all things ... an orphanage.'

Walker grunted. 'I was going to ask you about her. She seemed a little ... eccentric, but she was vehement in her story, so I sent for you. She mentioned the orphanage to me as well. You are going to Gading to assess the situation for yourself, I assume?'

'I am,' Hawksworth responded, expecting a further query, but when none came, he peered closely at Walker and saw him bunching his fists, flexing his forearms, the muscles in his jaws tensing.

'What is on your mind, Sergeant Major?'

'I have been thinking about the missing children and what the *orang asli* told you.'

'Go on.'

The normally laconic man spoke in a torrent, barely pausing for breath, 'I had a missus in Shanghai when I was a young man ... Just out of Gordon's army and wandering and lost. She was a ladybird, a girl from the market who took in sailors now and again to pay the landlord. Even after all that time in the East I never had seen a girl so pretty and lovely, and she were tough, too, did not need me to protect her, could protect herself well enough. Or so I thought.

I started to visit her room once or twice a week and then it were all week every night and before you knew it we were together just the two of us and she stopped taking in other men. Me, I was poor, out of the army, and taking jobs here and there, muscle work. I was breaking heads at night for a few dollars and she was selling rice porridge by the docks at Suzhou Creek. Her name were Ping but I called her Judy and we were together for nearly a year when she fell pregnant with my lad and I knew that I could not keep breaking heads so I reenlisted and hoped to stay stationed in Shanghai and with my experience they did, they kept me there. Yet, us not being wed in holy matrimony as it were, they stationed me in single men's barracks so I only saw Judy and my lad on my off duty. Then after this goes on about three months and we are settled to routine I come back to the town and she were gone. They told me half in Chinese half in English, 'cause I never could make heads nor tails of their language, they told me that she had been kidnapped. Chinese clan had come through the market one day and made off with her. She was still so pretty even after the boy maybe even more so … I never found her.'

'And the boy?'

'Dead. He was only a babe and they must have tossed him over the side because he was fished from the river next day and because the police knew me they fetched me to view his little body, still bundled as he must have been when he clung to her and they pulled her away. Nothing I could do, either, him being a bastard and me only regular army without any access to the powerful. The police said the clan sent women to Hong Kong and Burma and Singapore so I came to look and ...'

'You stayed in Singapore.'

'My final port of call.'

Hawksworth studied the man across from him, the shadows of the campfire deepening the crags of his face, and he could see the pain the Sergeant Major kept hidden there. In all the years he had known the man, he had never heard this story. Walker had never told another soul, Hawksworth realised, now he has told me, and I alone know the cross he has to bear.

'You became a policeman.'

'Aye, I did. But do not think I was looking to serve justice, because I do not believe in justice. I do not believe in it.'

'Why did you join the force, then?'

Walker spoke staring into the flames, 'To break heads without running afoul of the police, I joined the police.' He stood, rising above the flames, growling, 'and if there are bandits in these hills taking the children of these poor backward savages, then I swear to holy heaven that I will find them and I will split their heads and pour their brains on the ground. I swear it.' Then he stomped off to face his demons in solitude.

Hawksworth sat gazing into the cooking fire until the logs had burned to dim embers and their low light was extinguished. He fell asleep sitting upright by the ashes and awoke hours later to find himself alone in silent darkness. The light of the myriad stars shone coldly, their bright patterns offering no hint of fate or solace.

CHAPTER VI

Gading

ON THE VERGE between forest and cleared ground, they came upon a tree that seemed to be alive, shaking and writhing and screeching. A colony of giant fruit bats, *Pteropus vampyrus,* what English speakers called 'flying foxes' and the Malays *kalongs,* had infested a *duku* tree, feeding on the fruit. They were as big as dogs, with wingspans that could reach more than four feet. Their vulpine faces with large agate eyes looked especially inquisitive and intelligent, and it was easy to believe that they were shape-shifting humans. Yet the big bats ate only fruit, which caused their meat to be sweet. The locals considered it a delicacy. As the troop passed the tree, they could see two or three men gathering around the trunk, preparing slings and stones to try to knock some of the poor creatures from their roost.

The tree was the last totem of the wilderness before they entered a landscape dominated by human endeavour: before them stretched the wide, gently sloping plain that descended to the coast at Malacca. After being accustomed to the verdant lushness of the natural landscape, the outskirts of the town of Gading seemed particularly shabby. Unpaved roads were bordered by ditches filled with foul water, unpainted wooden shacks leaned against each other helter-skelter, banyan trees sprouting between them. Scruffy cats with knobs in place of tails chased scrawny chickens pecking in the dirt, while children wearing a ragged mix of native and Western clothes chased the cats and each other. One half-nude waif had a sorry looking puppy on a string who sat on its rump, scratching at the fleas in its ears.

When they entered Gading, the only difference was that the roads were loosely paved with crushed stone. The town had started out much like the camp at Labis: a group of itinerant workers had congregated near mining operations. Over time it had consolidated into a town. Now there was a main road lined with numerous brick-built shops. There was even a police station, but no post office or telegraph. In fact, Razin told him, there were plans to string a telephone line from Malacca; Hawksworth mused that the town would skip from the age of pen and ink straight to the age of electric voice reproduction. However, not more than two decades previously, this would have been a rough and tumble shantytown set amidst the *kampongs* that provided food for the men digging out the tin mines. It would have taken considerable grit and fearlessness for a woman to start an orphanage in such a situation.

In the town the men felt acutely dirty, their torn clothes, broken boots, and greasy hair marking them out as wayfarers. The first thing they wanted to do was find a shelter with beds and baths. There was no hotel but there were rooms above a Chinese eatery for Hawksworth and Walker. The constables and porters had to make do with the hospitality offered by their brothers-in-arms at the police station.

After a hot bath, a properly cooked meal eaten while seated at a table, and a night's sleep on a mattress, no matter how thin and uncomfortable, Hawksworth felt like a man returned to civilisation.

Walker immediately set about the task of provisioning his

men, while Hawksworth began to make inquiries about Isabella Lightheart and the orphanage. The Superintendent of the police station told him the grim news: the woman died two years before, and not long after that, the orphanage caught fire and burned down completely.

'Cause of death?'

'She died in bed with fever.'

'Was there an inquest?'

'No. The death was not suspicious so we did not call for the coroner to come from Malacca. There is no coroner here.'

'I see,' Hawksworth said, studying the man's face. He was Eurasian, in his late twenties or early thirties. As the Superintendent of an upcountry police station, he drew a salary that would be considered quite decent by local standards, but for which no European would work. Being Eurasian, he would feel compelled to spend more to live slightly better than pure-blood locals, to whom he would feel superior. To gain this extra income, he might very well take bribes from the type of people that would covet the land on which the orphanage stood. Suan Imm had told him the hills were swarming with nefarious parties from both secret societies and legitimate companies. The Superintendent's word, he decided, was not to be trusted, though it was the only source of information he had at the present time. 'And the orphanage fire? Any deaths?'

'There were no deaths as it was abandoned after Madam Lightheart's passing. We suspected arson, but an investigation turned up nothing. All the evidence was destroyed in the fire.'

'What of the missionary, Nathaniel Cooper?'

'Minister Cooper died of a blood disorder several years before Madam Lightheart passed.'

'Is there anyone in Gading who knew Lightheart? Who can

provide me with more information about her?'

It was now the Superintendent's turn to study Hawksworth's face intently. 'May I ask, sir, why you are so interested in this ... old news?'

'It is a personal matter, an errand for a friend in Malacca.'

The Superintendent sighed, 'There is a Malay woman, Miss Fatima, who was Madam Lightheart's housemaid and constant companion. She is still in Gading. Let me take you to her.'

'That would be good. And I ask that you show me where the orphanage once stood.'

The lot at the back of the town was empty except for weeds and *lallang* grass. A mound of ashes and a few blackened beams and the scorched trunk of a dead palm tree were all that remained. It had been a massive conflagration, he was told, and the volunteer town fire brigade had been helpless before it. Beside the empty lot was an abandoned chapel. The side that had faced the fire was black with soot, the structure now fallen into disrepair. Beyond it was a small Christian cemetery, and then foregrounding the rising hills was a newly built foundry for smelting ore.

'They want this land for building a factory for tinning, both fruit from the interior and fish from the sea,' the Superintendent told him. 'Now that Madam Lightheart is passed and the orphanage burnt, the cemetery is the only thing holding up the construction. But not for long,' he spoke without emotion. 'Either the graves will be moved or they will simply build over them.'

'Who owns the foundry?'

'It belongs to the Straits Mining Company.'

Hawksworth nodded silently, making note of the name. He was not a believer in coincidence.

'Madam Lightheart is buried here,' the Superintendent said flatly.

'Show me.'

The grave was a mound of dirt with a plain metal cross, painted white, her name stamped on a plate held by a single rivet. Beside it was a similar mound with 'Nathaniel Cooper' on the plate, the cross tilted at a steep angle, covered with devil's ivy creepers. In only a few years the markers would fall, the mounds subside, vegetation would obscure the graves, and they would be forgotten.

'Take me to the maid,' Hawksworth said. Casting a final glance at the two mounds side by side, slipping inexorably to oblivion, he felt nothing but an empty and dire perplexity.

* * *

She lived in Lightheart's house, a one story brick-and-plank box with a small veranda, only a stone's throw from the lot where the orphanage had once stood. The veranda was sagging; the house smelled damp. She was a slight woman, dressed in Western clothes a decade out of fashion, a plain full-length dress buttoned up to her chin. A silver cross hung at her throat over the yellowing lace of the high collar.

Her eyes were clouded with cataracts, which had turned them an eggshell blue, and her fingers were gnarled with arthritis, but as soon as she saw Hawksworth at her door, her hands flew to her face and she shrieked like a young girl. Then she spoke quickly in perfect English, 'Blessed be the Lord! You are Madam Lightheart's son, are you not? Come from Singapore? I always knew no matter how hard she tried to keep herself a secret from you, one day you would come to Gading. Please come in. You are welcome to stay as long as you please.'

'Thank you,' Hawksworth said, bewildered at the woman's

reaction. The house was as spartan as a Presbyterian church. There was a braided rug on the wooden floor, but otherwise there were no decorations or ornaments except for fresh cut flowers in a clear vase placed on a sideboard. Once inside, she reached up to him, for she was at least two feet shorter, and touching his face once, gazed at him. He recoiled slightly, staring into her face.

'You have her eyes, yes you do.'

'Excuse me, Miss Fatima, but I am more than a little in the dark about Madam Lightheart. You see, I have no memory of my parents. I believed for my entire life that that I was an orphan … And indeed I *am* an orphan. Forgive me, but I cannot share your enthusiasm until some of the questions I have are answered,' he said, then added, 'if they even can be.'

She answered him by shuffling to the side table then taking a bundle from its drawer: this contained a small locket, which she handed to him. Inside the locket was a daguerreotype of a woman in her early thirties, very plain, her hair covered. She was turned in three-quarters profile from the camera so that her gaze rested away from the viewer. 'That is my only picture of Isabella Lightheart,' Fatima said. 'You may keep it, if you like.'

The resemblance was remarkable, he had to admit. The woman in the locket had the same straight jaw line, the same slightly aquiline nose, the same elongated neck, the same intense cast in the grey eyes.

'How long did you work for Madam Lightheart?'

'From the time she first came to Gading, in 1854.'

'And how old was Madam Lightheart then?'

'Not more than twenty or twenty-one years old.'

Hawksworth took a deep breath. He had always been told his birth date was in 1851. 'Why did Isabella Lightheart believe that I was her son? No, let me ask again, what was the story she told of her son?'

'She told me that she had a child in England, and that she had to abandon that child in Penang when she came down with fever.'

Hawksworth felt dizzy, the floor beneath his chair seemed to twirl. 'Go on,' he whispered.

'She came here, to Gading, with Minister Nathaniel Cooper, whom she met in Province Wellesley. They came to establish the orphanage.'

'But how did she know …'

'We get the Singapore newspapers here, very out of date, but they come. Your name was mentioned in an article. This was years ago, when you were promoted to Detective Inspector. That was when she told me about the child she abandoned in Penang.'

'My name is Hawksworth, not Lightheart,' he said more sternly than he intended to. 'How did she know it was me? Unless she … unless she had been keeping track of me since my earliest days in Penang.' The implications were almost too much for him to bear.

'I do not know. I only know that she spoke of you with great sadness,' she said. 'And she always knew that it was you. She knew in her heart and by the divine providence of the Lord.' Hawksworth sat in stunned silence.

'How rude of me not to offer you a drink! Give me a moment, I will return. Do you take goat's milk?'

He nodded numbly, fingertips working the edge of the locket. He stayed like that until she returned with a tray holding a pitcher and two glasses. 'Here, drink this, you will feel better.'

'What of my father?'

'She never spoke of her former husband … Or of her former life. If it had not been for your name in the newspaper, then as far as I knew, her life began the day she and Mr. Cooper set foot in this town. You are the only link to her past.'

'Perhaps then that is why she avoided me,' he said mordantly.

From the bundle on her lap, the bent fingers produced a slim book bound in brown leather, tied with a faded yellow silk ribbon. 'Madam kept this diary when she first arrived. I do not think she wrote in it for many years after that, yet the secret of her heart may well be in it.'

She presented it to Hawksworth, who took the volume into his hands with a mixture of excitement and trepidation.

'May I ask – when Madam Lightheart passed, were there any suspicions?'

'I do not understand your meaning.'

'I have heard rumours that there was a conflict with a local mining company over the orphanage land.'

'I grasp your meaning now. Madam's passing was natural. I was with her right up to the end, sleeping in a chair beside her. She was old, Mr. Lightheart, and she was exhausted, but not from fighting these businessmen. Over the course of years your mother raised several hundred children in her orphanage, and she did this almost by herself. She had helpers, but they were paid very little and never stayed long. As for me, I stayed to serve her. Her selflessness was, and remains, an inspiration to me. I now draw my own strength of will from her inspiration ... and my guidance from the spirit of our Lord.'

His fingers were running over the old leather of the diary that had once belonged to Lightheart. So she raised hundreds of children, he thought to himself, but she had no time to raise me. He was about to say this aloud when he looked at the old woman before him; the shrunken body in the ill-fitting clothes, the tight lips in the withered face, the iron grey hair, thinning yet pulled back severely, the filmy eyes, the trembling hands. She was a perfect picture of sacrifice and devotion. He kept his thought to himself – perhaps things were not as they appeared, perhaps he would learn what had happened.

'I will not take much more of your time ...'

'Stay as long as you please.'

'Thank you,' he leaned back, sipping the goat's milk. It was warm and fresh, most likely produced that very morning. Nonetheless the sour taste was off putting and blended in his mind with the damp smell of the house. It was the smell of old age, infirmity. 'Allow me to ask about the burning of the orphanage.'

'Now that was no doubt the handiwork of the mining company. They wanted to clear the land.'

'You believe that it was the Straits Mining Company ...'

'I do not believe, Mr. Lightheart, I know,' she said fervently. 'The owner is named Loke Yew. He is the man who hounded us in the years before Madam's passing.' Her voice quavered as she spoke, choked with emotion.

'I have heard his name. Is he in Gading?'

'I would not know where he is, for I do not remark the devil. But I can tell you that the mining company office is in Malacca.'

'A final question Miss Fatima.'

'Yes?'

'In the many years that you knew her, did Madam Lightheart ever express any ... regret ... about leaving her son in Penang?' he asked, his voice unintentionally slipping into a falsetto, the high voice of a child.

The old woman leaned forward so that their knees nearly touched, then spoke in a rushed, hushed voice. 'All those children she raised, all those motherless children she cared for with her own hands. Each and every one of them was a shadow of you, the one that she could not care for herself. There was a sadness in

Isabella so profound that only the Lord was able to offer succour. You may not have been here with her, but not a moment of a day went by that she did not think of you. You may think me a simple-minded old woman, but believe me when I tell you that in your absence ... perhaps because of your absence ... you were her entire life.'

* * *

Sergeant Major Walker stood in the centre of the room, his hands held behind his back, elongating his legs by flexing his feet, putting his weight on his toes, so that he rose up several inches while keeping his upper body completely immobile. It was a surprisingly elegant movement for a man his size and age. 'Good afternoon, Chief Detective Inspector,' he said without interrupting his action. 'You look as though you have seen a ghost.'

Ignoring the comment, Hawksworth sat in an uncomfortable wooden chair, watching the Sergeant Major's body rise up and down, the leather of his boots creaking. Finally he asked, 'What the devil are you doing?'

'Stretching my new boots,' he said smartly. 'Also the motion helps to alleviate some of the pain in my knee.'

'I see.'

'Did you find the woman you came for?'

'In a way, yes. She is dead. But I spoke with her intimate friend who gave me a locket and a diary.'

Walker stopped his exercise, then walked ramrod straight to a sideboard, poured himself a glass of water, then turned to face Hawksworth. 'It is best to leave the past unexplored. We have the present to concern ourselves with.'

The uncharacteristically philosophical remark coming from

the Sergeant Major caught Hawksworth by surprise. 'Yet surely you will agree that the past affects the present?'

Walker grunted. 'I know where I have been, where I am, and where I am going. Which is what I mean to discuss with you. Once my expedition is refreshed, I would like to return to the hills.'

'For what purpose? Surely you do not think that the Resident's killers are still on the loose up there?'

'No, but a party of child hunters might be, and that is what I intend to discover.'

Hawksworth sighed. There was no use in arguing with the man – he was obstinate beyond measure. 'Once I have returned to Malacca, I will telegraph Singapore of your intentions. As we are not actively investigating the reports of kidnapping, I will tell them that you are staying to continue your pursuit of the Resident's killers. However, as we suspect that the two cases are related, I do not suppose I will be stretching the truth too far. When do you intend to return to Singapore?'

He knew the Sergeant Major would rather stay in the hills until he captured *someone*, for to return empty-handed would be difficult for his martial sense of obligation. However, he would need to come home before too long. He was needed at his post in Singapore, too.

'Give me an additional two weeks,' Walker said without a tone of request.

'Consider it done.'

Cooking smells wafted up from beneath the floorboards – the inviting scent of tea mingled with the heavy pungency of frying pork fat. 'That would be our lunch, I suppose,' Hawksworth remarked, realising suddenly how hungry he had become. He tucked the diary into his bag and slipped the locket over his head, around his neck – the safest place he knew. The string holding it was frayed and needed to be replaced, but all he had to hand was twine. Later in Malacca, he would pick up yellow ribbon to match the yellow ribbon Isabella Lightheart's fingers had knotted around her diary to keep it secure all those years ago.

* * *

The road to Malacca was wide and well kept, even if the pressed gravel had worn away in places due to the severity of the climate and revealed the red laterite dirt beneath. Hawksworth and the constables rode comfortably in a carriage through a landscape of paddy fields and neat little *kampongs*, the whitewashed estate houses of plantation owners perched atop low hills, surrounded by colourful hedges and fruit trees. The closer they moved to Malacca, the greater became the frequency of brick built buildings, though behind these were open plantation land or the waving green and gold of rice fields. It was a prosperous landscape, pastoral compared to the raw jungle through which they had been tromping. From down here, it was hard to imagine the strife taking place in the hills, the rough-and-tumble mining camps infested with Chinese clans, the impoverished villages, the land leeches waving and puckering like tiny blood-sucking monsters.

But the illusion of the peaceful valley faded when Razin said that they had chosen a good time to complete their expedition, for the northeast monsoon was coming, and the downpours that washed through the valley across the plains frequently made even this modern road impassable when the paddy fields flooded. It also meant that Ayer Panas would become virtually cut off by the new year and would stay that way for several months.

Then it came to him in a flash: like all hunters, the child thieves would have to stalk their quarry in season, and when the rains came, the hills would be difficult to traverse. The hunters would have to fill their bags before the heavy rains came – and that was *now*.

The Resident of Negeri Sembilan had interloped during prime hunting season. Surely this was not a coincidence. It also meant that the hunters were most likely still in the hills; the Sergeant Major's chances of catching the perpetrators were increased. He wished he had thought of this before, when they were still in Gading, so he could have shared the insight with Walker. In any event, he would check with Shaw when he arrived: perhaps reinforcements could be sent to assist before the worst of the rains came.

The approach to Malacca from the landward side was odd, like sneaking up behind someone. There were no landside defences, no gates or entry points as there had been when the old Portuguese fort was still intact. Instead, the fields slowly gave away to narrow lanes with houses side-by-side, the number of multi-storey stone-and-brick buildings increasing until they faced the main streets in an unbroken line. Suddenly, one was in the midst of a town. Glancing back, the fertile valley plains rose into the dark hills, and towering behind them was the stone crown of Mount Ophir.

The closer they drew to the seashore, the more somnolent the town seemed to become. Finally before the venerable Stadthuys, the air seemed to stagnate, as though a miasma had enveloped them. The familiar sense of sweltering lassitude overcame the tall man; it was as if time had not moved at all, as if he had only left that morning.

Shaw greeted him cheerfully and suggested that he refresh

himself before they take dinner – just the two of them – so he could learn all the Chief Detective Inspector had discovered. Hawksworth agreed, and was shown to the same room he had occupied previously. After a quick scrub in the porcelain basin, he collapsed into the deep cushions and clean sheets beneath the mosquito netting as though falling into a pond, and his consciousness was quickly submerged.

* * *

'And that, Mr Shaw, is what we now know about the death of the Resident of Negeri Sembilan,' Hawksworth said, dabbing curry away from the corner of his mouth before taking a draught of beer.

'When the body of the Police Superintendent came back I surmised that the Sergeant Major was alive. Is it a good idea to send him again so soon into the field?'

Hawksworth smiled, 'There is no place he would rather be.'

'This news of kidnapped children is distressing, but there seems to be little we can do with our current manpower.'

'It is a problem that should be dealt with at the source. We need to discover the reason the children are being kidnapped, why these children in particular, and where they are being taken, and then work backward. But with so many people roaming the territory, it will be next to impossible to catch the perpetrators before the rains begin. Whoever is doing it, I imagine that they are being controlled by a central command, most likely from here or from Tampin in Negeri Sembilan.'

Shaw nodded in understanding while eyeing a platter of pineapple drizzled with honey being set on the table – it was dessert. 'What of your own interest, the one that brought you to

Gading?'

Hawksworth scooped some of the fruit onto his plate, 'I did find what I was looking for, though not in the form I expected. There are further inquiries that I would to make. You mentioned before the Straits Mining Company and a man named Loke Yew. Is he in Malacca?'

'There is an office here. You can visit it in the morning,' Shaw popped a slice of pineapple into his mouth, munching. 'When do you intend to return to Singapore?'

'In another day or so. I would like to speak with Loke Yew about his operations in Gading, and I would like to speak again with Mrs. Lim Suan Imm. I have a message for her from an old friend.'

'I will send a boy to her home first thing in the morning. Loke Yew you can surprise. Coffee?'

'Thank you,' Hawksworth stifled a yawn. 'And is there something stronger? Brandy, or whisky?'

'We have brandy. I will have it sent to your room later. Trying to get a restful night's sleep?'

'Indeed,' said Hawksworth. Since he had arrived in Gading, he had been having his usual recurrent nightmares, of being lost in the jungle, of being chased by shapeless creatures covered in flames, of being burnt alive. The brandy, he hoped, would suppress them.

* * *

The office of the Straits Mining Company was located upriver from the Stadthuys, on Jalan Bunga Raya, the main road out of town into the hinterlands. Only a half mile beyond the line of two-storey brick edifices was the flat paddy land of Kampong

Java, the beginning of the cultivated countryside that lay between Malacca and Gading.

He arrived after the breakfast hour when the sun was just up, leaving half the street in deep shadow. The front of the office was tidy and neat, with only a young Chinese man seated behind the desk and a Bengali *punka* puller resting in the corner and fanning the room by pulling the curtain suspended from the ceiling with a cord tied to his big toe. The building was not wired for electricity. The young Chinese was in the process of eating a sticky rice bun that lay on a banana leaf before him when Hawksworth strode through the front door.

'*Selamat pagi*,' he greeted in Malay. 'Good morning.' The Bengali responded merely by opening his eyes. The Chinese half-choked on the bun, looking baffled. Walk-in visitors were unheard of in such an enterprise. Perhaps the *ang-moh* was lost?

'*Pagi*,' he replied without a trace of hospitality.

'I would like to see Mr. Loke Yew,' Hawksworth said in English.

'I do not speak English,' the young man said sanguinely in Malay, then said it again in Teochew, to test the white man.

The reply came in placid Malay, 'My name is Chief Detective Inspector Hawksworth of the Straits Police, Singapore.'

The young man stared gormlessly at him. Having never been surprised by a policeman before, it seemed that he was unsure of what to do, and thus thought the course of action that posed the least risk was to do nothing at all. Usually Occidentals would react to this sort of inaction with anger, believing that the Oriental was being intentionally obstinate. They would shout until hoarse, further befuddling the local, eventually causing a loss of face, after which point the situation would become irretrievable, for then the local would indeed turn obdurate. Being nearly native himself,

Hawksworth knew that the best method was to give polite yet direct instructions: 'Please inform Loke Yew that I am here. Then ask him if he is available now, for I would like to speak with him.'

The young man rose from his desk – he was neatly dressed in a suit of Western clothes, a starched white shirt with a high collar, though he still wore his hair in a short queue. He ascended a short flight of wooden stairs to the second floor, and then through the boards of the ceiling, Hawksworth could hear voices in Teochew. The young man returned shortly, saying in Malay, 'Mr. Loke Yew can see you now. Please go up. May I offer you tea?'

'Thank you, tea would be capital,' he said, then walked up the creaking steps. The upstairs office was as sparse as the downstairs, although here the desk was large, the chairs cushioned. A second *punka* was being pulled by a man who could have been the spitting image of the Bengali man he had seen on the floor below; he was on his back in the same ludicrous position, pulling the cord with his toe. The room was bright, lit by two big windows that looked down on the street, the hot early morning sun illuminating the face of the man seated behind the desk. He looked like the young Chinese man downstairs, only twenty years older and bald. He did not stand to greet the detective.

'How may I help you?' he said tersely in Malay, without preamble.

'Good morning, I am Chief Detective Inspector Hawksworth of ...'

'Yes, I know, my assistant told me. This is not Singapore. What do you want?' Hawksworth realised the man's surliness was meant to mask fear, but he was not in a mood to play along.

He had not had enough coffee that morning, and had a slight headache that the morning's blazing sun had made worse. He simply strode behind the man's desk and sat his rear on the edge, as close to the man as he could. He then leaned down into the man's face – a face that did not register any shock at the actions, though the fear shone in his eyes. 'There is always time to be polite, Mr. Loke Yew. To be otherwise demonstrates low breeding. Now, let us begin again. I am Chief Detective Inspector Hawksworth of the Straits Police on special assignment in Malacca to investigate secret society activities in the surrounding hills. I am especially interested in your operations in Gading.'

The man nodded, but remained quiet and impassive.

'Let us begin with the burning of the abandoned orphanage there. Your foundry abuts the land. The local police told me that they suspect arson at the hands of a clan. What do you know about this?'

'You cannot threaten me.'

'There you are wrong,' he said coldly, letting his jacket come open to reveal the short truncheon holstered there. 'I could arrest you now on suspicion of arson. It would be a long investigation, with travel not only to Gading but to Singapore at your own expense. All told, perhaps six months of your life would be lost as you shuttle between prisons and courts while we sort the facts. I suppose the young man downstairs can run your business operations in your stead.'

Loke Yew frowned up at him, then gave a sigh of resignation. He spoke slowly, 'The fire at the orphanage was an unfortunate accident, but it is true that we have since acquired the land to expand our operations.'

'And the adjoining Christian cemetery?'

He was silent.

'I do not think that a man of business like yourself need do any more than hire thugs to burn things down for you. But I am told that you are in the process of selling your shares to a larger enterprise, which I do believe has access to organised criminal elements.'

'My business is my business.'

'Perhaps they would not buy your shares if they were not confident of your expanding operations in Gading. And perhaps they first put pressure on you to clear the land, and when you were not capable of clearing it yourself, they supplied the muscle? A loss of face, surely.'

'You think you know much about my business.'

'I know that you will not be able to handle the competition from the Singapore firms that are expanding into Malaya, so you will be smart, and instead of fighting them, you will join them. And to join them, you must prove yourself capable of holding your own. Otherwise they will totally consume you.'

'What are you really here for, Detective? This is not about Gading, is it?' His voice was beginning to quaver. Hawksworth knew the man's resistance was breaking down.

'Further questions,' he snapped. 'Is the Straits Mining Company sending surveying parties into the hills?'

'I will tell you,' the Chinese said in a hoarse whisper. 'My grandfather started this business. He was a miner with no education and he came here and worked the ground with his own two hands. He fought other Chinese, and he fought British East India Company officials. Eventually he laid claim to a mine. Then his son, my father, started the business proper. We were called the Gading Tin Company back then. Now we are faced with extinction because of these enterprises coming in from Singapore. So as you say, either we join them, or we fight them – and if we fight, we perish, because we lack the money and muscle to win the fight. My destiny was to run my grandfather's company, send my own sons to school, build our prosperity. But now … Now I take orders from men I have never met, men who sit in a city I have only visited once. They are not content with Gading. They want continuous mining operations from Johor to Ipoh.'

'I understand.'

'No, you do not,' Loke Yew slapped his hand on his desk, raising his voice defiantly. 'It is not only the "big brothers" in Singapore who are coming. It is also European companies who want the land, the ore, the manpower. And it is local enterprises, too. The Malays and Klings are gaining power and prestige. They are making claims to our land. Not just old families like the Alsagoffs, but young families, families of shopkeepers. They are joining with European interests to compete with the Chinese. I will not see my birth right taken over by …'

Even in his rage, Loke Yew cut himself short, not wishing to offend the detective leaning over him, but Hawksworth could finish his thought for him: 'taken over by white men, brown men, black men … barbarians. It is far better to sell out to other Chinese.'

Loke Yew was silent, his face turned to his desktop. He spoke in a calm voice. 'If you want to know who is sending men into the hills, speak with Suliman Amjad bin Ahmed Alsagoff. The Solomon Company sends men all the time, but the company owns no mines.'

'Alsagoff? He told me he is looking to expand his business into agriculture. I should not be surprised if he were sending surveying teams into the jungle.'

Loke Yew shook his head to indicate that Hawksworth had not understood his meaning, 'He sends men into the hills, but they bring no surveying equipment.' He looked up at the detective.

Hawksworth scrutinised the man's broad face, which was creased with years of worry. 'Then what are they doing?'

'No one knows what they do, but they stay in the hills a long time. As I said, ask Mr. Alsagoff about this. They are his men, after all. As for my operations,' he shrugged the Chinese shrug that indicates genuine resignation, 'you already seem to know everything you want to know.'

* * *

'Alsagoff is an eccentric fellow, surely, but I do not think he is involved in any criminal enterprises in the hills. And we would certainly notice if large numbers of kidnapped native children were being shipped through Malacca. My guess is that his surveying teams keep their equipment at an outpost in the backcountry. If Chinese men are with them, it would only be to keep the peace with any other Chinese they may encounter. The hills are overrun with them these days,' Shaw said to Hawksworth over afternoon tea – the same bitter, gut-wrenching faux Earl Grey they had every afternoon.

'I am not so certain. I am curious to speak again with Alsagoff. I would also like another interview with Mrs. Lim.'

Shaw said he would send word to Alsagoff, then informed that Lim was off visiting a niece who had taken ill. 'She left the day after you started your expedition, but she did leave a letter for you, believing that you would pass back through town before she returned.'

He found himself unexpectedly nervous holding the letter in his hand. He pulled open the envelope, shaking out the single page inside. His trepidation was misplaced, for the letter was merely a polite excuse for missing him, though she did expect to return to Malacca in a few weeks' time and would be very pleased to meet him to hear news of her old friend in Gading.

'Happy news, Chief Detective Inspector?'

'No, no, I am afraid not,' he said, his eyes resting again on the antique map he had noticed on his first day in Malacca. 'I should return to Singapore as quickly as possible. When is the next ship?'

'The steamer *Dancy* should be calling tomorrow midmorning before heading directly to Singapore on the mail run. I will arrange to have you aboard. Will you join us for dinner tonight?'

'I will be pleased to join you,' he rose to leave, then asked over his shoulder, 'Point of curiosity ... Is the *Dancy* an Alsagoff ship?'

'I do believe she is, sir. The Singapore side of the family, not part of the Solomon Company owned by our local Alsagoff.'

'It seems that they are everywhere,' Hawksworth said testily.

* * *

His intuition later proved all too accurate. As he was taking his usual brisk walk around town before his siesta, he was ambushed near the old Kling mosque on Blacksmith Street. An expensive two-horse carriage, lacquered black with glass windows, suddenly pulled directly in front of him, blocking the way between the street and the stone wall of the mosque. The door swung open and from inside he heard a voice call his name. It was Alsagoff's voice.

The carriage stopped long enough for him to climb inside. The man sat on plush cushions, his black *songkok* firmly in place. 'Your expedition was a success, Chief Detective Inspector?'

Hawksworth studied the man's impassive face, the soft dark eyes that masked the outsized self-assurance. 'Shaw sent word I wished to speak with you?'

'He did. So *I* found *you*.'

They were rocking slowly as the carriage made its way along

the strange silence of the street, the houses and shops closed and boarded as always, as if the town were under siege.

'Thank you, you have saved me the inconvenience of waiting. I want to ask about the teams you send into the hills. What is their purpose?'

'Ah. That is simple. They survey.'

'I hear reports that they bring no equipment with them.'

'Your reports are incorrect. My men are surveying for rubber plantations in the hills above Gading.'

'Then I hope they are careful. You heard of the two surveyors killed at a camp near there?'

Alsagoff smiled knowingly. 'The hills are a dangerous place to be, as your Resident of Negeri Sembilan discovered. Rest assured, my men are well protected.'

'By whom?'

'By me. For I am the one who supplies the weapons and training they use. What else did you discover at the Chinese camp at Labis?'

Hawksworth cocked his head and stared hard into the man's eyes. The loud clop of the horses' hooves and the creaking turn of the carriage wheels filled the emptiness between them. 'How are you so sure I visited Labis?'

Smirking, Alsagoff merely shrugged then peered out the curtained window. He spoke toward the street, the foothills beyond. 'Very little happens in those hills that I am not aware of, Chief Detective Inspector.'

Hawksworth found himself growing angry, his voice turning thin and harsh, 'Then you are aware that children are being kidnapped from villages throughout the neighbouring districts.'

Turning again to face him, the smirk intact, Alsagoff said, 'The natives say a *pontianak* is to blame. But what do you think?'

'I think,' Hawksworth spat, 'that whoever is responsible for the killing of the Resident and the kidnapping of the children will shortly be brought to justice.'

'I do hope so,' Alsagoff sneered, 'for murder and kidnapping are bad for business, to say nothing of ghouls and lost police patrols.'

The carriage jerked to a halt and Hawksworth became aware that they were before the Stadthuys. Alsagoff had merely taken him about in a circle. 'Your temporary abode. I trust you will have a comfortable night's rest. You are to depart tomorrow morning on the *Darcy*, no? You are required in Singapore, even if your Sergeant Major is not.'

'We are not through.'

'And yet, we are. I am afraid that I must leave on urgent business to the Klang Valley and will not return for a week at least. I am so happy, however, that we had time to have this chat before my long-scheduled departure.'

The carriage door was flung open for him. Hawksworth opened his mouth to retort, but before he could, Alsagoff leaned in close. 'Did I not warn you that this town is cursed, Chief Detective Inspector?' He smiled, his eyes hooded, then hissed, 'Bon voyage'.

With a grimace, the tall man exited the carriage into the tepid air of the late tropical afternoon. He heard the door being slammed shut behind him, and the horses snorting as the whip snapped over their heads, then the metal wheels turning and crunching gravel as the carriage drove away.

He could see the flat hazy cerulean line of the sea past the palm trees, the harbour empty, the tide high. The sound of the small rollers came to him, washing the shore placidly. A cicada started its drone nearby. Drawing a deep breath, he held himself erect, eyes fixed on the horizon. He had no choice. He would pursue Alsagoff and his Solomon Company from Singapore, where he was on familiar ground and the advantage would be his. Curses be damned.

* * *

His siesta was not refreshing. He awoke from intense dreams and did not feel rested – the dreams themselves remained ciphers, for he could not recall their content or structure, just a sharp image of a skull with living eyes, as though a person were somehow inside it.

Despite his fatigue, the dinner was pleasant. It was only himself and Mr. Shaw. They spoke mostly of politics and current events, and the fare was the familiar curried fish with rice and garlic fried fresh vegetables, simple yet delicious. The dessert was a sweet coconut and honey confection. It was convivial company, the sort that officers in barracks live and come to love, and for a time he forgot the troubles and anxieties of the world outside.

After dinner, Aloysius of noble Portuguese blood led him quietly with a lantern along the dark passage to his room, where a bottle of brandy awaited him. As he followed the dim light, he became aware of an uncanny sensation that the stone floor was sloping into the darkness, as though they were walking not straight ahead but downward, into the ground itself.

CHAPTER VII

Home Again

IT WOULD BE A MOONLESS NIGHT. They rounded the Raffles Lighthouse on Coney Island and entered the Straits of Singapore as the purple evening was fading to fluid darkness. The sea was flat like a sheet of molten lead into which the ships had been frozen, their red and green lamps flickering as they sat still in the motionless water. Moving through the black ships toward the harbour entrance was like crossing a watery stage set, funnels and tall masts and rigging painted on the scrim of an artificial sky.

Slowing so as not to leave a wake, the steamer entered the narrow mouth of New Harbour. The big guns of Fort Siloso on Pulau Blakang Mati to their right, and the smaller battery at Fort Pasir Panjang on Labrador Point to their left, appeared as galaxies of burgundy lights against the dark mass of the land. There was much activity on the shores. Handheld lanterns and inarticulate yelling marked the location of men. He caught fleeting glimpses of silhouettes through the foliage.

Ahead the docks and slips and godowns of New Harbour were bathed in blue gaslight, and here and there shone the brighter white of electric bulbs. The ship was headed for the Tanjong Pagar Dock Company wharf. The main engine was cut and they drifted into the slip where teams of coolies grabbed the ropes tossed from the deck, twisting them around man-sized cleats.

Hawksworth walked down the gangplank with his valise gripped in his hand and pushed into the scrum of people: touts and rickshaw *wallahs* and procurers and a few family members and friends assembled there to meet loved ones or associates.

There was no one there to meet him.

Across the street, sunk in shadow, was an impromptu hackney carriage station, with a few coaches waiting. He stepped into one and gave instruction to be driven to Geylang.

As he rode along, into the heart of the town, he heard the ringing of temple bells and of gongs; smelled the strong stench of fried shrimp paste in the Chinese district; heard shouts in Tamil near the goat's milk stalls of Upper Cross Street, and swearing in Cantonese along with loud laughter near the canal; saw illuminated against the distant night sky the bright white steeple of the Armenian church and, later, the brick walls and wooden roof of the Sultan Mosque near Haji Lane.

Just outside of the city on the far side of Rochor River they rolled past the *pasar malam*, the night market, at Kallang. The food stalls and grocery section was closest to the road and he could smell meat frying in fish sauce. In the yellow circles of light cast by paraffin lanterns tied to the rough wooden piles he could see heaps of onions and potatoes from Bengal; piles of purple brinjals and of bright red chillies; brown mottled blue duck-eggs massed in baskets; mounds of ground spices in a calico pattern of colours spilling from burlap sacks; dried and salted fish stacked on wood boards, surrounded by buzzing flies; an embankment of pale green durians, their spines interlocked. He could smell the pungent fruit, akin to rotten meat, for the next quarter mile.

Then they were in the rolling darkness of the outer districts. It would not be much longer now.

They were soon in the cool palm plantation, the spiked trees standing in serried rows on either side of the road, looming in the gloom, the carriage lanterns their only earthly illumination. Then against the starry sky he could see the dark crown of the massive banyan tree in his front garden, and then the dim lights of his own home.

She was waiting on the front veranda – she had stood there every night since he had left, waiting. The carriage rolled to a stop and he got down and was striding up the front path, but she was already running down to the garden to greet him. Despite his dirty clothes and sweaty smell she leapt into his arms. He dropped the valise and held her up, feet dangling an inch from the ground, so she could burrow her face into his neck, rub her nose along his cheeks, plant kisses on his lips. Over and over she whispered in Siamese *khid thueng mak mak*, 'I missed you so very much.' Her clean scent, like of sandalwood, filled his entire head.

He carried her clinging to him into the house, and to their room, and dropped her onto their bed, lifting up its draping of mosquito net. Without igniting a flame or even stopping to bathe, they stripped each other, and she pulled him toward her and on top of her, and then he felt her soft moist warmness enfolding and gripping him. They stay entwined under the net as though lying in a cocoon, he slipping inside of her again and again, until the first pink light of dawn streaked the morning sky. And then they finally fell asleep in the steamy heat, their breathing shallow but steady.

*   *   *

He watched her chest rise and fall as she slept, naked and dusky, pliant to the touch. Her face was slack yet serene. Gently stroking her fragrant hair, he let the dark strands run through his fingers.

128

He could smell himself, his body unwashed after the voyage, his odour musky after the long bout of lovemaking. He had come inside her quickly the first time – he had been unable to help himself – and then had continued to do so each time they coupled. Normally he pulled out. They used no other method of prevention (unless she did something unbeknownst to him) and he wondered if perhaps this time they had conceived.

His mind skipped ahead to hiring a midwife and a maid to help in the early days, fitting out a corner of the house with a crib, bringing in special food (he had no idea what babies ate) and other things his child might require – he knew next to nothing, he suddenly realised, about the birthing and caring of babies.

He kissed her cheek then rolled out of bed to have a wash.

When he stepped out dressed for work, she had already risen and prepared a light meal of spicy shrimp-and-vegetable soup with rice noodles and coffee. Before he sat down to eat, he gave her the present he had bought in Malacca: a picture postcard set showing the Stadthuys, the ruined chapel on the hill, the old mosque, a Chinese temple, the Resident's bungalow, and a market square. After he supped, she sat on his lap as he described each picture to her in detail, animating it with descriptions of what he had seen and done in town. He kissed her on the forehead and was walking out when she ran after him, intercepting him in the garden just as she had the night before, and, jumping up, kissed him passionately on the mouth. Instinctively his palm spread on her belly, fingers gripping and kneading the soft flesh there.

*   *   *

By noon he was standing in front of the Central Police Station on South Bridge Road. The facade was undergoing construction, repairs to the front of the building due to the heavy damage sustained from an explosion earlier in the year when several pounds of gunpowder had detonated without warning. It was only an accident, but a dozen men had been killed and Hawksworth himself had been maimed when the heavy desk he had been sitting at landed on his foot. The explosion had blown a large hole in the front of the building and caused the paint to blister and peel across the exterior. A square clock tower was being erected where the hole had been, and the entire façade was getting thickened and extended. The result was a building that looked less like an administrative office and more like a fortress. It also meant that Hawksworth's office window, which once looked over the street, would now be recessed inside a colonnaded corridor that ran the length of the second floor of the building.

As part of the reconstruction, an office for the Adjutant to the Chief Detective Inspector was added to his own. He stepped silently through the shared doorway, expecting to find his adjutant hard at work.

Detective Inspector Dunu Vidi Hevage Rizby was sitting stretched far back in his chair, his feet propped up on his desk, his head and face completely obscured by the dashing figure of a cowboy on a charging mount. Stepping closer, Hawksworth could see the fine details of the illustration on the magazine cover: the words 'Beadle's Half-Dime Library' were printed at the top, and the title of the story in which the Detective Inspector was so engrossed was printed beneath that, 'Wild Bill, the Pistol Dead Shot, or Dagger Don's Double', and the author's name across the bottom, 'Prentiss Ingraham'. For the last several years, during his breakfast, Rizby had slid into a similar pose, totally lost in the latest American cowboy serial magazine.

"'Well, pards, what has happened?'" Rizby was reading out

loud in a bad American accent.

'"He killed Manton, and I am just as sure that he killed Hugh, who lies here at my feet. Buffalo Bill believes Weston dead; but I do not! So here I vow to take the life of Wallace Weston, and thus avenge my brothers."

"He raised his right hand as he spoke, pressed his left over his heart and so registered his vow of revenge. Then, mounting his horse, he rode away upon the trail he had before followed."'

'If he had already followed the trail once before, what could he possibly hope to discover by retracing his steps?' Hawksworth asked his adjutant loudly.

Rizby jerked in surprise and his feet slipped clumsily from the desk as the chair's spring snapped upright, and he loudly thumped his elbow on the arm. When he righted himself, the tall man's face was beaming with mirth.

'Chief Detective Inspector, I did not hear you come in! You startled me!'

'I am sorry to interrupt your after breakfast entertainment.'

Rizby laughed and sprang to his feet, his face beaming, his hand extended in greeting. 'Welcome home, sir. I am so glad to see you.' The two men pumped hands, then Rizby rubbed his elbow in pain. The chair had thumped him harder than he had thought. 'How was the journey? Did you find what you expected to find?'

Hawksworth provided a brief outline of the grisly murder of the Resident, the unexpected search for the missing Sergeant Major, the rumours of the *pontianak*, the encounter with the *orang asli*, discovery of the children disappearing from Malay *kampongs*. He did not mention the recovery of what was quite possibly his mother's diary. Their relationship hinged on professional, not personal, matters.

'Do you think the missing children are somehow connected to

the death of the Resident?'

'I do. The Sergeant Major is tracking through the jungle a party of men whom he suspects to be the kidnappers of the children as well as the murderers of the Resident. Walker may require reinforcements. I will enquire with Superintendent Fairer about that possibility.'

'May I ask, what of the *pontianak*?' Rizby's eyebrows arched.

Hawksworth gazed quietly at his adjutant before answering him with measured words, 'We found no evidence that such a creature is involved. I am rather inclined to believe what the *orang asli* told us, that the kidnappers are creating the appearance of a phantom to camouflage their activities. If there is competition for the land – for rubber and tin and even possibly gold – children might be kidnapped to frighten natives out of the territory. I believe that the Resident uncovered this scheme and was nosing about on his own there. Whatever the cause, we must get to the bottom of it. What I do firmly believe is that this slippery Suliman Alsagoff is thoroughly entwined in all of this.'

Rizby nodded in understanding. 'By the bye, since you mention children, I must inform you that last night the corpse of a girl was brought to the morgue. A gang of coolies came upon two men digging a grave near a plantation road not far from the *kampong* at Seletar. The men panicked and ran, leaving behind the body.'

'What more do you know?' Hawksworth pointed his nose directly at Rizby, his face set.

'She was not European, and we are waiting for the coroner's report as to the cause of death. Because of the remoteness, the Coroner did not visit the location himself but sent the Assistant Coroner. That is all I know. Two men from Detective Inspector Dawnaday's squad are at Seletar today examining the crime scene.'

'So it is Dawnaday's case?'

'Yes, sir.'

'I will have a word with him. In the meantime, look into this Solomon Company that the Alsagoff brother in Malacca owns. What are their interests? Who is on the board? What are the connections to Singapore? Be stealthy about this investigation as they are a powerful family and not officially suspects – at least not as of yet. Now it is time for my coffee,' Hawksworth rose. 'And Detective Inspector?'

'Yes, sir?'

'You are a representative of Her Majesty's government and an officer of Detective Branch. Please do leave the wild west to the cowboys – at least until after duty.'

* * *

Detective Inspector Dawnaday was not in his office nor could he be found anywhere in the Central Police Station. Hawksworth did not care for the detective, a younger man who did nothing to hide his ambition and who chafed under the Chief Detective Inspector's command. Coming from the mother country, Dawnaday considered the Malaya-raised Hawksworth something of a country bumpkin and did little to hide his contempt for his superior. However, although he lacked Hawksworth's knowledge and connections in the native communities, he excelled at dealing with Europeans. Except as the duty of his office required, Hawksworth tended to leave Dawnaday to his own devices and usually dealt with the man by ignoring him. That he was given the case of the dead native girl the Chief Detective Inspector put down to himself having been unavailable. Sipping the last of his coffee, he decided to visit the morgue to view the body. His intuition told him that it might have a bearing on the case of the dead Resident.

A steam tram rumbled past Central Station, raising a cloud of dust. The day lacked the usual steamy heat; it was high and fine under a vivid blue sky with cirrus clouds white and bright stretching across the eastern horizon. The sun shone steadily so that even his solar topee did not quite shade his eyes, bleaching colour from the world. Still, it felt good to be putting one foot before the other on the familiar street.

When he turned at the Chinese burying ground at the end of South Bridge Road onto Neil Road – a slight rise ahead that would take him to the dead house at Sepoy Lines – his intuition crackled. He was being shadowed.

The lower stretch of Neil Road consisted of street-front shophouses one or two storeys tall, with the usual covered arcade of the five-foot-way. He paused behind a column, half hidden in shadow. A passing rickshaw provided the opportunity of cover and he dashed to the opposite side of the street, taking up a position next to a dumpling stand. No one showed themselves, so he continued up the rise, toward a row of townhouses in various stages of construction. The top of the hill had become a fashionable neighbourhood for old Peranakan families and second generation Singapore-born Chinese. Without the cover of the arcade, he paused against an unfinished garden wall in the hot, flat sunshine, waiting to see if anyone emerged from the shadows across the street. No one did.

Another rickshaw passed and he ran along beside it, hiding his movement behind the spinning wheels. He was now under the shade of another five-foot arcade at the top of the hill, pressing his back against the decorative glazed tiles of a doorway. Two servant women in formless shifts walked past him chattering in Hokkien.

His gaze was on their backs when a voice suddenly spoke into his ear, '*Selamat datang*. Welcome home, Chief Detective Inspector.'

Beside him, materialised as if from the air, stood Tan Yong Seng. The purple lips smiled at Hawksworth, who smiled in return, then the two started walking side by side, Yong Seng's long black *changshan* swishing as he moved. He wore no vest in the afternoon heat. A straw boater was on his head, adorned with a long flowing black ribbon band. His queue was plaited tightly and ran straight down his back nearly to his rump, swaying like a pendulum in counterpoint to his stride. His eyes were covered by small round glasses with lenses as black as pitch. Hawksworth could see his own face reflected darkly where Yong Seng's eyeballs should have been.

The men kept stride together, picking their way along the five-foot-way. After a short distance, Yong Seng stepped toward the swinging outer doors of a brand new townhouse. Beside the *pintu pagar*, literally a 'door fence', a tough-looking Chinese was sitting in a bamboo chair, fanning himself. He also wore dark glasses, through which he regarded them briefly without breaking his fanning rhythm. Yong Seng greeted him with a nod before pushing his way in, Hawksworth striding after him.

The front room was illuminated only by the sunlight that filtered around the *pintu pagar* and through the frosted green glass of the street-facing windows. Hawksworth took note of the comfortably expensive furniture – Chinese rosewood inlaid with mother of pearl, as well as a Western-style cushioned daybed in damask.

Joss sticks smouldered before a gilded altar to Tua Pek Kong, the red-faced, white-bearded deity of wealth and good fortune. He had been a living man, a Hakka merchant, some say, who was tossed from a shipwreck onto the beach of Penang Island two hundred years earlier. Over time, he had been transmogrified into a venerated saint, his idol dressed in fancy robes and placed on altars across Malaya – his cult was unknown in the motherland. In addition to the joss sticks, a bunch of flowers and a small stack of oranges and a bottle of rice wine had been placed before him. The oranges still appeared dewy and fresh, but the cut flowers placed in a vase had already begun to wilt in the equatorial heat.

A gruff voice called out in Hokkien from a side room, asking who was there. Yong Seng answered by calling back his own name. Hawksworth could hear the sound of pots and pans being rattled in the back of the house, and a faint smell of cooking oil. Lunch was being prepared.

'Where are we?' he asked. As always, the two men conversed in a mish-mash of Malay and English, with the occasional Chinese word tossed in the mix.

'This is the house that Chong Yong Chern bought for Shu En.'

'An entire house? The Mother-Flowers are becoming prosperous if the boss can afford a brand new house for his girl.'

Yong Seng laughed, 'Aiyah! He had no choice! She asks and he gives. She has power over men,' he added in a teasing voice, 'as you well know.' He looked directly at the Chief Detective Inspector but did not remove the eyeshades despite the dimness of the room.

'I have heard that Shu En is now the brains of the Mother-Flowers. Yong Chern merely supplies muscle. True?' An image of the moon-skinned Hokkien gamine came to his mind, the usual lusting desire coming with it. Gentle-faced and beautiful, but as deadly as a cobra in the garden, he thought.

Yong Seng shrugged a sharp Chinese shrug that means, 'think what you want, I shall neither confirm nor deny because the question itself borders on the impertinent'. 'We heard that you were in Malacca.' It was a statement, not a question.

'Yes. Why would that interest you?'

'We take an interest in all our friends on the police force, and we take special interest in our oldest and greatest *ang-moh* friend. The trip was profitable for you?'

'It was … revealing. I am now pursuing a case and perhaps you could help me.'

Another shrug, more rounded, this one meaning, 'go on, I am interested and listening'.

'The Resident of Negeri Sembilan was murdered near Mount Ophir. There are several companies sending men into the region to survey for rubber or tin mines.'

'Or gold.'

'Have you heard something?' the Chief Detective Inspector asked too quickly.

Yong Seng smiled. 'One hears much about gold in that region, but it is only *fool's gold*,' he used the English expression.

'Malay and *orang asli* children have gone missing from the same region. The locals think it is a *pontianak* but we suspect they are being kidnapped by men. We do not know for what purpose.'

Another shrug, this one slow and gentle, which meant, 'what does any of this have to do with me?'

Hawksworth continued, 'And there is a rather shady little man in Malacca named Alsagoff, a scion of the Singapore family, with his own company and interests there. I do not trust him.'

'You are wise not to trust him. The Alsagoffs make their money from import and export. I have been told that they import and export people, too.'

'A common enough trade in Singapore.'

'Hhmm … But these people are different.'

'What do you mean?'

'We bring coolies and girls from China for labour. The Klings do the same from Chennai. The Arabs are different.' He paused, searching for the correct phrase. 'They bring in people for other people.'

'You mean slaves?'

Yong Seng shrugged the lopsided shrug that indicated genuine lack of knowledge. 'Who knows? We hear things. But they do not cross our business, so we do not cross with theirs.'

Hawksworth smiled inwardly at the practicality of the Chinese. 'You might be interested to know that this Alsagoff in Malacca owns an outfit called the Solomon Company, and I have a notion that they are up to dirty business in Singapore. Could you look into it and let me know what you discover?'

'I will be happy to, but it is becoming difficult to make discreet inquires without causing unpredictable suspicions.'

'Perhaps if I could offer an appropriate form of gratitude?' He used the Malay word *rahmat*, which means a 'gift from on high'. It was an offer of grace from the police.

'That would make it much easier for me to ask delicate questions.'

What Yong Seng wanted was an exchange of information. In the past, Hawksworth had notified the Mother-Flowers of an impending raid, not even necessarily on their own people but sometimes on a rival clan, which they could use to their advantage. Once or twice he had even contrived for his men to look the other way when the Mother-Flowers went about their business, though that level of cooperation was not something he wanted to make a habit of. 'I will see what I can arrange.'

That being settled, Yong Seng relaxed, his tone lightening. 'Do you have time for tea? Or perhaps,' mischievousness crept into his voice, 'we will drink some European brandy. We have not been naughty in a long time, my old friend!'

Hawksworth pulled his watch from his pocket. 'Good lord, man, it is only past noon!'

'Why deny the attraction, brother? I know a house nearby with beautiful girls. It is a clean house, newly opened, one-of-a-kind. It is run by the Low family, a competitor, but we can sneak in. They specialise in *variety*,' he used the English word, then lovingly sketched the options: 'They have fair-skinned Sundanese girls, Tonkinese girls with big breasts, petite dark Javanese girls, girls from Shanxi with smooth pink lips, Japanese girls with slender necks, and Siamese girls with gentle fingers, Russian girls with skin the colour of cream and eyes like opals. We could drink some wine, hear some music, have ourselves a good time. What do you say?'

The heavy perfume of the joss sticks on the altar mingled with the savoury odour of ginger and fish frying in the unseen kitchen, filling Hawksworth's nostrils with a musky smell. It was a tantalisingly suggestive mixture, and despite the previous night's incessant sex, or perhaps because of it, the thought of spending the afternoon sprawled on cushions, enfolded in wine and music, entangled in the soft and stroking arms of a cuddlesome stranger was very tempting indeed.

But the temptation was fleeting. His mind was on the case. 'I think, my dear Yong Seng, the earthly paradise you have described will have to wait until another day.'

'Put business before pleasure too long, and soon life is all business and no pleasure.'

'That is true, old friend, but our pleasure will wait until this case is resolved.'

'Why are you so dedicated to this case? What do you care

what the Alsagoffs are doing?'

'I have a feeling – nothing more – that the case of the murdered Resident has something to do with … with my family.' Then his mind fixed on his destination, he said for emphasis, 'And it is my sworn duty to preserve law and order in this Settlement, whether the law is just or not.'

Yong Seng studied him for a moment. 'You have always been a serious man. Do not become stiff and rigid before it is time. But if this is for your family, then do not let me keep you.'

'We will indulge ourselves soon, I promise.'

Yong Seng smiled from behind the eyeshades, 'In the meantime, I will take your share of *variety* girls for myself. And you will owe me their cost when next we go to the house!'

* * *

He left feeling good. He had not realised how much the trip to Malacca had put him out of sorts, but being back on home ground was restoring his spirit.

Less than an hour later his disposition was changed when Dr. Robert Cowpar pulled back the sheet to reveal the little brown face of the dead girl. She looked not more than ten or eleven. 'She was most likely strangled,' said the coroner, pointing to thick bruises all around the thin neck. 'Whoever did it used his own two hands, not a garrotte or noose of any kind.'

'I am given to understand that the body was found while it was in the process of being buried. Can you say how long she had been dead?'

'About twenty-four hours. Not long before they tried to bury her.'

'Any other damage inflicted?'

He pulled back the sheet completely to expose the body on the slab. She was covered in bruises and abrasions. One arm was broken, the elbow bent the wrong way, as though it had been deliberately forced into that position. The nipple of one breast was missing: it looked like it had been chewed off. There were knife cuts, precisely spaced and very deep, along the inside of both thighs, the flesh of which had been flensed. Her pubic area had been mashed and pounded into a fleshy pulp.

Hawksworth could not tear his eyes from the trauma inflicted on the body. It was as bad as he could ever remember seeing ... perhaps worse.

'She was beaten and tortured and raped, both vaginally and anally, before she died,' Cowpar explained. 'In fact, if she had not been strangled she would have soon perished from the internal wounds sustained during the penetrations, which were violent in the extreme. Between the beating and the penetration damage, her internal organs nearly liquefied.'

'Holy god.' Hawksworth took an involuntary step backward.

Staying close to him, Cowpar spoke in a low voice. 'Chief Detective Inspector, I must tell you, as a medical man I have seen many dead children. As you know, native children die in this colony every day from disease, usually in gross agony. But this child, sir ...' The normally emotionless professional struggled for words. 'Hawksworth, this is the most heinous murder I have come across in my entire professional life. It was methodical and deliberate yet passionate and furious, and it was perpetrated on a defenceless child. It is the work of a seriously depraved mind.'

Hawksworth remained silent, then slowly pulled the sheet to cover everything but the girl's head.

Regaining his composure, Cowpar continued, 'Those cuts on her thighs did not happen yesterday. In fact, to judge by the clotting and scabbing, the incisions took place over several days. And to judge by the trauma to her ... nether regions ... she was violated repeatedly over a similar period.'

'If the death was a culmination of a prolonged episode, how long ...?'

'Many days, perhaps weeks. If I may point out, Chief Detective Inspector, if those two coolies had not stumbled upon the men trying to dispose of the body, then she would have laid in the ground a very long time before she was discovered – if she were ever discovered.'

Hawksworth tore his gaze from the girl's face to look at Cowpar. 'Are you suggesting there are likely more victims?'

'Given the methodical nature of the crime, I do not believe that this is the first time the perpetrator ... Well, I mean to say that this person has most likely done something like this before, perhaps many times before. As you can see, there is a method here, and developing a method requires practice.'

Hawksworth crossed his arms over his chest. 'Yes, I see all too well. I would suggest excavating the ground where she was found. There may be more remains buried nearby. What did Detective Inspector Dawnaday have to say about this?'

'Dawnaday?' Cowpar's eyes opened wide in surprise. 'He has not been here. I thought this was your case.'

'What? The man has not viewed the body? But it is his case!'

'Perhaps he is visiting the scene of the crime. Seletar is quite a long way away, and I was told the burial site was far down a plantation road,' Cowpar said calmly.

'Perhaps.' Hawksworth made a note to track down Dawnaday immediately and question him about his obvious disregard for procedure.

'Another point, Chief Detective Inspector. I am having

trouble identifying her race. She was obviously neither European nor Chinese, nor Kling. My Malay assistant used the word *sakai*, but he seemed completely unnerved by the body and fled the room before I could ask him any further questions. Do you have any idea what that means?'

'That word means "slave".'

'Slave?' Cowpar asked, genuinely puzzled.

Hawksworth gazed down at the girl's lifeless face, the flat Negroid nose, the kinky hair laying in bundles of tight curls, smooth skin the colour of caramel, full lips now covered in bruises and scabs, almond shaped eyes beaten closed. '*Sakai* is a derogatory term the Malays use for her people.'

'If not Malay, what is she, then?'

'Write in your report that she is *orang asli*.' He pulled the sheet over her head, then added almost inaudibly, 'one of the "original people".'

*   *   *

He was at Dawnaday's office door, which was open for the heat. The man was seated behind his desk, head bowed over a paper, but he was not writing. He was stabbing at the paper with a pencil as though throwing a dart.

Without preamble, the tall man entered the room. 'I am surprised to find you here, Detective Inspector.'

Dawnaday looked up, startled, the grip on the pencil visibly tightening. He was shorter than Hawksworth but strongly built. Light brown hair was thinning on top and receding on the sides, forming a widow's peak above a long sloping forehead. Dawnaday's eyes were soft brown, yet the jaw was sharp and jutting, so that on the whole he looked like a man damaged on the

143

inside, a man living in a shell. A moustache of sweat constantly dribbled from his smooth upper lip, so that his stubby fingers were incessantly brushing his face and coming away moist.

'Why surprised, sir? This is my office.'

'You share it with Detective Ramsfield, if I am not mistaken, but my surprise is that you have not been to the dead house to see the corpse brought in from Seletar. I understand the case is your own.'

The pencil was dropped so the pudgy fingers could wipe sweat from the upper lip. 'Yes, well, sir, I was going to view the body after lunch. My men are in Seletar now, looking over the ground where the body was found. I was just now preparing my report.' He pointed at the paper before him. Hawksworth could see that beside the dark stab points made by the pencil, the paper was blank. Dawnaday asked tersely, 'Have you seen the body?'

'I have. Doctor Cowpar told me you had not.'

'I apologise, sir,' Dawnaday stiffly replied. 'As I said, I intend to view the body after lunch, and my men are going over the ground ...'

'I want the ground excavated. There is a strong possibility that there are more victims buried there.'

'Sir?' Dawnaday's fingers wiped again at the chafed upper lip. 'Is that an order? I mean, this is *my* case.'

'Had you gone to view the body yourself then I have no doubt you would have come to the same conclusion. As is, consider this a professional favour, Detective Inspector. Have the ground excavated or I will send my own men to do it.'

He could see anger flash across Dawnaday's face, which then slipped into a firm grimace. 'Yes, sir, I will do so,' the voice was defiant even if the words were not.

'And you will then report to me your findings,' Hawksworth

snapped, then softened to add in professional courtesy. 'I believe that our cases may be linked. Perhaps the dead native girl and the murder of the Resident of Negeri Sembilan are connected. We should keep one another closely informed of the other's progress.'

Hawksworth was certain that he saw fear flicker across Dawnaday's face for an instant before the grimace of a defiant subordinate returned to it. The stubby fingers did not wipe away the moustache of beaded sweat on the red chafed lip as he glared up at the taller man. 'Yes, sir, I could not agree more. Let us keep one another closely informed.'

CHAPTER VIII

The Golden Chersonese Club

AT THE END OF THE DAY, word came to Hawksworth by the usual channel – a nondescript Chinese boy in pigtails and a worn blue cotton *changshan* waiting for him just beyond the front gates of the Central Police Station – that Tan Yong Seng wanted to meet him. He was to go at sunset to a tea stall near a wharf on Boat Quay.

When he stepped out from the station the sky was coloured lavender, shot through with streaks of gold from low clouds blocking the direct rays of the sun. The effect was stunning, and even the usually bustling quayside warehouses seemed calmed by the soft apparition above them. It was the idealised sky painted on the walls behind the idols in Taoist temples: the sky of heaven.

The choice of location was no accident. When the Mother-Flowers were first coming into their own among the criminal underworld, Yong Seng had been forced to meet with Hawksworth clandestinely. This was not just to keep his access to a detective secret from the other *kongsi*, but also to keep his friendship with a white man hidden from the Chinese community at large. If it had become known, he could have been considered a conspirator or a traitor – or worse. But now that the Mother-Flowers were the most powerful Hokkien gang in Singapore, with numerous smaller gangs under their umbrella – and now that Hawksworth was the Chief Detective Inspector – Yong Seng liked to meet Hawksworth as openly and as obviously as he liked. The tea stall was visible to all the coolies and *towkays*, the bosses, on the quay, and it was firmly in Mother-Flower territory. Nonetheless, they still met in the murky light of early evening, partly because Yong Seng rose very late in the day and partly because their relationship was to remain both seen and unseen, hovering as it were between reality and rumour.

By the time the Chief Detective Inspector had made his way to the riverside, the sun was fully beneath the horizon and the streaks of holy gold had vanished. Lavender had darkened to plum, casting an eerie green light, making it seem as if the town were at the bottom of the sea.

He spotted Yong Seng standing by the tea stall – little more than a bamboo lean-to beside the front entrance of a go-down where river bumboats could tie up and have their cargo quickly unloaded. An old shirtless man was serving tea to the coolies, his kit a simple tripod brazier with boiling water and a stack of rough ceramic cups. Despite the dirt and squalor of the working wharf, Yong Seng was expensively attired. A black silk vest brocaded with the motif of two crossed cranes was tightly crossed over his thick chest, above the draping material of a flowing violet *changshan*; on his head was a straw boater hat with a black silk band, his queue twisted around his neck. It was high fashion for Chinese gangsters from Hong Kong to Shanghai to Malaya. Seeing him now, Hawksworth recalled that when they first became friends, the man had been able to afford little more than a padded cotton shift.

Both men held their steaming hot cups of tea and watched the last violet light fading from the sky above the dark river. A nearby gas lamp was lit, casting yellow light into a weak circle of chartreuse shadows.

'A lovely evening,' Yong Seng said in Hokkien.

'The weather is very fine. Neither humid nor still,' Hawksworth replied in English.

They exchanged one or two more casual pleasantries then after consuming their second round of bitter tea, Yong Seng finally came to business. 'I have news of your Alsagoff. He is involved in more than shipping and people smuggling.'

'Go on.'

'My cousin is a violin player and sometimes works in a European club here, performing for *ang-moh*. Alsagoff's company owns the club. There are rumours that it is also a brothel.'

'Are you certain is it owned by the Solomon Company?' Hawksworth asked.

Yong Seng nodded affirmatively, sipping at his tea. 'It is owned by the company of the Malacca brother, not the Singapore brother.'

'What is the name of the place?'

'The Golden Chersonese.'

'I know it,' Hawksworth said. 'Rather above my level, I think. It serves mostly our captains of industry and some of the more highly placed government officials. Very exclusive and difficult to join, I am told.'

Yong Seng set down his empty cup. 'We have tried to infiltrate the club, but other than my musician cousin, we do not have anyone on the inside. They only hire Malays.'

'And what of these rumours of a brothel? It is unlikely a jemmy club like that would become involved with simple prostitution.'

'I do not think that what they offer is "simple".'

'Ah. Something more than the usual? A European version of an Oriental pleasure house?'

Yong Seng shrugged the Chinese half shrug that indicated he had no further information but he believed that his interlocutor's suspicion was probably correct. 'I will share with you what I learn about The Golden Chersonese.'

'Thank you, Yong Seng.'

'But you also have a promise to keep. I have a special *rahmat* to ask.' Yong Seng pointed at the bumboats tied together, ready to unload their goods into the go-down controlled by the Hokkien. 'Tonight those boats are filled with raw sugar. In two days they will be filled with opium that we will sell in Java. The opium will be stolen from a British-owned warehouse on Magazine Road. One of your men, a Kling named Lakshmanan, works at night as a private guard there and unfortunately he is too righteous in his dedication to service.'

'You mean he will not accept money to look the other way when your boys arrive.'

'*Dui*,' Yong Seng nodded. The Mandarin word for 'correct' had become part of Singapore street slang.

'And you would like me to have a talk with him and convince him to take ill that evening and remove himself from the premises.'

'*Dui*.'

Hawksworth gazed out at the bumboats. They were so closely packed that they acted as an extension of the quay; one could almost walk across the river by stepping from gunwale to gunwale. They bobbed with the dark river tide in a reptile movement, like the rippling of scales above coiling muscle.

'The man's name is Lakshmanan?' he said to confirm. 'Consider it done.'

Yong Seng smiled and tucked his arms into the silk sleeves of his *changshan*. 'Join me for some rice wine? We have a house near the canal, very close to here. Pretty girls!' he cooed, indicating that he was done talking business for the evening.

Hawksworth studied the dark eyes sparking with mischievous delight. He thought of the corpse he had seen that afternoon, the cuts and bruising on the little body, the skin already discolouring with the rot of death. He needed some rice wine very badly. 'Tonight, my old friend, I shall not refuse your offer.'

* * *

He woke the next day stiff and sore. It felt as though something small and furry were nesting inside his parched mouth. His finger bones cracked as he flexed them, and his neck felt as though a weight had been pressing on it all night. When he rolled over to take in the room, his head spun and he felt dizzy and slightly nauseous. Despite this condition, he found that he was incredibly aroused: the mere scent of Ni's body had excited him and his erection was pushing painfully against his pyjamas.

But Ni was not in bed – only her scent lingered there to tease him. He swung himself slowly off the edge, pushing his legs out of the mosquito netting.

It was already late morning – he had overslept – and the thought of heading directly to his office was unappealing in the extreme. As he washed himself in the brick closet, open to the air, sluicing warm water over his body from the clay vessel, his thoughts drifted to his conversation with Yong Seng, and he decided to drop by The Golden Chersonese Club on Jalan Sultan Road on his way to town. He was in the mood to shake a snake basket just to see what would come tumbling out.

* * *

As his carriage rolled past the Hajjah Fatimah mosque on Java Road, he took in the tomb's peculiar blend of Oriental and Occidental styles, which reflected the mixed Malaccan sensibilities of its namesake and founder, whom Suan Imm had said she had known as a girl. Skewed from the street to face Mecca, the main minaret featured Doric columns, yet the roof was lined with green porcelain Chinese tiles. Erected on sandy soil, the minaret was listed about six degrees off-centre, earning it the inevitable moniker of 'leaning tower of Singapore'. Hawksworth recalled that not only was Princess Hajjah Fatimah buried there, but her son-in-law Syed Ahmed Alsagoff, father of the very man whom the Chief Detective Inspector was investigating, was also interred on the grounds.

His mind was on the case at hand, yet gazing at the leaning tower, at the fanciful mausoleum of this prosperous family, the image of the grave in Gading, sunken and covered in devil's ivy, rose unbidden in his mind: Isabella Lightheart's last resting place, where she lay beside Minister Cooper. He felt no connection to these strangers who lay unregarded and nearly forgotten. Something nagged at his hung-over mind. There was a connection between the mysterious Lightheart and her burnt orphanage and the recent spate of kidnapped children he felt sure existed but was unable to discern.

Moments later his carriage rolled to a stop in front of the painfully bright exterior of The Golden Chersonese Club. Housed in a bungalow property that had been walled in, the façade consisted of a long whitewashed wall that ran the entire length of the road, set back from a low drainage ditch with a small bridge leading up to massive wooden doors. Potted plants, burgundy veined crotons, bird's nest ferns, and yellow-pink bougainvillea rising on trellis around the dark wood of the doors were the only ornamentation. From the outside, the club resembled a Moorish fortress.

A gnarled frangipani tree rose from behind the garden wall, covered in blooms of the 'graveyard flower', *Plumeria obtuse*. He recalled that in Malay stories, the flower's scent was also that of the *pontianak*, and he suddenly found himself on his guard. Ignoring the feeling of unease that was quickly filling his stomach, he gently rapped on the heavy front door and when that elicited no reply he pounded on it, albeit carefully, because the door was covered with metal spikes. After further pounding – which caused a pain in his throbbing head – the door finally swung open to reveal a gorilla-sized man in dark pantaloons and white blousy shirt. A red fez matched a red cummerbund. He looked costumed like a Turk for a fancy dress party, though his heavy and scowling face was anything but comical. They were roughly equal height, but the man weighed at least seventy pounds more.

'*Selamat pagi*,' Hawksworth greeted. He could hear tinkling music coming from behind the giant.

'*Belum buka*,' the man said gruffly, 'we are not open yet', and made to shut the door.

'*Saya faham*,' Hawksworth responded, 'I understand,' stepping into the doorway. 'I am Chief Detective Inspector Hawksworth of the Straits Police, and I would very much like to come in.'

The tinkling music stopped suddenly, then a feminine voice called out from inside the house, 'Ahmed, who is it?' The voice spoke in English but with an accent, French or Italian, he was not sure.

'*Adalah mata-gelap*,' Ahmed used the slang for detective, *mata-gelap*: 'eyes in the dark'.

'Then you had better allow him in.'

The giant studied Hawksworth's face for a moment, then stood aside, opening the door wide. The detective found himself in a spacious foyer – what most probably had been the main room of a bungalow house once – ornamented with potted palms and brass lamps.

The music he had heard indistinctly from outside was being played again in a farther room. It sounded like a *gambang kayu*, a gamelan percussion instrument with a glassy resonance. It was sparsely elegant music, the harmony propelled by vertical sheets of sound, like the tintinnabulation of a fountain, and he felt drawn to the source, moving toward it as if in a trance. Rounding a large potted palm standing by a rattan room-partition, he was startled to find that the source of the music was a petite grand piano.

The music ceased abruptly when he became visible to the seated player. Her hair was covered by a light shawl. A pair of hazel-green eyes set above high sharp cheekbones regarded him coolly from a smoothly sculpted face.

'Please do not let me interrupt your playing, it is lovely.'

'Thank you.'

'I have never heard a piano played like that. I thought perhaps it was gamelan.'

She smiled at him with a trace of condescension. 'No, it is Erik Satie, *Gymnopédies*. I ordered the sheets from Paris, and they arrived only this week. And who are you, sir, who admires modern music?'

'I am Chief Detective Inspector Hawksworth. Please pardon my intrusion.'

Her right hand toyed with the keys as she spoke, 'This is the final *Gymnopédie*, my favourite of the three. It has a sense of the mysterious that I find enchanting.' She played now with her left hand as well, and the aural fountain again filled the room.

Then she let the melody trail off incomplete, and the fountain evaporated. 'Do you play, Detective?'

'No, I am afraid I do not. But I do enjoy music.'

'It is the most evocative of the arts. But if you do not play, well then ...' The woman rose to an impressive height, her slim body taut and firm yet supple, like young bamboo. 'I do not suppose we will perform a duet.' She remained behind the piano as she spoke, looking directly into Hawksworth's eyes. 'How may I help you? Is this official police business?'

'No, no, purely personal, I assure you. I am interested in joining this club.' He spun his topee in his hands awkwardly. Not being accustomed to opulent living, he was rarely comfortable in such luxury.

As though sensing his unease, she slowly pulled the silk scarf from her head to reveal a mane of strawberry blonde hair, curls spilling to frame her face with delicate tendrils. 'We would be delighted to receive an application, but you must know, Chief Detective Inspector, you will need an existing member to pledge you, and our membership list has some of the most prestigious names in the Settlement.'

'Yes, so I was given to understand.'

'However, we are always happy to accommodate members of our esteemed civil service. Point of fact, there are already several members of the police force on our list. Perhaps you would like to inspect the premises before you give the matter further thought?'

He relaxed slightly, and only then realised that he had stiffened up earlier, when she had first stood up and shown herself to him. 'Thank you. That would be most kind.'

'Normally I ask my assistant Ahmed to give visitors a tour of our club, but seeing that we have already met, and that you are a lover of music, I will show you myself.'

'With all due respect, you have yet to tell me your name.'

She laughed amusedly as she moved toward him from behind the piano. Her silk dress clung to her, revealing long curves. 'Camille Sodavalle. I am the manager of this club.'

'Who is the owner?' he asked too quickly.

She stopped a few feet from him, a frown pulling down her lips. 'I thought you said you were not here on police business.'

'My apologies ... Force of habit.' He felt very hung over and susceptible as he looked into her witch hazel eyes.

Her face slipped into a smile revealing large pearly teeth, with a prominent gap. 'Perhaps when I say "manager", I misspeak,' she said breezily. 'I run the day-to-day operations, behind the scenes, as it were, but it is my brother who is the rightful man of the establishment.'

They walked past a rattan room screen painted with an oasis motif, camels and date palms in desert sand, which cleverly blended into the material. It was blocking off a side room with a skylight, two potted palms flourishing under opaque glass. 'Our tea room,' she said, gesturing toward the blocked room. 'We offer high tea with musical accompaniment.'

'Do you perform during the recitals?'

She laughed lightly. 'No, my music is only for myself. Sometimes I will perform for our evening guests, but that is only on special occasions.'

'You play very beautifully,' he said, looking at her. She merely smiled in reply. She was nearly as tall as he was, and Hawksworth was not used to looking into the face of women who stood his height. As they walked he noticed the swell of her breasts moving beneath the sheer material of her dress and the unrequited desire of his morning bed flared again.

They paused in a sunken room that was piled with heavy

couches and easy chairs, its walls lined with potted palms and ferns, its floor covered in Persian rugs. The pungent smell of stale cigar smoke hung in the air. The décor maintained the Arabic flavour. The furniture was upholstered in Moroccan leather with colourfully brocaded cushions nestled in the armrests. Heavy brass lamps with perforated shades were placed in the corners of the room. They were wired for electricity, he noted, and would throw dramatic shadows at night. The walls were curved upward to a single point of intersection of four arched beams so that the ceiling appeared peaked, like a Bedouin's tent.

'Our main club room,' she said, sweeping into it soundlessly. 'In fact, we will open for lunch in only an hour more, so our tour will have to conclude soon. Do you like what you see so far?'

'Very much so,' he said, gazing at the oblique curve of her legs, the rising swell of her breasts, the tangle of strawberry curls.

'Good. I do hope you will consider joining us.'

'I would be interested to learn more. I have heard that there are … special arrangements the club can make for members?' he spoke tentatively.

She bit into her lower lip while eyeing him carefully. 'And this is not police business?'

'I assure you, it is not.' He smiled warmly to show he meant no harm.

She studied him a moment more, then said quietly, 'In that case, I do have one more room to show you.'

Sodavalle led him down a narrow corridor, the entrance obscured by potted palms. He could see that it opened into a garden through an arched portal barred by an ornate gate. Two arches of similar size were set into the wall on either side of the gate; before one of these, Camille paused. Then she swung it open and damp air from an unused room rushed out.

She stepped inside and he followed. From the gloom emerged a den-like space, with leather upholstered sofas lining the walls. The same brass lamps were here, and the intricate Persian rugs, but at the centre of the room was a slightly raised stage, on which were haphazardly stacked wooden stools and benches. Some of these, he noted, had metal rings anchored to them. Further nooks were visible beyond the light from the hall, half hidden behind rattan screens.

'This is our private entertainment room, for only the most esteemed members of the club,' she said, moving close to face him, barring him from further entering the space. 'We call it the Ophir Room.'

She then brushed his shoulder lightly, with the same touch, he thought, that she had used when she was toying with the gamelan-like Satie melody. It was brief, but enough to electrify. He turned to see her smiling, her plush lips lusciously inviting. Her hazel-green eyes gazed into his, compelling a response.

He spoke low. 'The Ophir Room. What an interesting name.'

'Yes, we strive to make all our members feel as rich as King Solomon himself.' She moved closer to him, strawberry-blonde curls shedding perfume. 'They say he had seven-hundred wives and three-hundred concubines.' She purred, her hand resting on his shoulder. 'His life must have been endless rounds of pleasure.'

'And the desert *djinn* taught him the speech of the birds. I know about old king Solomon. You are owned by the Solomon Company, are you not?'

She turned cold, her face sliding into a scowl. 'I thought you said that you were not here on police business. Why so many questions?'

'Again, my apologies. Habits die hard,' he realised even as he spoke that his voice was unintentionally harsh.

'So you said before,' she said icily, stepping away from him. 'Please do not pry: it would make me very cross and I would kick up a shine with your superiors.' She did not need to add that some of those superiors were already members of The Golden Chersonese Club for the threat to stick.

'My apologies. I assure you that I am here only on personal interest. This is not an investigation.'

She nodded without smiling, seemingly satisfied with his explanation.

'May I ask you something personal, Chief Detective Inspector?' she moved in closer again, her face relaxing. He could smell her private scent, a musky mixture of honey and clove.

Parting her lips to reveal her gapped front teeth, she whispered, 'Why did you become a detective? Are you merely serving your queen and her empire? Or is it something more philosophical, like peace and justice, you believe in?'

'To serve her Majesty, I do my duty, which is to preserve order so that peace and justice are the rule, not the exception.'

She moved close enough to kiss. The desire to embrace her, to throw her down, strip her clothes and ravish her was powerful. 'You know of the Queen of Sheba, and how good King Solomon was to her?' she whispered, hazel eyes searching his.

'Are you offering to be Sheba? Is that part of the entertainment?'

'Only if you are a good man, Chief Detective Inspector Hawksworth.' She leaned back from the waist, eyelids fluttering, moist lips parted.

In a flash he caught her wrist, gripping it enough to hurt her. She winced, but did not utter a word of protest. 'I am good,' he said, breathing heavily, 'when my duty requires it. Are you good when you offer your services to your clients?'

She tried to pull back but he held her tightly. Stamping her foot she shrieked, 'I am a businesswoman, not a whore. If you do not release me I shall register a complaint!'

'Whores are businesswomen.' He pulled her to him, exhaling his stale hangover breath into her face, then pressed his lips against the moist softness of her parted mouth. He held her against his hard body tightly, inhaling her, then twisted her wrist once more before letting her go.

She fell back, stunned for a moment, rubbing the pain in her thin wrist. The commotion had attached the attention of Ahmed, whose bulk now appeared in the hallway. 'Is everything in order, madam?'

Regaining her composure, she touched her fingers to her lips, tracing where he had kissed her. 'Yes, Ahmed. But I would like you to show this gentleman out. He was just taking his leave.' To Hawksworth she said briskly, 'I hope you do join our club, Chief Detective Inspector. I do look forward to appreciating your company more … intimately.' She raised a single eyebrow above the gapped-tooth pout. 'Perhaps I will even teach you the speech of the birds.' She laughed before twirling away, strawberry curls catching the air like feathers.

Once he had walked out the massive front door, it took him a moment to adjust to the heat and light and noise and dirt of Jalan Sultan. From the nearby Hajjah Fatimah mosque came the sound of the muezzin's call to *zuhr*, the midday prayer. He hailed a passing rickshaw. 'Take me to Central Police Station.' But when the chair had been tipped back and they were under way, he barked, 'Change of direction. Take me to the Straits Club, Hill Street.' To himself he muttered, 'A *stengah* of whisky will go down nicely. Women like that are what drive men to drink.'

CHAPTER IX

The Fate of Fenella

ON HIS DESK, beside the cup of *kopi-o kosong* – black coffee no sugar – and a plate of curry *prata*, was a copy of *The Straits Times*. While he sipped and chewed, his eyes scanned the lines of an article titled 'The Prospectus of Peace' regarding the negotiations between China and Japan taking place in Seoul: the Chinese were willing to negotiate a peace settlement while the truculent Japanese were less inclined to do so. Hawksworth's eyes shifted to the advertisements and announcements on either side of the page. He noted that the John Little department store was selling beverages bottled by the local firm of Gowns, Alexander and Company. Tennent's Pale Ale was $1.75 a pint. Cider was going for $3.50 a quart.

Above this advertisement was an announcement that the North Borneo and Labuan Revenue Farms were now open to tenders for sale. The opium, tobacco, spirit selling, pawn broking, bird's nest collection and sale, and wharf duty collection operations, were all up for grabs. The most lucrative farm would be the one for opium selling; that the profit would be split between several rival factions was hinted at in a proviso, so as to parcel out the spoils so that they had fewer reasons to compete with each other: 'Tenders for the opium farm may be made for the whole Territory or/and Labuan, or for each province separately.' The effect would be to drive competition to the black market, so that British administrators could maintain an illusion of controlling vice for profit while the Chinese clans could make their money without relying completely on the foreign administrators. He envisioned the packets of cash being passed furtively under tables to ensure that such order was maintained.

According to an adjacent two-line announcement, the SS *Port Melbourne* had just docked in Singapore with a cargo of 'beautiful Australian apples, in capital condition', which could be purchased for $1.00 per basket, with twenty-five apples in each.

Kelly and Walsh, Limited, of No. 6 Battery Road was selling 'new and popular novels'. *Under the Great Seal* by J. Hutton was on offer for $1.20. *The Fate of Fenella,* 'a story by twenty-four different authors, male and female', including Bram Stoker and Arthur Conan Doyle, the advertisement explained, could be purchased for $1.35.

Hawksworth's eyes paused at another notice: 'The Undersigned have on hand for sale several Hadji Promissory notes at the cheapest price. Whoever intends to purchase them please apply to Alsagoff and Company, No. 5 Battery Road.' The company was located on the edge of Raffles Place, only a short distance from Johnston Pier, on the other side of Fullerton Square.

The announcements set his thoughts running over the case, and he found the name 'Fenella', from the adjacent advert, fused with the image of the dead *orang asli* girl, as if it had belonged to her. Now, in his mind at least, she had a name.

A knock came at his office door. When it opened, a grim-faced Superintendent of Police stood behind it. Hawksworth quickly wiped the last of the curry's orange sauce from his mouth and pushed back his chair to stand at attention.

'Superintendent Fairer, good morning, sir.'

'David,' the older man said in a gentle voice that contrasted sharply with his mashed-potato face and his surly bulldog demeanour, 'be seated'.

'Thank you, sir.'

The Superintendent pulled up a chair on the other side of the desk. The two men had known each other a long time and maintained a casual if distant relationship.

'Welcome back from Malacca. You discovered our missing Sergeant Major, I understand. Rather a Doctor Livingstone moment, was it not?'

'Yes, sir. Bit of a ramble in the jungle.'

'And now you are back in Singapore working diligently.'

'Yes, sir. Several cases, when my administrative duties permit.'

'Including the case of the Resident's purported murder at Ayer Panas?'

'Yes, sir. As indicated in my report, the Sergeant Major found ample evidence of murder, and I believe that the case is connected with interests in Singapore. As I was the one who found the Sergeant Major, it only made sense that my squad would take on the case – as it states in my report, sir.'

'I am wondering why you went to Malacca in the first place? "Family matters", you said.' Fairer paused, and tapped his foot resonantly on the wooden floorboard.

'Yes, sir.' Hawksworth glanced at Fairer's face, trying to read the man. He detected an uncharacteristic evasiveness in his long-standing superior.

'May I ask if it was the case of the murdered Resident that brought you to The Golden Chersonese Club yesterday morning?'

Hawksworth straightened his back and met the Superintendent's intent stare with his own. His visit must have stirred the pot more than he had anticipated. He realised suddenly that Camille Sodavalle's come-on had been an act, a test of his intentions. Despite his rushed kiss, he had acted too much like a policeman and not enough like a man interested in the seductions she was offering. He had failed her test. 'Yes, sir. After receiving a lead from an informant, I thought it best to pay the place a visit in person.'

Fairer sighed, running a hand over his short cropped hair, then gazed out at the square of blue sky framed within the office's window. Cries in Hakka came from the street below: a sweet bun seller, hawking his goods.

'Chief Detective Inspector, The Golden Chersonese Club is a well-known and respected institution. Several prominent persons in our community are members there, including both the Attorney General and the Colonial Secretary as well as several members of the Colonial Council, at least two of whom are close friends of His Excellency the Governor, not to mention, of course, our own superior, the Inspector General of Police. And now I have word from that very man that the proprietress of the club complained to him about you. She had stated that you demanded entry before opening hours and generally made yourself a nuisance. Would you mind telling me why you believe that such an esteemed establishment is somehow involved with this sordid business in Malacca?'

Hawksworth waited, studying the Superintendent's face: the lines were taut like a ship's rigging under sail. 'It is based on a conjecture, sir.'

'*Conjecture*? Is that what I am to tell the Inspector General? Explain yourself.'

'I believe that a man in Malacca named Alsagoff, who owns a company that is involved with mineral or other exploration in the lands around Ayer Panas, is complicit in the murder of the

Resident. His company also owns The Golden Chersonese Club.'

'You are referring to the Solomon Company, which, you may be interested to know, is not wholly owned by Mr. Alsagoff of Malacca, but also by other vested interests here in Singapore, including European.'

'European, sir?'

'The Sodavalle family, from Marseille, I believe. Who have long-standing ties in Singapore with the Alsagoffs, among others. I will also point out to you what you already know – that the Alsagoff family is highly respected in their own community as well as the European and Chinese communities.'

'The Sodavalle family?' Hawksworth's voice lingered on this information, but Fairer was not to be taken in by the redirection.

'David, I will be blunt,' he snapped. 'You must tread very carefully. When it comes to The Golden Chersonese Club, I will not be able to protect either yourself or your men if you should step over the line.'

'Protect, sir?'

'Do not be thick with me!' Fairer raised his voice, the higher octave simultaneously gruff and whining, like a millstone cracking grain. He had not used it on Hawksworth in a very long time, and the detective found it chilling.

Then softening, the Superintendent continued, 'Your methods have always been … unorthodox. But as they create positive results, I am able to defend you to *my* superiors when they question your techniques. But when it comes to the friends of my superiors, and indeed my superiors themselves, I cannot shield you. So allow me clarify the situation for you. The Resident of Negeri Sembilan was *not* a member of The Golden Chersonese Club. The Resident was small beer, and no one let him into the place. He, and his unfortunate demise, are not connected to this club or its owners in any way whatsoever.'

'Superintendent, sir, are you suggesting ...'

'I am *instructing* you, Chief Detective Inspector, to not enter The Golden Chersonese Club again. I will not be able to protect you in the event that certain highly placed people decide to take your investigation in the wrong spirit.'

'Wrong spirit, sir?' Hawksworth retorted quickly. 'It is a murder investigation of a British official.'

'Then do your job,' the millstone voice ground out again. 'If you continue to snort about like a bloody rampaging elephant then you might well find yourself the sole police officer of a station far upriver. Very far up river indeed.'

'I understand, sir.' Hawksworth realised there was no point in arguing any further. Fairer was not only sending a warning, but was safeguarding his own position. The threat, he knew, was coming from high up in the ruling hierarchy.

'I do hope so, for your own sake, David. These are not people to be trifled with, not even by the police.' Superintendent Fairer rose from his chair. Hawksworth followed suit, standing sharply at attention behind his desk.

'Good day, Chief Detective Inspector,' Fairer said in a grave voice.

'Good day, sir.'

* * *

'Good morning, Chief Detective Inspector!' A bright voice called out. It was Rizby, freshly arrived. 'I saw the Superintendent in the hall – he seemed somewhat grim.'

'Good morning, Detective Inspector. Yes, the Superintendent was just here to politely warn me away from further visiting The Golden Chersonese Club in any official police capacity.'

'What?' Rizby looked both discomfited and confounded. 'Begin from the beginning, sir. What were you doing in a jemmy establishment like The Golden Chersonese Club, and why in heavens would the Superintendent warn you away from the place?'

'The Alsagoff I met in Malacca owns the club. I had a suspicion that the place is not what it seems. I am now convinced of it. While I was there, I met a woman named Camille Sodavalle who claimed to be the sister of the manager. The Superintendent inadvertently dropped that her family is from Marseille, which, if the tip Lim Suan Imm gave me in Malacca is to be trusted, would indicate that they belong to the Alsagoff bloodline.'

'And the warning?'

'My visit must have ruffled some feathers because Sodavalle complained to the Inspector General of Police, himself a member of the club, who in turned sent Superintendent Fairer to warn me away.'

Rizby was silent, his fox-like head cocked to one side, fingers tugging at his earlobe, deep in thought.

'What I would like you to do,' Hawksworth continued, 'as quietly as you can, is to find out all you can about the Sodavalle family and the Solomon Company. What are their connections to each other and to The Golden Chersonese Club?'

'Yes, yes, I will,' he said, then added pointedly, 'This business about the Inspector General is worrisome.'

'There is more. The girl whose body was discovered in Seletar was *orang asli*. I suspect that she is one of the children who have gone missing near Ophir.'

'What was an *orang asli* girl doing in Singapore?'

Hawksworth was quiet. He felt the sweat running down his spine, beneath his neatly creased shirt – pressed by Ni only the night before – to pool near his tailbone before cascading down further, to soak the seat of his trousers. The climate of the torrid zone sometimes did strange things to the minds of men who were not born into it: he knew from experience that the unrelenting heat and moisture, the broiling sun and hot-house nights, occasionally drove men to extremes of sex and violence that they never would have been capable of back home in London or Paris or Amsterdam. The social structure of the colonies, with the explicit hierarchy of races and privileges, only added fuel to the fire.

'I do not know what she was doing here,' he spoke meditatively, 'but I do believe that the murder of the Resident and the disappearance of the children are connected. And I believe that the slippery Alsagoff in Malacca is only one end of the thread that runs through this grotesque arras, with the Sodavalles and The Golden Chersonese Club at the other.'

There was a knock at the door, and Ah Fong, the coffee boy, entered with hot sweet tea for Rizby and another pot of black coffee for Hawksworth. He was dressed in his usual cotton tunic and a pair of loose trousers that ended at the ankle. His queue was iron grey, long and well kept, and he projected an air of indifferent acceptance. Hawksworth mused that in all the years he had known the man, he had not once seen him smile widely or frown deeply. He knew that it was this narrow spectrum of expression, mixed with an oblique approach to the vicissitudes of fate that caused foreigners to describe the Chinese as 'inscrutable'.

After the steaming cups were placed on their desks, Hawksworth thanked Fong, who performed a perfunctory bow. The Chief Detective Inspector knew that for decades he had been informing on police movements to the Hainanese *kongsi*, the clan of his people, but that was only to be expected.

Turning again to the morning paper, another announcement caught the Chief Detective Inspector's attention: arrived the previous night at New Harbour was *The Archimedes*, a passenger steamer. It plied a route from Calcutta to Singapore – her homeport – with ports of call along the coast from Burma to Malaya. This was nothing unusual; many ships owned by many companies plied the same route. What was odd was the penultimate port of call: Muar.

'What do you make of that, Rizby?'

'Perhaps it is not so unusual. If no other company sends its ships to Muar, then whoever owns *The Archimedes* might find a lucrative niche by stopping there.'

Hawksworth sipped his coffee, drumming his fingers on his desktop. 'Who owns the ship?'

Rizby leaned forward. 'What is the sudden interest in Muar?'

'Muar is the nearest port to Ayer Panas, where the Resident was found dead, and not far from the area where the native children have gone missing. And as it is in Johor, there are no Straits police present.'

Both men grew silent, considering the implications.

'Detective Inspector,' Hawksworth began, 'we have been specifically instructed by our Superintendent to cease any investigation into The Golden Chersonese Club. We have been asked to not go anywhere near the place, is this not so?'

'Yes, sir.'

'And yet we have been asked to pursue our investigation into the murder of the Resident.'

'Yes, sir.'

'The Golden Chersonese Club is far from New Harbour, is it not?'

'By Singapore travel standards, yes sir, it is,' Rizby started grinning, catching Hawksworth's drift.

'So if you and I were to take a rickshaw to New Harbour and make inquiries about this ship whose last port of call was Muar, then we would not be investigating The Golden Chersonese Club at all, would we?'

'Not as far as I can see, Chief Detective Inspector.'

He finished off the bitter coffee in one last flourish. 'Fancy a day by the seashore?'

Rizby laughed. 'Shall I invite any of the other men?'

'No, no need.' He cocked his hand like a revolver, then pushed the brim of an invisible cowboy hat up his brow with the barrel, and speaking in his best American accent, said 'We're pard-ners, ain't we, Tex?'

Rizby laughed aloud again. 'In that case, shall I bring my pearl-handled six-shooter?'

Hawksworth paused, and then answered in all seriousness, 'Yes.'

*   *   *

The proximity to water did nothing to allay the midday heat. The sprawling Tanjong Pagar Dock Company facility at New Harbour was almost completely empty under the sun's furnace.

Hawksworth adjusted his topee to reduce the nearly unendurable glare and spied a group of young Malay boys diving into the water from a small sampan in the harbour not far from the quayside. Their lean hard bodies glistened – most wore only light shorts to protect their modesty, and some had dispensed even with those. They were diving into the translucent water to look for coins the passengers from the ships tossed overboard; the latter liked to watch with delight as the taut brown boys, smooth as seals, slipped to the bottom to pluck their livelihood from the sand and coral.

Spying a familiar round figure in black making its way down the quayside, the tall man cried out 'Mr. Bosworth!'

'Chief Detective Inspector! What a pleasant surprise!' Bosworth responded jovially.

The two men approached each other, keeping to the shady side of the quay. Once met, they greeted each other warmly. 'Mr. Bosworth, allow me to introduce you to Detective Inspector Dunu Rizby,' to whom Hawksworth explained, 'Mr. Bosworth was with me at Malacca and Ayer Panas.'

'A pleasure to make your acquaintance, sir,' Rizby said. 'When did you arrive in Singapore?'

'Just now. A quick trip to Malacca to supervise the final stages of the surveying report and collect some samples, and now I am back – thankfully.'

'May I ask which ship you took?'

'*The Archimedes*,' he said, gesturing in the general direction of the sea. 'I am overseeing the unpacking of my equipment on the quay. Time for lunch, now. *Makan tengah hari*, as the locals say.'

'Were you aboard when she called at Muar?' Rizby asked.

'Yes, indeed I was, and I was put in mind of the adventure I shared with the Chief Detective Inspector.' He shook his heavy jowls. 'None of that for me again, thank you. After you left Ayer Panas, my portmanteau was invaded by white ants that devoured all my clothes in a matter of hours.'

'They are a constant problem, especially in the rural areas. Lead chests lined with camphor can prevent them, but even that method is not always effective. I am curious … Did you notice anything unusual while you were stopped at Muar?' Hawksworth asked.

'Not any *pontianaks*, if that is what you mean,' Bosworth

said archly.

Hawksworth smiled. 'No, no. I meant any unusual passengers or cargo taken aboard?'

Bosworth paused to think. 'There was something, he said. 'We were only at Muar for a short time. I assumed it was to pick up more passengers as the ship was a quarter empty. Instead, I saw them hoist aboard a large wooden crate, and it was only an hour or more after it was secured that we sailed. It would seem that we stopped at Muar for the sole purpose of collecting this thing.'

'A crate? Was there anything odd you noticed about it? Distinctive markings, perhaps?'

'There were holes drilled in the top. As you would expect for carrying a large animal.'

'Did you stop between Muar and Singapore?'

'No. We sailed straight through. Although we did spend the night at anchor in the roads while waiting for an available berth. Why are you so curious about this journey, Chief Detective Inspector? Working on a case?'

'Any idea, Mr. Bosworth, who owns *The Archimedes*?'

'I am disappointed to say that it is owned by our pretentious little friend, Alsagoff. It is a Solomon Company ship.'

Hawksworth turned to see Rizby's fox-like face grinning up at his, a knowing glint shining in his agate-coloured eyes.

Bosworth noted the silent exchange. 'What do you think it is? Is he transporting some sort of dangerous exotic beast?'

'Something very much like that, Mr. Bosworth, something every much like that, indeed.'

'Well, I wish you the best of luck with your investigation. Any damage done to Alsagoff would help my own prospects in Malaya. Forgive me, but now I must make haste. Unless you care to join me for lunch, I must be going.' He added sincerely, 'It has been a pleasure to see you again, Chief Detective Inspector – and I am sure we will meet again before the year is out.'

With a slim smile, Bosworth continued his sweaty way down the quayside toward the hackney carriage station. The detectives turned the other way, toward the end of the quay and the block of low wooden sheds where the dock master worked and lived.

His name was Marcus Kneer, of German extraction, though he had been in Singapore since anyone could remember. His face was lined and tanned like old leather, from the years working under the equatorial sky, and his voice was ravaged too, sounding like a razor on a strop. The speculation was that he was a ship captain before he started the less strenuous job of administrator for the Tanjong Pagar Dock Company, but no one ever knew for certain. He had simply blown in one day on the tide, and after attaching himself like a barnacle to the New Harbour dock, he had never left.

His office had a peculiar marine smell, of fuel and creosote and rot. It was made of thin clapboard, the windows lacking glass. Daylight shot through the gaps between the wooden slats, casting a sharp pattern of bright spots and deep shadows across the room. Combined with the sounds of the dock and the cry of the gulls, the overall effect was that of being aboard a ship at sea. Rizby stood by the door, which was left open for light and air, while Hawksworth spoke with Kneer.

His voice sawed away: '*The Archimedes* is indeed owned by the Solomon Company. She arrived last night and spent the first night in the roads. She berthed to disembark passengers and unload cargo just past dawn, then she went back to anchor. She is due to depart in another three days.'

'You seem very sure.'

Kneer bristled, blue eyes momentarily blazing. He was not a man used to being questioned. 'It is precisely my job to know such things.'

'Of course. And do ships usually go out to the vessels that are waiting in the roads?'

'Yes, tender boats make trips to supply the ships in the roads,' he mumbled.

'And do vessels unload cargo while waiting in the roads?'

Kneer frowned. 'You know as well as I do, Chief Detective Inspector, that cargo is smuggled from vessels in the roads. It is not a condoned practice, but it is common.'

'There must be a disembarkation manifest of some sort for *The Archimedes*. I should like to see it.'

There was the shuffling of papers on his desk accompanied by much grunting. Eventually the document was produced from atop a cabinet. There was a list of the passengers who had disembarked and the cargo that had been unloaded, along with the details of the port of embarkation. He spotted Bosworth's name and his itemised freight; both had boarded at Malacca. There was no indication of either passengers or cargo being taken aboard at Muar.

'There was no unaccompanied freight from Muar disembarked at Singapore?'

'*Richtig*, yes, none,' Kneer said gruffly. 'This is the final port of call. The vessel is completely emptied of all passengers and cargo.'

'The outbound voyage is the same as the inbound – she will stop at the same ports along the way?'

'She calls at all but one.'

'Which?' Hawksworth asked, though he already knew the answer.

'Muar,' the voice rasped. 'That ship only calls at Muar on her voyage home to Singapore.'

* * *

Back in the bright heat of the quay, Rizby positioned himself to stand in the taller man's shade. 'Should we go out to the ship, sir?'

'I doubt that we will find anything still aboard. Nonetheless, send Anaiz and Rajan. My suspicion is that the crate was unloaded by quiet of night when she first arrived, while she was anchored in the roads.'

'What next?'

'The captain of the ship is most likely still in Singapore, and perhaps he can explain to us the mystery of the crate from Muar, though I already have my suspicions.'

Rizby was quiet before he said softly, 'It is almost too frightful to contemplate.'

'I fear things will only become uglier the more we learn,' Hawksworth sighed then stepped back into the shade of the overhang. His topee back on his head, he stared across the glittering emerald green of the harbour at the muscled bronzed bodies of the Malay boys as they dived silently into the water. Their flesh was young and resilient, while his own felt heavy and careworn, perspiring under his clothes. The need for a strong drink was suddenly intense. 'I will search for the ship captain. He will most likely be put up in Sailor Town.'

'Do you want me to accompany you?'

'I can handle Sailor Town all on my own,' he said confidently. 'I ask you to discover all you can about the Solomon Company's business dealings, and try to be as discreet about your enquiries as possible.'

CHAPTER X

Victoria dei Gratia

HE CROSSED INTO SAILOR TOWN long after the sun had set, and though the blaze had fled the sky, the land remained steamy and hot as at midday. The streets were thronged with the usual motley gang of seamen and prostitutes, street vendors, and temple-goers. The stench and press of human flesh could at times be unbearable, and there was the constant undercurrent of violence, as though the place were strung with bare electrical wires. He watched a Russian sailor kick a legless Indian beggar off his wooden platform; the latter flopped over, flailing, revealing dark unwashed genitals that looked like a knot of wood. The Russian's companions laughed loudly, jeering and pointing before moving on. It was a small act of degradation the likes of which would be repeated all night in Sailor Town.

There was a lean-to shack near the Thian Hock Keng temple on Telok Ayer, little more than a heavy plank and stretched canvas over a narrow space between two shophouses. The assemblage of flotsam and jetsam was an institution, the home and place of business of Toddy Jock, a Cornish sailor long since shipwrecked in Singapore.

The Chief Detective Inspector took a seat – the stump of a log – before the low table at the front of the shack, and spoke loudly at the hunched figure resting half hidden in shadow: 'Good evening, Jock. How goes business?' The man was blind in one eye and twisted by arthritis; legs rendered slender as twigs kept him bound to a wheeled board, which he used to push his himself along. He had sold strong homemade toddy from his lean-to for as long as anyone, including Hawksworth, could remember, and he knew all that happened on the streets in Sailor Town.

The wizened face turned toward him, the blind eye milky blue and gelatinous like an oyster. 'Chief Detective Inspector Hawksworth, hav'n seen you here in a long while. What brings you to Sailor Town on a night like this?' His voice was high pitched yet rough as if it had been sanded down and sawed off. It was not a pleasant sound.

'What kind of night is this?' Hawksworth asked, genuinely perplexed.

'Careful as you go. The dead will walk the earth tonight, Chief Detective Inspector,' he held up a white paper lantern crudely painted with a black grimacing face. 'It is All Hallows Eve, even if these heathens all around do'n know it.'

He had not been invited to any of the fancy dress parties and masked dances held in the European districts, and the significance of the date had passed him by. A half-formed question flickered through his mind: was there a fancy ball that night at The Golden Chersonese Club? He pictured Camille Sodavalle's long nude lines wrapped in diaphanous veils that billowed and furled behind her like the tail of a Siamese fighting fish while she swayed through the room, entertaining her many guests.

'I had forgot. But never you mind the dead, Jock, it is the living that pose the greater threat. I am looking for the captain of *The Archimedes*, recently put into port from Muar.'

'Aye, Muar, aye, but she sails inbound from Calcutta. She calls in Rangoon and Penang and Malacca and others more,' Jock drank down a drought of toddy from a wooden cup, smacking toothless gums.

'What do you know of her captain?'

'That would be Garnett Martin. Australian. He puts up at The Kenning Mate.'

'Thank you.' He reached into his pocket and pulled out a fistful of coins, poured them onto the table.

'Hold about, Chief Detective Inspector. I am a businessman, not a charity,' the voice scolded.

He watched as Jock dipped a ladle into a bucket of frothy orange liquid, then poured the contents into a dirty wooden cup that he offered to the detective in a claw-like fist. Hawksworth took it, frowning at the rim darkened with many mouths, then held his breath as he drank down the noxious brew in two gulps. It tasted like coconut and tar water and burned his throat. Jock smiled crookedly at him, and Hawksworth smiled back before lurching out of the lean-to, his stomach already feeling sour. He wondered if the stuff was what kept Jock alive, pickled like a specimen in brine.

* * *

The Kenning Mate was a new establishment, a rooming house above a tavern built on the damp ground of reclaimed land. Across the street from the tavern, the mudflats stretched vacantly, already laid with a grid of streets ready for buildings, the lights of ships bobbing in the inky water beyond the shore. Two paper lanterns were strung up outside the front doorway, painted with garish faces, much like the one Toddy Jock had shown him. Leaning against the wall was a Tonkinese woman, nodding off, one breast with a dark purple nipple bared before a sleeping infant. She regarded him with the rheumy eyes of an opium addict as he walked past.

Hawksworth could hear the music before he stepped into the narrow smoky room. There was an empty space at the back in which two singers with guitar and fiddle kept time by stomping on the planks of the floor. He recognised the tune, one apt for All Hallows Eve. It was a ghost tale about a bride locked in a chest during a game of hide-and-seek in a country mansion. Undiscovered, she dies, her skeleton found only years later. Hawksworth remembered first hearing it in his youth in Penang, but the rowdy players of the joint had changed the lyrics:

The beds were all made in the bawdy house fine,
And the whores were rejoicing in gin and wine,
And the old bawd herself, dressed out so gay,
Was making them drunk on Christmas day.
And there was Peg Watkins, the brothel's delight,
Got lewd on a cove, as was there that night.
And said she to herself: 'If I don't have a go,
I'll content myself with the old dildo.'

It was a crowded room, with a short bar along one wall. To judge by the voices, most of the drinkers were Australians, and to judge by the general cleanliness of the place, they were captains and officers. He asked the bartender, a swarthy moustachioed man in a surprisingly clean white apron, for his man.

'And who are you?' he said with a pronounced accent, lighting a cheroot.

'I am Chief Detective Inspector Hawksworth. Is the man here?'

Without a change in his expression, the bartender pointed

with his chin at a very drunken blond man slumped over the bar.

'What is he drinking?'

'Grog.'

'One more for him, and one for me, and allow me to pay,' Hawksworth said, then pushed into the space beside the man. Sweat was already pouring down his back, unpleasantly soaking his shirt.

The bartender placed two mugs of grog – arrack mixed with ale – in front of the blond man, paying no mind to the Chief Detective Inspector. 'Captain Martin?'

Bloodshot eyes glared from a face closing in on middle age.

Hawksworth spoke, but his voice was muffled as the singers belted out the song's chorus: 'Oh! the old dildo, oh! the old whore's dildo!' Voices in the bar loudly joined in the ragged harmony.

'Are you Martin, Captain of *The Archimedes*?' Hawksworth repeated himself over the bar noise.

'Aye and aye. Who are you?' Hawksworth slid the mug of grog before him. 'I am Chief Detective Inspector Hawksworth of the Straits Police.'

The red eyes lingered on him for a moment, while the hand lifted the mug to the thin lips. He said nothing while gulping down the liquid. Replacing the emptied mug and wiping the back of his hand across his mouth, he narrowed his eyes and said, 'Rack off.'

Hawksworth's arm was swift: he gathered a bunch of the man's straw coloured hair at the back of his head then forced his face downward into the bar. The thud was covered by the chorus of voices, 'Oh! the old dildo, oh! the old whore's dildo!' The bartender, noticing the fracas, hurried over.

'Two more mugs of grog,' Hawksworth ordered sharply. The bartender looked at him a moment as if to say something, then thought the better of it.

'That was not polite, Captain Martin,' he said, looking down at the reeling man. 'Let us begin again. I am only here for a friendly conversation. Now, here is a second mug of grog, if you would be so kind as to join me.' He pushed the mug over to the captain.

'For the Lord's sake, you nearly broke it!' the Australian shouted, holding his wounded nose. But he seemed ready to answer Hawksworth's questions now.

'What kind of work do you for the Solomon Company.'

'I drive them their ship.'

'So I am aware. What sort of cargo do you carry?'

'Whatsomeever they pays me to carry.'

'Do you ever carry any gold?'

Martin looked at him, raised the mug, and drained it back. The next round of drinks arrived, and he pushed one before Hawksworth. Then both men raised their mugs, and drank.

She flew with the treasure into her room,
Its size was the handle of a broom.
Oh! what ecstatic moments she passed there,
As she threw up her legs on the back of a chair.
Through each vein in her body the fire lurked,
Surely and quickly the engine worked;
Face her, back her, stop her no! no!
Faster and faster flew the old dildo.

'Aye, gold and jewels and camels and elephants. *The Archimedes* is a passenger ship, our cargo is second trade for us, set by the company. I never see it.'

Hawksworth swallowed more of the burning stuff, his eyes calmly watching the captain. 'You are lying.'

'Are you going to break my nose? There is nothing to tell, I

180

tell you.' There was a small quaver in his voice, enough to give away his fear.

Backing off, Hawksworth said earnestly, 'You are in no trouble here, Captain. I am asking after your employer. Do you know if they ever use their ships to transport illicit cargo?'

'I am no dobber.'

'I am sure you are not. Have another grog. Compliments of her Majesty's purse.'

The captain thought for a moment, then shrugged.

Away they all flew to Peggy's room.
But, ho! 'twas filled with smoke and fume,
And a terrible stench came forth from the bed,
Where poor Peggy lay all burnt and dead.
Sad, sad, was her fate, when, instead of a fuck,
With the old dildo she had tried her luck;
And when at the short digs she so hard did go,
It caught fire with the friction – the old dildo.

Two more mugs came, accompanied by the last mirthfully shouted chorus of 'Oh! the old dildo, oh! the old whore's dildo!'

Laughter and applause roiled the room. The musicians took a break, rubbing their hands. Hawksworth and Martin drank another round – then another. The musicians returned to play more rigadoons and clap-along jigs. Girls, dark-skinned Malays and Tamils garbed awkwardly in Western dresses, appeared and danced with the men.

He let the man talk: 'Aye, I was taking … the thingummyjig …'

'Whaleboat, you said.'

'Whaleboat, yes, the whaleboat we was sailing in Cavvanbah

Bay and a mermaid, I swear on the Lord's blood, it was a mermaid … This was in, oh about, eighteen hundred and seventy nine …'

'Captain, I was wondering something about *The Archimedes* …'

'Grand ship. Best I have driven in the Orient.'

'Why stop at a little outpost like Muar if you have already called just up the coast at Malacca?'

Martin grew silent. Very drunk and swaying in his seat, he watched a Tamil girl stomp her feet on the floor. Already the tavern was emptying, the girls and officers disappearing up the stairs to the rooming house or out into the steam of the night. He leaned closer to the bar, hunkered down and whispered, 'Not my bowl of rice'.

'Excuse me, Captain?'

'I have stopped at Muar only for the past year.' He rolled an empty grog mug back and forth on the bar top, his head lolling as he tried to follow it.

'Why do you stop at Muar?'

He sighed heavily. 'To collect cargo.'

'What cargo?'

'One crate. With holes bored in the top. And it stinks like a thousand shits.'

'What is it?'

'Live animals.'

Two more mugs of grog appeared. The Chief Detective Inspector's stomach was already churning from the booze.

'Tigers? Monkeys?'

At this question Martin began to laugh loudly and harshly. Only now did Hawksworth notice that the musicians and dancing had long since stopped. They were nearly alone, with only two or three other very drunken patrons slumped at tables.

'What is funny, Captain?'

The laughter subsided and turned into sobs, then tears.

'Children,' he said the word so quietly that it was little more than an exhalation.

'Did you say "children"?'

'At Muar. Our cargo,' he gulped, clumsily reaching for the last mug. A sound like a whimper escaped the man's lips, then his head rolled back and he started moaning, swaying, weeping to himself 'May the Lord forgive me, may the Lord forgive me'.

* * *

It was late night, or early morning, when he left: the bars were ejecting their last inebriated patrons like dogs shaking off lice. The streets were filled with drunken men and stoned sailors, some in groups, others solitary, of whom the youthful pickpockets and prostitutes made quick work. Noisy brawls were breaking out around him; inert bodies lay in his way. He tried to maintain his balance on the heaving ground, convincing himself that the earth remained flat beneath his feet. He stumbled once, and struggled to keep a Tamil prostitute at arm's length when she stepped toward him – his wallet and truncheon and shackles all remained on his person when he leaned against a wall to check.

He made it as far as Amoy Street. A group of laughing white men who were giving each other piggyback rides knocked him to one knee. He was rising when he was struck behind his ear, toppling him over. Rough hands dragged him through the dirt of the street, then pulled him to his feet and propelled him into a space between shophouses. They shoved him into the alley, pitch black except for white moonlight filtered through the trees of Mount Erskine. A punch to the stomach brought bile into his mouth as he doubled over. Then he was on the ground, struck by another blow behind his knees. He puked on the way down. As he lay sprawled, choking on vomit, they stomped on the foot that had been injured in the police station explosion earlier in the year.

He managed to get his hand on the ankle of one of the assailants, and with a violent tug brought him down, but then a kick to his ribs made Hawksworth roll onto his side in agony. He heard Chinese words – Teochew – then another kick rolled him onto his back. His ankles were held fast; hands pulled his wrists above his head while a rag was stuffed into his mouth. His jacket was torn open, a knee pressed into his chest as hands plucked away his truncheon and shackles. They smacked his face, then, laughing, shackled his wrists together. They pressed something in his palm, making him grasp it tightly, and were in the process of binding his feet when he heard a voice bellow, 'You there! Stop!'

They were gone in a flash. He could hear their feet as they ran down the alley. A face was now hovering over his own, a brown face in a red and white striped turban: a uniformed Sikh policeman. The rag was pulled out from his mouth. When he sat up, vomit and bile spilled from his mouth down his front.

'Sir, are you alright?' the Sikh asked.

'I am Chief Detective Inspector David Hawksworth. Take me home.'

The patrolman was taken aback and unsure if he should salute, but given the pathetic, beaten figure on the ground, decided it was pointless. 'Sir, you should be in hospital.'

'No, no, I need to be home.'

'Yes, sir, very good, sir, a moment, sir.'

'Bloody hell man, help me up!'

He was lifted upward and leaned against the wall, his hands still shackled.

Two more patrolmen had now shown up, along with their commanding officer. 'Chief Detective Inspector Hawksworth?'

'Yes, who is that?'

'Sergeant Jennings, sir, Sikh Rifle Patrol.'

'Jennings, help me get home. And get me out of these blasted shackles.'

'Sir, are you sure you do not require medical aid?'

'I doubt it. Once the alcohol wears off, I will know for certain, but for now I need to be cleaned up and placed in my own bed.'

A patrolman who had been sent after the assailants returned, his lantern swinging.

'Did you find them?' Jennings asked.

'No, sir. They disappeared into the darkness.'

'Come, help me get the Chief Detective Inspector into a carriage.'

Back on Amoy Street, they paused under a gaslight while the two patrolmen called on the street for a hackney carriage. Hawksworth finally opened his fist: the object that had been pressed into it was a gold half-sovereign coin.

* * *

Two days he recovered at home, Ni tending to him. His ribs were sore but not broken. In fact the injuries were largely superficial: bruises and wounded pride. The worst of it was a swollen lower lip and the acute pain in his injured foot, the place where the bones had not mended correctly. Feeling the metatarsal, he was sure it was not broken again but very badly bruised.

By noon the day after the attack he had sufficiently recovered his senses to sit upright, and though his head swam, he sipped coffee at his table. The journal that had been given to him in

Gading, Isabella Lightheart's diary bound in yellow ribbon, was open before him. Beside it was the locket with the faded picture of the woman herself, the woman whom he resembled enough for strangers to believe them a family.

He had tried reading the diary, but what he saw inked neatly on its yellowed pages was code, strings of numbers separated by precise spaces, or the occasional capital letter placed before or after a series of numbers. He recognised it as a book code, but without knowing the source book and the key to which the numbers and letters corresponded, it was impossible to decipher.

Why on Earth would a missionary woman running an orphanage upcountry feel the need to write her journal in a secret code? Once he was fully mended, and all this dirty business with The Golden Chersonese Club was finished with, he intended to take the journal to his old friend Theophilus Green, the Chief Librarian of the Raffles Museum and Library. What he needed most now was rest, and several days of sobriety.

He woke up early the morning of the third day and realised that he would need a walking stick for support: his foot still hurt immensely. He had a fine one made from Borneo ironwood, hand carved with geometric designs by Iban tribesmen in Sarawak, and hard enough to act as a cudgel. But he opted instead for his ivory-handled cane sword. A twist would release the concealed steel blade from the shaft made of hard Malaccan rattan. On the handle was carved a hawk's head, of which the Chief Detective Inspector was particularly fond. That dim morning, in the light of the paraffin lamp, he cleaned and oiled the blade so it would slide from the scabbard with ease, then headed into town. By the time he was at Central Station, the heat was already intense, the humidity oppressive.

The station was unusually hectic, with men running up and

down stairs or chattering anxiously in clumps, eyeing him warily. Only one or two greeted him on his way in, and none seemed to notice his use of a cane. He made his way upstairs to Rizby's adjoining office.

'Good morning, Chief Detective Inspector. Welcome back! All in one piece I see.'

'Good morning, Rizby. What is the excitement today – surely not due to my return?'

'No, sir. I suppose you would not have heard the news in your convalescence. The Colonial Secretary has been murdered.'

'Good Lord! When?'

'It happened last night in front of his house in Tanglin. He was assaulted as he stepped out of his carriage in his own driveway. The only witness is the driver, who said he saw two men attack the Colonial Secretary before dashing off into the night. We are keeping the information out of the newspapers as long as we can to avoid a panic, on order of the Inspector General, but most of the men know something is amiss.'

'Any clues as to who did it?'

'It was a rough piece of work. They used a hatchet. Cut the carotid artery with two blows. It looks like the work of a *kongsi*, perhaps the *Chiong Sau*.'

'Bosh! The Long Hands,' he said, using the English translation of their name, 'are made up of Cantonese *sinkehs*, newly arrived in Singapore. They would have no reason to attack the Colonial Secretary.'

'But they operate with the sanction of the Hai San. Perhaps the ruling *kongsi* is using the Long Hands as expendable proxies?'

'No *kongsi* would dare attack such a high official so brazenly, not even the Hai San. And the Hai San would not be so clumsy as to leave a witness alive.'

'Still, if such a rumour were to gain wider notice, the European population may well panic.'

'They are given to panic as a regular course,' he said dryly. 'Are you interviewing witnesses? Have you been to the scene of the crime?'

Rizby cleared his throat, then looked down at his desktop.

'What is it?' Hawksworth asked impatiently.

'Detective Inspector Dawnaday has been put in charge of the investigation.'

Hawksworth stared into the fox-like face of his adjutant. 'Why?' he asked icily.

'The official reason is that you were convalescing and that no one knew when you would return.'

He rapped his cane hard on the wooden floor. 'Something stinks here, Rizby. I am being shunted aside. Who issued the orders?'

'Superintendent Fairer himself ordered Dawnaday to take the case.'

'I shall look into this situation, first with Superintendent Fairer. In the meantime, keep your ears and eyes open. I want to learn as much as I can without being seen.'

'I thought you may have said so, sir. One of the detectives on Dawnaday's squad is a friend.'

'Good. What about *The Archimedes*? What did you find?'

'There was no evidence of smuggling aboard her, sir, just a crew of Javanese sailors frightened by the presence of police.'

'Not a surprise. I did however learn from the Captain that, as we already suspected, native children are being smuggled from Muar on the Solomon Company ship.'

'I did learn more about the Solomon Company.'

'Go on.'

'Other than Suliman Alsagoff, the only investor is a Frenchman named Estève Sodavalle. No other member of the Alsagoff family is involved.'

'That stands to reason. I gathered that Suliman is out to best his own brother. I met Sodavalle's sister at The Golden Chersonese Club, but who are they?'

'He and his sister have been resident in Singapore for a number of years. The origins of their wealth are somewhat murky, but he is apparently well connected, for he is a member of several clubs, including exclusive European ones like the Island Club and the Cricket Club.'

'Any rumours of impropriety?'

'Nothing beyond the usual rich man's vices: gambling, high-priced whores. One thing, though.'

'Yes?'

'The address of The Golden Chersonese Club is not a registered business address. The land and the residential building registered there were owned by the Alsagoff Company, then sold to the Solomon Company. Legally, they are not allowed to operate a business on that property. Also, the Sodavalles have given the club's address as that of their residence.'

Hawksworth nodded, tucking that information away. 'Any word on the excavations carried out on the plantation at Seletar where the *orang asli* girl was found?'

'Ah. That is the most interesting news! The speed and spread of the excavations have been increased because—'

A knock came on the frame of the open door, causing both men to turn. It was Superintendent Fairer. 'A word, Chief Detective Inspector.'

'Of course, sir.' He stepped into his own office, pulling the door closed behind him. The two men were alone. Hawksworth sat behind his desk, leaning his cane sword against the side.

'How are you today, David? Recovered from the nasty business of the other night?'

'Indeed, sir. I am feeling fit and ready for duty.'

'I suppose you have heard about the Colonial Secretary?'

'I have, sir.'

'Terrible business. Mrs. Fairer tells me that the gossip mill is already churning out all sorts of noxious rumours. We need to bring this case to resolution as quickly as possible. In the meantime, the Inspector General of Police has ordered a total blackout on the press.'

'Sir, I have been told that Detective Inspector Dawnaday is to lead the investigation into the death of the Colonial Secretary.'

Fairer nodded his bullet-shaped head grimly. 'That is correct. We were unsure when you would complete your convalescence. Fear not, Chief Detective Inspector, you will maintain oversight of Dawnaday as is your role, but the day-to-day work will be handled by his squad.'

'I see, sir. But I am now fit for duty and can lead the investigation myself.'

'This is an order direct from the Inspector General. It is to be Dawnaday's case.'

Hawksworth was silent as he considered this information. He wondered if he was being bypassed or if he were simply overreacting?

As if reading his thoughts, Fairer spoke, 'If truth be told, David, there has been some concern expressed about your state of mind.'

'My "state of mind", sir?'

'No one doubts your loyalty or your abilities, but perhaps you need some recuperation time. You have never taken leave, at least not as far as I know.'

'Yes, sir, that is correct.'

'To speak plainly, it is your drinking that is causing worry. You have been seen at the Straits Club in the middle of the afternoon once too often. And you were intoxicated the other night in Sailor Town to the point of being incapable of defending yourself.'

'It is a hazard of the professional life, sir. I was speaking with … With someone who had information about the murder of the Resident of Negeri Sembilan.'

'And it was necessary to become so intoxicated that a gang was able to assault you? Where was your pistol?'

'I do not carry a pistol, sir, as you know. As regards that night, it was unfortunate. I had not taken dinner before going into Sailor Town and the drink got the better of me.'

Fairer exhaled, folding his hands together so that his fingers formed a pyramid. 'You know how to do your job, David. I am sure of that. But since you mucked around at The Golden Chersonese, you have come under the special attention of the Inspector General.' He added with genuine concern, 'Please do be careful.'

'I understand, sir.'

'I hope you do. I cannot warn you again without docking pay, or worse. Now tell me about what happened on October 31.'

'Is this an official statement, sir?'

The Superintendent's faced relaxed and he snorted a laugh, 'Yes, it might as well be. I will call in our shorthand recorder. Detective Inspector Rizby can act as witness. But this must be done quickly. This awfulness about the Colonial Secretary takes precedence.'

Once the men were settled, and Ah Fong had provided them with a pot of tea, the deposition began. Hawksworth remained behind his desk, with the Superintendent and Rizby facing him. The shorthand writer, a Tamil lad wearing Western dress, a tight collar squeezing a face pocked with acute acne, sat behind them, taking quick but copious notes while the Chief Detective Inspector narrated the preceding events, beginning with his visit to Tanjong Pagar, along with Detective Inspector Rizby, to inspect *The Archimedes,* and ending with the information the Captain had given him of native children being smuggled into Singapore.

Fairer was silent as he heard it all, a look of surprise crossing his face, then asked, 'Native children?'

'Yes. I believe that they are used for ... nefarious purposes.'

'You will have to be more specific than that.'

'I believe, sir, that they are being used in prostitution rings that are especially violent. The murdered *orang asli* girl we discovered the other day is, I believe, a victim of this smuggling.'

'Have you shared this suspicion with Detective Inspector Dawnaday? That is his case.'

Hawksworth winced at the man's name. 'Not as yet, sir. There was no time to do so after I was ... during my convalescence.'

Fairer was staring at Hawksworth, weighing what he had heard. 'What happened after you obtained the testimony of the ship's captain?'

'I left the Kenning Mate, intending to make my way home. I was aware of how inebriated I was, however I did my best to think clearly and act correctly. It was near the corner of Amoy and Japan Street that I was attacked.' He described the attack up until the point that the Sikh patrol discovered him.

'How many were there?' Rizby finally spoke.

'I am not sure, but I think between three to four. They were Teochew Chinese. It was not a random assault. I believe I was deliberately followed.'

'You believe that you were targeted?'

'Yes, sir. I was professionally handled: they did not injure me except to restrain me. Nor did they take my wallet. In fact, they were hog-tying me when they were interrupted. I believe it was to humiliate me and to serve me a warning … And, perhaps, even a message.'

'Message?'

He pulled the gold half-sovereign from his pocket and handed it to the Superintendent. 'That was pressed into my hand.'

Fairer examined the coin before passing it to Rizby, who placed it on the tip of his thumb and flipped it into the air, catching it on the back of his hand. The profile image of the Queen faced him. 'Victoria dei Gratia,' he mumbled, reading the inscription.

'Victoria by the Grace of God,' Hawksworth translated.

'What do you think this means? Quite an expensive trinket to leave behind.'

'It is perhaps related to gold mining at Mount Ophir. Perhaps it is a warning, there but for the grace of God go I. Or perhaps it is a red herring.'

Fairer frowned. 'Interesting hypothesis, but all very vague, Chief Detective Inspector.'

'One more thing, sir. The attackers knew of my foot injury.'

'You walk with a limp. Anyone can see that.'

'True, but a limp may be caused by injury to the knee or ankle. They knew to go straight for the bones in my foot.'

'So you are absolutely convinced it was a personal attack?'

'I am.'

Fairer was about to speak when a knock came at the door. A constable stuck his head inside, then saluted when he saw the Superintendent. Speaking excitedly, he said, 'Apologies for interrupting, sir, but we have just received word that more bodies have been unearthed at the plantation in Seletar. They are bringing them to the dead house now, and ...' the man's voice wavered, 'they all appear to be children, sir.'

The men exchanged glances. 'We should conclude this for now, then, Chief Detective Inspector. Do you have more to add to your statement?'

'No, sir.'

'Then we are done.' Fairer left hurriedly with the constable.

Once the shorthand writer was gone, Hawksworth turned to Rizby. 'Do we know who owns this plantation in Seletar?'

Nodding grimly, Rizby explained, 'It was one of the reasons that we quickened the pace of the excavations. The plantation belongs to the murdered Colonial Secretary.'

CHAPTER XI

Empress Shu En

IT WAS THE MONDAY BEFORE DEEPAVALI, the Hindu festival that marked a time when the forces of light triumphed over those of darkness. Many of the Tamil constables and several of Hawksworth's detectives had risen long before dawn to partake in the ritual event known as *Theemithi*, the fire walk in honour of Princess Draupadi, a reincarnation of the Goddess Mariamman, known as Mother Rain, the South Indian goddess of fertility.

The men would congregate at the Sri Srinivasa Perumal temple on Serangoon Road to walk barefoot over the rough and filthy streets, a yellow string with turmeric and a spray of margosa leaves knotted at their wrists. They would process nearly five miles to the Sri Mariamman Temple on South Bridge Road, only a few hundred feet from the Central Police Station.

The previous day, a massive bonfire had been built in a nine-foot-long trench in the centre of the temple complex. At its height, the smoke rose in a column over six stories high, billowing out over the Chinese Quarter. The heat grew so intense that the brick and plaster walls of the temple had to be cooled with water, enveloping the ceremony's many acolytes in hissing steam. The fire was tended as it burned to coals so that by dawn the following day, the trench was glowing red for the bare feet of the firewalkers. A pool of rancid cow's milk waited at the end of the fire pit, into which devotees plunged their feet to cool them. It was said that those whose feet are scorched have not partaken of the ritual with purity of heart and have thus been punished for their vanity. Those who walk the fire without injury receive the manifold blessings of Mother Rain.

Normally non-believers were not allowed inside the sacred space of the temple to observe the ritual. But given Hawksworth's station plus his general popularity with his Tamil subordinates, he was invited to attend every year, and every year he did so.

In the deep velvet darkness of pre-dawn, the two-story tall temple doors beneath the elaborate *gopuram* tower swung open, and the first of the devotees entered the compound, swathed in saffron robes. The chief priest walked slowly and deliberately over the smouldering cinders with a *karakam*, a sacred pot containing water balanced on his head.

The ceremony had begun.

The line of men shuffled forward to stream individually across the bed of coals. One or two lost their calm midway and dashed toward the end of the trench, splashing into the milk pool. Others strode so slowly that the singed hair on their legs and arms smoked and shrank then shrivelled into nothingness. These men held a beatific look as they moved, as though transported to heaven.

Years before, Rizby had told him, 'You are aware, sir, that there is no trick. It is simply that the coals are not hot enough to burn the feet if one moves swiftly enough. Slow walkers will feel only slight pain so long as they continue to move, but those who panic and stop will burn. The only one in real danger is the priest who first tests the embers, which is why he carries the pot of water on his head.'

'But how would a good Sinhalese Buddhist like yourself know

so much about Hindu ritual?' he had playfully asked.

'One of our legends says that the Tamils must fire walk for refusing shelter to Skanda-Kumara, the guardian deity of Ceylon. For us, the fire does not prove purity of devotion but acts as a punishment for transgression.'

He studied Rizby's fox-like face before stating matter-of-factly, 'You have done it.'

The shorter man rubbed his earlobe. 'Of course,' he grinned as he spoke. 'As I said, there is no trick.'

The spectacle unfolding now before the Chief Detective Inspector belied any trickery. He could feel the heat coming from the bed of coals, and occasionally the whiff of burned flesh would trickle into his nose – or was that the rancid milk heating up? He wondered if he could do it himself, walk barefoot for miles then across a burning trench. It must help to have a rain goddess to believe in.

There were several hundred participants that year, but Hawksworth waited until each of his men had completed the ritual before he decided to leave the temple. It was well past sunup by then and the rest of the Settlement was already going about its business. The rickshaws on the street buzzed past the steam tram, like mosquitoes harassing an elephant.

A coffee stand, the only one in the Chinese Quarter, was on the corner of Cross Street, only a short distance from Central Station and the police courts. It was another mild day, the sun shone bright and clear, and despite the matter weighing on him, he felt his spirits lifted. The black coffee in a wax-paper funnel was hot in his hand as he greedily drank it down.

He sat on a bench in Hong Lim Green behind the courts, facing the octagonal building of the Chinese social club, smelling the residual stench of rancid milk that still clung to him. His thoughts had begun to drift again: he saw a *pontianak*'s glowing red eyes on the sylph-like face of an ancient Chinese woman morphing into the strawberry-haired Camille Sodavalle, laughing, dancing the seven veils of Salome for him, changing abruptly into Ni's lithe naked body, laying against his own. He was pulled back to reality when a Chinese boy tugged on his sleeve. He recognised him as one of the messengers Yong Seng usually sent. The boy was shy, not more than eleven or twelve years old, with a shaved head and the beginnings of a pigtail forming at the back.

'Yes?'

The boy spoke nervously in thickly accented English, 'Yong Seng. Neil Road house. Today.'

'What time?'

The boy pointed at the sun, then flipped his hand palm downward.

'I see,' Hawksworth said, before placing a few coins into the boy's skinny fingers. The lad smiled and bowed before slipping away into the crowded street. Hawksworth followed the blue smock with his eyes as long as he could, but lost him behind the wheels of a bullock cart. He rose on aching legs and made his way toward his office to face another long day of paperwork and meetings.

He knew the boy's gesture from his own youth in Georgetown, where he had learned it on the street when he was running with a tawdry little gang that pilfered fruit and tobacco and pocket-sized treasures from street carts. They had a whole vocabulary of sign language they could flash to each other from across densely packed market places. He was amused to find that the gestures had not changed in all these years. The boy's gesture had meant 'after the sun turns down'. Night time.

His happy mood was dispelled when he walked into his office to find Dawnaday seated before his desk, cleaning dirt from under his fingernails with the metal pick on a folding pocketknife. After each pick, he flung the minuscule amount of filth toward Hawksworth's desk, then examined his nails before picking at them again.

'Detective Inspector Dawnaday, to what do I owe this pleasure?' Hawksworth said grimly.

Startled, Dawnaday nearly dropped the pocketknife, then stood as his superior strode in. 'Hello, Chief Detective Inspector. I came to congratulate you. Your intuition proved correct. The bodies of three more children were uncovered at the Seletar planation.'

'Native children?'

'Cowpar reckons all three are ... were ... Malay. Two girls and a boy.'

'Ages? Time of death?' Hawksworth asked moving behind his desk. He did not invite Dawnaday to sit.

'Their ages are unknown due to advanced decomposition, but less than fifteen and over eight years old, at best guess. They have been in the ground a long time.'

'All were buried at the same time?'

Dawnaday shifted from one foot to the other. 'Not likely, as the decomposition is varied.' He cleared his throat noisily, 'Now, Chief Detective Inspector, you have no doubt heard that the bodies were found on property that belongs to the estate of the late Colonial Secretary, whose murder case has been assigned to me. From here forward, the two cases are to be treated as one,' and he added a perfunctory 'sir'.

Hawksworth said nothing, merely eyeing the man narrowly.

'In short, the Inspector General has asked me to handle this case exclusively.'

'You will continue to report to me as your superior officer.' It was a command, not a question.

'Yes, well, you see, the Inspector General … he asked me to bring this note to you personally. He is too busy to come down himself. When you read it, you will discover that given the gravity of the persons involved, on his orders, I am to report directly to him, and only to him, regarding this case.' The stubby fingers went to the moustache of sweat and when they came away he was unable to suppress a triumphant sneer. The other hand held out a folded note.

'Put it on my desk.'

Dawnaday did so, the sneer still on his face.

'Now get out.'

Dawnaday sauntered away, not bothering to shut the door when he left. Hawksworth took the room in two strides behind him then slammed the door so hard that plaster from the ceiling cascaded down in a fine loose powder.

*　*　*

It was night when he finally approached the house on Neil Road. There were now two men guarding the front entrance, one in the bamboo chair, the other standing with his back to the column of the five-foot-way. Both were dressed in black cotton *changshans* that did little to conceal the long knives strapped inside. Evidently they were expecting Hawksworth for as he approached, the seated one reached up to rap his knuckles on the coloured glass of the window.

The door opened to reveal Yong Seng's smiling face. His head was bare, the sleek hair pulled back into a queue. He was scrubbed and clean and sober and dressed casually. Hawksworth wondered if Yong Seng was spending the night in the house of his *samseng*'s girl.

'Welcome, Chief Detective Inspector, come in.'

The two men stood in the front room. It was expensively lit by an electric chandelier.

'I heard you were beaten in Sailor Town. Not too bad?' Yong Seng asked, eyeing the cane Hawksworth was leaning on.

'They put me down for a few days, but I am recovering steadily. More than I can say for the Colonial Secretary.'

'Who did it?'

'You mean ...?'

'I mean *you*. I do not give three farts for the Colonial Secretary.'

'I am not sure. They attacked me in the dark, but I can tell you that they spoke Teochew. And that they knew the exact place where my foot was wounded.'

'I have already begun to make inquiries.' Yong Seng smiled.

'I thank you for that. Is Yong Chern here?'

'Yong Chern is in Johor Bahru, but we have news for you.'

Hawksworth began to speak but stopped short when Shu En noiselessly entered the room.

Her hair was piled in a high bun, held in place by ivory picks, her body wrapped in a shimmering robe of blue and yellow silk that flowed like liquid. Her feet were hidden and silent as she glided into the room, a servant dressed in plain cotton rushing behind her.

'Good evening, Chief Detective Inspector,' she spoke in halting English, with a directness that startled him. Her smile was devious, and her dark eyes sparkled as she examined him. The scent of her perfume filled the room, and he could almost taste her, like sipping cool rose water. He recalled the secret morning they had stolen together, the slim suppleness of her neck, the slightness of her knees, the fragrant pink petals between her legs. Was this the same woman?

She seemed a different person from the sweet pale-skinned gamine he had first encountered, a recently purchased *mui tsai* girl, little more than a love toy for Yong Chern. There was a hardness about her that had not been there previously. Her face was still delicate, the coral lips succulent, the petite body seductively doll-like, but now she held herself with a ruthlessness that commanded respect: a concubine become empress. It was not time that was responsible for this transformation, he realised: it was power. So the rumours he had heard were true – Shu En truly was running the Mother-Flowers now.

'Good evening, Shu En, it is a great pleasure to share your company again.'

'The pleasure is all mine,' she said with a sly smile only he could see. 'I was concerned to hear that you were attacked recently, but you look to have recovered.' When her freshly acquired English failed, she switched to Hokkien, which Yong Seng translated for him. 'Please, sit.' She indicated to one of the upholstered chairs. She sat opposite him, Yong Seng standing directly behind her. Her slippered feet, Hawksworth noted, barely reached the floor. Tea was brought and placed on the table between them.

'Forgive me for disturbing your calm house, Shu En. I believed that I was to meet with Yong Chern today.'

'Your presence is never a disturbance. In fact there are still times I long for your presence in the most immediate ways,' she said mischievously. Yong Seng shifted his weight uncomfortably from foot to foot. There were some things the servants should not overhear. 'As Yong Chern is not available, would you share your thoughts with me?'

'What is on my mind is the kidnapping and murder of children.'

'Not the death of the Colonial Secretary?'

'I believe the two are related.' He noted that she knew of the official's death even before it was announced in public, but that was no surprise. The Mother-Flowers, like all *kongsi*, had spies throughout the colonial administrative apparatus.

'The police believe that one of the *kongsi* is behind the murder.' It was a statement, not a question, that Shu En put before Hawksworth.

'The *Chiong Sau* are suspected as the culprits, at the direction of the Hai San.'

'So we were informed,' Yong Seng spoke above Shu En.

'Personally, I doubt that the Hai San ordered the murder. Nor do I think the *Chiong Sau* would be capable of it themselves,' Hawksworth spoke slowly for the translation.

'The Hai San would not risk a war with the police by attacking such a high-profile European,' Yong Seng said. Shu En nodded her agreement then whispered something to him in Hokkien. He rang a small brass bell for a servant.

'We also want to learn more about the murder of the Colonial Secretary. If *kongsi* are to be blamed for the death of highly placed officials, we will have a problem. Are the Hai San being deliberately targeted?' Yong Seng asked.

'I do not know. The Inspector General of Police has personally put Detective Inspector Dawnaday on the case. I am being deliberately shunted aside.'

'Dawnaday?' Yong Seng asked. As he spoke, a servant

arrived with a thin-stemmed ceramic pipe for Shu En. It was not opium but bhang, a smokable compound made from the buds of marijuana plants. It was an Indian habit that often became an addiction amongst newly arrived Chinese in Singapore.

'He is also leading the investigation into the death of a kidnapped and murdered *orang asli* girl. As I said, I believe the two cases are related.'

'Dawnaday gambles in one of our houses. He owes a small amount of money but since he is police, we do not pressure him for payment.'

The information was not a shock to Hawksworth. Because of the nature of their work, most of his detectives kept close ties with the underworld, and this often translated into some harmless participation in vice. It was part of the attraction of the job.

'Dawnaday's investigation of the Colonial Secretary's death will not get far. I have a feeling that there are larger forces at play here than the Hai San and their dogs. The Colonial Secretary was a member of an elite club called The Golden Chersonese.'

Shu En had begun to slip into a reverie, a cloud of odiferous bhang smoke emitting from her lips, but at hearing the name of the club she sat upright again. She turned her glassy eyes on Hawksworth. The expanded pupils made them appear black and depthless, and he thought she never looked as perversely attractive as when she was gonged out her head.

'The Golden Chersonese! I have only learned of it,' she spoke with delight.

'What is your interest in it?'

She laughed chromatically, nestling the bhang pipe in her silken lap. 'I want to open such a club.'

'Ah. But you have brothels under your control now.'

'Disgusting dens of sin that attract only sailors and policemen,' she said quickly, and Yong Seng smirked. 'What I want, my dear Chief Detective Inspector, is to put The Golden Chersonese out of business. I want to run my very own social club that caters to high-society *ang-moh* men and powerful Europeans.'

'Men like the Colonial Secretary?'

'Or the Inspector General of Police,' Yong Seng added.

'I want to have a puppet show like that,' Shu En said, raising her chin defiantly.

'Puppet show?' he asked.

The little empress raised her pipe and pulled deeply, letting Hawksworth's question hang in the air. Then he all too clearly saw the answer. Camille Sodavalle supplied the men with whatever vice they desired so she could leverage it later for blackmail.

After exhaling, her words confirmed his suspicions, 'We do not intend to sell black market opium and smuggled Canton girls to coolies, *sinkehs*, and sailors for the rest of our lives.'

Hawksworth spoke sharply, 'I believe that The Golden Chersonese is not just a clandestine brothel. The girl I saw was hideously tortured before being killed, and she was perhaps not killed merely to silence her agony, but because her death was the culmination of her killer's passion. Even the worst of the *kongsi* would not make a regular trade of such barbarity.'

'What do you know of barbarity?' Shu En snapped, her reddened eyes flashing. 'My mother sold me when I was only eleven.'

Hawksworth was silent, trying to comprehend the frightened child she must have been then, and the pleasure she had given him, and the wraith-like woman she was becoming. He spoke quietly, 'I can only tell you that the girl I saw was raped repeatedly, mutilated, and then beaten so badly her organs liquefied.'

Yong Seng placed his hand on the back of Shu En's chair to

silence her before speaking himself. 'So it would seem that we both want The Golden Chersonese closed. Maybe we can work together. Tell us what you know.'

The Chief Detective Inspector sighed loudly, shifting in his chair. 'May I have something stronger than tea?' he asked. Yong Seng nodded then tinkled the little bell again. Shu En puffed and exhaled, her gaze drifting to the ceiling. Brandy in a decanter with two filigree crystal glasses was brought forth for Hawksworth. After the servant poured, he rose to clink glasses with Yong Seng, who pulled over a chair so both men could now sit facing each other.

Hawksworth swallowed several mouthfuls of brandy then spoke in a rapid-fire voice, 'I can tell you that The Golden Chersonese Club is owned by the Solomon Company. I can you tell you that the company is jointly owned by Suliman Alsagoff in Malacca and that the Singapore arm of the Alsagoff family does not appear to be involved in the club operations. The remaining shares in the Solomon Company are owned by a Frenchman named Estève Sodavalle, who is resident in Singapore and seems to be the man in charge. I can tell you that Camille Sodavalle, Estève's sister, is the woman who manages, or so she claims, The Golden Chersonese Club, and I can tell you that some of the most powerful men in Singapore are members.'

He paused to gulp more brandy, then continued, 'I can tell you I have evidence that the Solomon Company kidnaps native children in Malaya and smuggles them into Singapore, and I can tell you that I believe those children meet a nasty end. I believe that this has something to do with the deaths of both the Resident of Negeri Sembilan and the Colonial Secretary. Finally, I can tell you that despite all this knowledge, my hands are completely tied. I have circumstantial evidence linking the Solomon Company to these crimes yet I am being actively hampered by my own superiors who have warned me away from investigating that evidence.'

Yong Send nodded then looked at Shu En who peered back at him with glazed eyes, her face serene. 'Tell him,' she said.

'Hawksworth, we have been friends a long time,' Yong Seng said, refilling their glasses.

'Go on.'

'We know Estève Sodavalle. Like Dawnaday, he is a gambler, and he owes us a great deal of money.'

'How much?'

The amount Yong Seng said was more than the salary Hawksworth would be paid for two years' work. He whistled low in appreciation. 'That is a large sum ... Large enough for you to use your usual means of collection, even against a European. What is preventing you?'

'He is protected by his stature in society. Most specially, he is protected by the Alsagoffs.'

'He has shared business interests with them, but I do not think the more devout Singapore side of the family ...'

Yong Seng shook his head. 'You do not understand. He is the son of Syed Ahmed Alsagoff by a mistress, a woman in France.'

Hawksworth's face tightened. 'So the rumours about a second family from Marseille are true. To be clear, you are telling me that the Sodavalles are the half-siblings of Suliman Alsagoff?'

'Alsagoff himself is never to be seen in Singapore, but he owns that European social club and uses his bastard siblings to run it. So you see why we let Estève Sodavalle run a debt with us. He is an obnoxious man who flaunts his connections. But if you were to perhaps keep the police away, we could settle our score without interference.'

Hawksworth nodded, 'That is true, but how would it help

you put The Golden Chersonese out of business? There would still be Suliman Alsagoff.'

'You need to shut down the Solomon Company. If their crimes are as terrible as you believe, surely you can find a way. Then we can reclaim our money from Sodavalle and open our own club.'

Anger jolted through him like a current, blood rushing to his face hotly as he considered the implications. He spoke sharply, doing all he could to contain his fury, 'You ... You have already *planned* all this? And you simply expected me to *participate*?'

'Chief Detective Inspector, it is growing late and you have a long road ahead of you,' Shu En spoke decisively as she rose from her seat. She was not much taller than the chair she had been sitting in. Both men stood with her, a courtier and a counsellor showing obedience. 'It has been a true pleasure to see you again,' she said, her moist gaze meeting Hawksworth's red-rimmed eyes.

Knowing that the interview had come to a close, and knowing better than to show his anger, he softened, though his nostrils remained flared. 'The pleasure has been mine, Shu En.'

She stepped toward him on invisible feet, as though she were floating. 'Hear me, dear Hawksworth. The Golden Chersonese will be closed before the end of the Christian year. Then I will open my own club. We will do whatever is required. I know you feel the same.' Before he could reply, she wafted out of the room in a cloud of bhang smoke.

Yong Seng walked him out, past the *pintu pagar*, into the hustling noise and the bluish light of the gas lamps on Neil Road. The smell of ox dung was strong, mingling with the dust that rose from the street and the pungent woody smell of a tropical night. Running his hand over his scalp, Hawksworth felt that it was damp with sweat brought on by the brandy.

After bidding good night, the tall man strode down the street, turning over this new information in his mind. The music of a bowed Chinese *urhu* floated from the second story of a shophouse, followed by a crashing sound and raucous male laughter. Then the *urhu* started again, light, high, lovely.

A knot was forming in his stomach as he walked away. He knew that against all his better instincts, he would have to enter the belly of the beast. The rot was pervasive and went right to the top, but it all seemed to emanate from The Golden Chersonese Club. Tomorrow he would find Estève Sodavalle and thump the Frenchman until his secrets spilled out.

CHAPTER XII

Tastes and Colours

THE STONE NEEDLE of the Dalhousie Obelisk appeared like a gigantic upended aubergine on the grass of the Padang. The inscription at the base of the needle was written in four languages, Jawi, Chinese, Tamil, and English.

Erected by the European, Chinese, and Native inhabitants of Singapore to commemorate the visit in the month of February 1850, of the Most Noble the Marquis of Dalhousie, K. T., Governor General of British India, on which occasion he emphatically recognised the wisdom of liberating commerce from all restraints under which enlightened policy this Settlement has rapidly attained its present rank among British Possessions and with which its future prosperity must ever be identified.

Beyond the needle sat the two-tiered pavilion building of the Singapore Cricket Club, at the western edge of the Padang, adjacent to the massive structures of government officialdom crouching around Empress Place, at the mouth of the river. Popular legend held that Dalhousie had stepped ashore precisely here with his proclamation that the guiding lights of the colony now and forever would be liberal commerce and enlightened prosperity.

Rizby had learned that not only was Estève Sodavalle an honorary member of the Cricket Club, but that he was known to lunch there on weekdays. Hawksworth found himself standing in the foyer, prepared to force his way inside.

'I am Chief Detective Inspector Hawksworth. I am looking for Estève Sodavalle,' he said as pleasantly as he could to the club captain, a stout Geordie in a buttoned-up linen suit, coal black hair turning lank in the heat, who stood blocking his path.

'Mr. Sodavalle is taking his lunch on the upper floor,' the captain said without budging.

'I would like to speak with him,' Hawksworth said tersely, his jaw set.

The captain studied the tall man a moment, sizing him up, then nodded and disappeared in search of Sodavalle. Hawksworth waited, his eyes roaming over the oil portraits of former club presidents strung on the walls. One of them was Cecil Clementi-Smith, the current Governor of the Straits Settlements. The incumbent was A.P. Talbot, to judge by his portrait, an athletic man, not particularly old, quite intelligent looking. Hawksworth vaguely recalled that he had come out many years previously in a medical capacity and was currently the Assistant Colonial Secretary and Clerk of Council, which meant that he held access to the highest governing authorities in Malaya. Talbot was the type of clever man who made himself rich through his connections and then made his connections rich, too – the type of man for whom the cricket club was specifically created. A foreign businessman like Sodavalle could only have been made an honorary member of the club if he had access to such men. Hawksworth wondered if Sodavalle reciprocated the favour at The Golden Chersonese Club, if men like Talbot were 'honorary' there, too.

The captain returned with an obsequious smile. 'Mr. Sodavalle would be very pleased, sir, if you would join him for lunch at his table,' he said in a voice slick as oil.

The man was seated alone on the upper floor of the pavilion, which was open to the air on three sides and offered a sweeping view across the Padang and out into the maritime roads where the ships were riding at anchor with the tide. His back was to the entrance, to better appreciate the view, but when the captain told him that the Chief Detective Inspector had arrived, he rose from his seat to greet him.

He was not what Hawksworth had expected, though after seeing him, he was not sure exactly *what* he had expected. The man standing before him was about his own age, nearly a caricature of a bon vivant. Portly as are the well fed, he was a large man, though the immaculate seersucker suit he wore rendered the fat appealing. Sodavalle was smiling widely, one hand already open and offered to Hawksworth in a gesture of friendliness. He had his sister's hair and eyes and cheekbones, but fleshed out, as though puffed in the tropical humidity. His nose was red from both sun and alcohol.

'Chief Detective Inspector Hawksworth, it is a supreme pleasure to make your acquaintance. Please, join me.' The voice was smooth with traces of grit that lifted it so that it sounded sonorous and merry at the same time.

'Thank you, Mr. Sodavalle. Forgive my intrusion. I hope I am not interrupting your lunch.'

'Not for a minute, Chief Detective Inspector, not for one minute. Allow me to order you a drink … You do drink, do you not? Bass ale?'

'Sounds capital.'

The portly man nodded to the captain as two waiters quickly set a place for Hawksworth.

'Thank you, Mr. Sodavalle. It is very kind of you.'

'You are lucky to catch me, for I was just about to leave after I finished my *vinho do porto*. However, I will join you in a beer.' He leaned closer to whisper conspiratorially, 'In truth I enjoy beer much more, but my sister tells me that a little port after an afternoon meal will aid my digestion, and it helps to keep up appearances. Beer, she informs me, is déclassé.'

Hawksworth was about to say, 'And yet you ordered it for me,' but bit his tongue. Instead he said, 'Your sister is partly the reason I was hoping to speak with you.'

The beer arrived in chilled glasses as Sodavalle spoke, 'My sister? Yes, she had mentioned that you met at The Golden Chersonese. I do hope, Chief Detective Inspector, you are not falling in love with her. I warn you out of sheer altruism that she is a beautiful woman, yes, but has a cold heart. Many suitors have perished at her hands.'

'Nothing about love, I assure you, sir. In fact, there was an unfortunate misunderstanding regarding my intentions when I first visited your club. Perhaps the early hour coupled with my, my manner, which was perhaps unintentionally coarse ...' he stammered, making a show of struggling to find the right words.

'I believe I understand what you are trying to say, Chief Detective Inspector.' Sodavalle apparently bought his act, his voice and face exuding kind charity. 'But tell me, how may I be of help to you today?'

'To be blunt, I am interested in joining your club, sir. I hope our past misunderstanding has not completely ruined my chances. Your sister, I believe ...'

'My sister often responds with unnecessary emotional force. It is her Spanish blood.'

'Spanish? I was rather under the impression that you are

French.'

'Ah, yes. Camille and myself were born in Marseille, but our ancestry is Spanish, with a long sojourn in the city of Oran, in the Mahgreb,' Sodavalle explained in a melodious voice. The statement was threadbare from use.

'You are a Mohammedan?' Hawksworth asked incredulously.

Sodavalle laughed heartily, setting his ale on the table. 'Hardly. My ancestors fled Oran when the Ottomans took the city from the Spaniards in the eighteenth century. Business connections in Marseille offered us sanctuary. We settled there and eventually adopted a local name, but we proudly remember our Spanish heritage.'

'Your origins perhaps explain the decor of the club?'

'You are also interested in aesthetics? You are a man of broad interests, Chief Detective Inspector.'

Smiling at the false compliment, he sipped his beer then said in a low voice, 'I have heard that the club offers something ... out of the ordinary.'

Sodavalle laughed warmly, though his eyes did not shift from piercing Hawksworth's own. 'Do not talk around your desire like a temperance warrior, Chief Detective Inspector. Come out and ask for what you want. There is no shame here. As they say in Marseille, "*Des goûts et des couleurs, on ne discute pas*".'

'Apologies, I do not speak French.'

'"Tastes and colours cannot be discussed", which I take to mean that what is blue for you is not necessarily blue for me. Each man has his own preferences in sensual matters.'

Hawksworth sipped his beer. 'I am not as worldly as yourself. I have some difficulty in expressing my ... desires.'

'There truly is nothing new under the sun! But I understand your predicament. After all, I am only a man, too.'

Hawksworth set down his empty glass. His fingers had left sticky prints along the outside, each clearly visible in the bright light.

'I say,' Sodavalle continued, gesturing to the waiter to bring another round, 'perhaps the best thing would be for you to come to the club and see for yourself what is on offer. By chance, we have a performance tonight that you might find enlightening.'

'That would interest me greatly.'

Sodavalle's face changed into a sudden scowl. 'Of course given your position, Chief Detective Inspector, we will need to be certain that we can take you into our confidence.'

'What can I do to convince you of my sincerity?' Hawksworth asked, forcing a note of desperation into his voice.

Sodavalle turned away from Hawksworth to scan the horizon before turning back to say in a low rumble, 'Actually you need do nothing except remain aware that many powerful men are our members of long standing.'

'I understand.'

'Then you can appreciate that your authority is also based on the same mechanisms that grant these men power.'

Hawksworth nodded to show his appreciation of the circumstances.

'There is also the question of wealth. The Golden Chersonese Club prides itself on exclusivity.'

Hawksworth shrugged. 'I am only a police official.'

'For our members in government service, we usually offer a steep discount. Police are always welcome at our club – so long as they come as friends and not as officers.' Sodavalle smiled without showing teeth, his eyes locked on Hawksworth's own.

'Of course,' Hawksworth replied casually.

'Good!' Sodavalle clapped his hands, his tone brightening.

The next round of beer arrived, along with a tray of chilled fruit, mango slices and iced rambutans. 'Let us toast to our new friendship!' He raised his glass in a pudgy fist.

When the glasses clinked together Hawksworth watched him closely, trying to spot some indication, even a modicum, of malicious intent, yet the mask of the seasoned bon vivant betrayed no insincerity.

* * *

The main club room of The Golden Chersonese Club offered no indication of impropriety. In fact, he noted, despite the garish decor, the place seemed absolutely staid. A few tight-lipped men in white linen suits sat casually in armchairs, newspapers spread before them, cigars in their mouths, glasses of brandy placed beside them on side tables. It was a placid scene to be found in any gentlemen's club in the empire, from London to Bombay to Kingston. Hawksworth and Sodavalle stood by the long bar, sipping whisky and water. 'The show will begin soon,' Sodavalle assured him in a whispered voice. 'In the meantime, we can relax.' Hawksworth shifted his sword-cane – other than it, he had come unarmed – into his other hand as he replaced his glass, expecting a refill.

The evening's music was being played by a Filipino string band in ill-fitting dinner jackets, set up near the piano in the corner where Hawksworth had first encountered Camille Sodavalle. The sound covered the room like aural wallpaper.

'Is your sister here? I would like to make amends for my behaviour from the first time we met.'

His face beamed as he said, 'Oh, yes, she is most assuredly here, but you will not see her until the show begins.'

Hawksworth scrutinised the man: it was like peering into the eyes of a crocodile.

'Sodavalle!' a voice called out. They turned to see a stocky middle-aged man with a ruddy face and a head of grey hair sprouting in several directions coming toward them. His eyes were glazed and his breath stank of gin.

'Mr. Powell! It is good to see you. Enjoying yourself?' Sodavalle's voice rang out.

'As always at The Golden Chersonese,' Powell gestured with his drink, sloshing some over the side.

'Allow me to introduce Chief Detective Inspector Hawksworth of the Straits Police.'

After the two men greeted one another, Sodavalle politely asked, 'Are you in for a long stay at Singapore, Mr. Powell?'

'Not this time, I am afraid. We depart tomorrow for Hong Kong.'

Sodavalle turned to Hawksworth to explain, 'Mr. Powell owns a company involved with the import and export of ... What was it again, Mr. Powell?'

'Tea is our primary commodity, although we do on occasion undertake special consignments to ship opium and other goods. Would much rather stay here in Singapore but my duties require my presence in Victoria City.' The man burped, then excused himself tipsily before saying, 'Rather subdued here tonight, eh, Sodavalle?'

'The recent death of our Colonial Secretary has damped our spirits.'

'Ah, of course. I heard. Terrible news.'

'He will be greatly missed,' Hawksworth added, sure to stress his sadness.

'Is it true, this story about his being murdered by a Chinese clan?' Powell asked Hawksworth.

'Whoever the perpetrators are, and whatever the motivation, we will uncover them. Rest assured that one of our top men is working on the case,' Hawksworth said with practiced ease.

'*Dker lkelb o wejjed zerwata*!' Sodavalle suddenly spouted in Arabic, quickly adding, 'Speak of the devil and he doth appear! Here is Detective Inspector Dawnaday,' Sodavalle gestured at the detective heading toward them.

'Good evening, Mr. Sodavalle. Chief Detective Inspector, I did not expect to see you here,' he said in a gruff voice.

Dawnaday and Sodavalle were staring at him now, the bon vivant smiling, the younger detective with eyes of ice. Hawksworth flashed them a wan smile. The fact that he was standing there unarmed and without any partner or support, against the express wishes of his superior officers, amidst the very men he believed were responsible for truly heinous crimes, weighed upon him suddenly. He was certain that they were watching him with as much suspicion as he maintained of them – and supposed that they had allowed him into the club merely on a pretext to lure him into a trap. But he had little choice save to confront the beast head on.

'Good evening, Detective Inspector. I was just explaining to good Mr. Powell here that one of our best men was pursuing the killers of the Colonial Secretary, and who should appear but yourself.'

'And I can assure you, Mr. Powell,' Dawnaday spoke, the beads of sweat trembling on his upper lip, 'that my squad is dedicating all its resources to bringing the killers to swift justice.'

The string band fell silent and a gong sounded from deep within the building.

'Ah, Mr. Powell, please excuse us, but we have a reserved

engagement for our friends from the detective branch.'

'Of course. It was a pleasure to meet both of you,' said Powell before turning to the long bar to order another gin.

'Are you going to the Ophir Room?' Dawnaday asked Hawksworth, his eyes narrowing in suspicion.

'We are indeed,' Sodavalle answered. 'Your superior has evinced an interest in our ... special entertainment.'

Dawnaday stared Hawksworth in the face, his chin jutting provocatively. 'I am sure you will find it enlightening, Chief Detective Inspector,' he said in a tone that fell just short of threatening.

'Come, *jalan*, as our Malay friends say,' Sodavalle spoke with high spirits to defuse the situation. 'Mr. Dawnaday, will you be joining us in the Ophir Room?'

'Not tonight, Mr. Sodavalle. I did not reserve a seat.'

'Very well. Enjoy the rest of your evening.'

Sodavalle lightly gripped Hawksworth's arm to call him away. The Chief Detective Inspector creased his face into a slight smile before following Sodavalle. Dawnaday, he noted, did not smile in return. The hairs on Hawksworth's neck stood on end, and he gripped the handle of his sword cane tightly.

On their way to the Ophir Room, they passed a heavy metal door he had not noticed on his previous visit. It looked extremely sturdy, like the door to a bank vault. Noticing his interest, Sodavalle breezily said, 'Our office,' before entering the hall with the arched doorways that Hawksworth recalled from his earlier visit. 'Do you mind if I call you by name? The use of titles is so formal, and we are in an informal place,' Sodavalle asked as they walked.

Hawksworth nodded his assent, despite realizing that Sodavalle was stripping him of yet one more layer of official prerogative. 'That is grand! We are sure to be fast friends!' Sodavalle proclaimed loudly, his eyes twinkling. He paused before the arched door to the Ophir Room, where Ahmed, the ape-like doorman, was standing guard in his faux-Turkish costume. 'In you go, Mr. Hawksworth.'

The den-like space was lit only by paraffin lamps in red glass, while the stage was illuminated by electric lights in brass backs. The overall effect was to create a *chiaro oscuro*, the stage lit in a ring of sallow light, spectators on wooden benches obscured in the murky red lamplight beyond. He could see perhaps a half dozen men already seated in the room, some on the banquettes around the walls, others on wooden chairs and benches closer to the stage. Some of the men were wearing masks to conceal their identities. Further back, hidden in the shadows of the recessed alcoves, he could hear still more men.

Sodavalle indicated two plush chairs with a full view of the stage, but were hidden from the other spectators by a rattan screen. A boy in an apron brought them a fresh round of whisky. The bon vivant held his glass up for a cheers, and after they clinked together, he said, 'Here is to a long life,' as a hush fell over the room. 'The show is about to begin. You are sure to be delighted, Mr. Hawksworth.'

He noted that the door opened and Ahmed slipped inside then drew a heavy bolt. There was no other exit he could discern in the dark. Sodavalle breathed heavily beside him, and he could tell that the man was as much watching him as he was the stage.

A pulsing buzz suddenly filled the air. A man with an *oud* sat cross-legged near the stage, strumming a hypnotic rhythm punctuated by percussive knocks on the instrument's body. Camille Sodavalle slid onto the stage dressed in a flowing gown, much like an Arab *abaya*. As she moved through the light and shadow, her strawberry hair glowed in the amber of the stage lights, and the outline of her curves could be glimpsed through the material. 'Gentlemen, thank you for coming.' Her swan-like white throat seemed to elongate as she spoke. 'Tonight we offer for your delectation a foretaste of the rewards that are promised in heaven. Tonight, gentlemen, we give you seven plus two dark-eyed *houris* ...'

Seven girls and two boys walked onto the stage. Each was shirtless but wrapped in a thin sarong. All were scrubbed clean, their hair glossy and set into elaborate headpieces meant to resemble Javanese crowns. There were several sighs of male appreciation from the shadows, and a light round of applause went up.

Hawksworth struggled to keep still in his seat. The children being paraded not more than five feet from him were Malay, though at least three of the girls, to judge by the tight curls of their hair, were *orang asli*. Here were the missing children! As he watched the little bodies on the stage, his impulse was to leap up and scream and fight, but he knew he would be brought down fast. He had no choice but to keep his seat, clenching his teeth together while the vein in his neck throbbed.

The children stood around the circle of light on the stage, and to judge by the choreography, they were well rehearsed. They were not fresh from the wilderness – they had been in Singapore for some time, he supposed, noting that none betrayed any fear, though they were moving sluggishly, obviously drugged.

'The show is by special pre-arraignment only, but the performers are available all week for special club members.' Sodavalle patted his knee. 'See anything you fancy?'

So this humiliating extravagance was meant to showcase the wares on offer, the children who were being kept as slaves for the profit of the Sodavalles and Suliman Alsagoff. The image of the dead girl's face, the girl he called Fenella, came to him, and he fought again to keep his rage in check. 'I do not know what to say,' he croaked.

Sodavalle kept his hand lightly on his knee, 'A common reply the first time members see the show,' he said mirthfully. 'There is no rush, Chief Detective Inspector,' he patted his knee again. 'Enjoy the show, then we will discuss your pleasure.'

Four children left the stage, leaving two girls and one of the boys with Camille. The girls swayed to the side, then stayed still, their bodies stiffened into poses that resembled ritual dance, legs akimbo, supple necks bent, little fingers curved backward. Camille ran her fingers slowly along the boy's torso as she guided him to centre stage. He offered no resistance as she first bound his wrists with silk cloth, then lifted his arms over his head to suspend him from a hook set in the ceiling. He was tall enough that his feet touched the ground, but his body was held taut between floor and ceiling, effectively immobilised. Camille plucked away his sarong in a single swish, leaving the boy naked, quivering. She clapped her hands once and the two girls shifted their pose, their sarongs falling away, too. A second clap of command and they broke their pose and sashayed toward the boy, taking up new positions in front and behind of his suspended body.

Hawksworth watched in concentrated horror as the Sodavalle on stage began to massage oil onto the boy's tawny frame, while the girls gyrated around him like belly dancers. She then caressed the buttocks of the girls, smearing them with oil as well, and pushed them against the boy. Camille stepped aside, letting the girls rub themselves rhythmically against the skinny boy sandwiched between them.

All this time the *oud* player continued the flow of pulsing music, which was now accompanied by gasps and heavy breathing coming from the men around the room. Hawksworth could sense sensual movement in the shadows of the alcoves now – apparently some of the spectators were not merely watching passively.

Estève Sodavalle nudged his shoulder. A fresh drink was in his hand, another whisky and water, which he offered to Hawksworth with a smile. The detective hesitated. He did not want to become too inebriated, and he did not trust the hand offering the drink.

Sodavalle cocked his head inquisitively, holding the glass out again, curious as to why Hawksworth should refuse. Sensing that his cover story was coming unravelled, Hawksworth grabbed the whisky and gulped it down in two swallows. Sodavalle's mouth curved into a slim smile, and Hawksworth forced a smile in return. He sensed the lurking danger and knew that he had boxed himself in.

On stage, the girls had moved aside to expose the boy again. Even though his head hung limply in a narcotic stupor, their rubbing had coaxed an erection. The woman spun the boy around slowly to show the entire crowd, then she clapped her hands and the two girls moved to their knees before the boy. Despite his drugged state, it was only a short while until his thin body shuddered with an orgasm.

The *oud* music stopped and the room was filled with a thunder of unrestrained applause. The children left the stage – the two girls dragging away the boy – while Camille Sodavalle stretched her arms up, momentarily holding herself in the same position as the boy had been, her adult body visible beneath the diaphanous material.

'Remarkable, was it not?' Estève whispered excitedly beside him.

Hawksworth was gripping the whisky glass so tightly that it

could have shattered in his fist. Sodavalle noticed the empty glass and motioned to a servant. A full one was in Hawksworth's hand before the next group of children took the stage attired in similar faux-Javanese costumes.

The *oud* played long glissando passages, and two girls proceeded to strip while performing a pastiche of ritual dance. After they were completely nude, they started circling Camille, bending their bodies in serpentine movements. The girls fell to her, as though attacking, pulling at her diaphanous robe until it fell apart. Her white flesh glistened, red pubic hair catching the light like fire. The excitement in the room was palpable, the seats creaking beneath the shifting, restless audience. Estève Sodavalle emitted a low whistle while watching his sister performing with the girls. 'This is new,' he mumbled, seemingly to himself, as the act finished.

Hawksworth was getting woozy. Another whisky – the third? Fourth? – was in his hand. The windowless room was stifling. The lamps gave off a smoky residue that mingled with the smell of hot bodies. The combined elements created an odour with which he was very familiar: the seedy human smell particular to brothels. He realised he was very drunk as the next act took the stage: this time two boys and one girl, and the seemingly indefatigable Camille. This one involved the wooden bench with metal rings embedded in it he had seen on his first visit, but now he was too drunk to keep track of the action.

The glass in his hand was refreshed again as the *oud* droned on. He had completely lost count of the drinks. His legs felt heavy, his vision blurred at the corners. He wondered if they had dosed his drink, but the thought came to him as if from far away, echoed through the hypnotic music. He shook his head to try and clear it, knowing that now was the time he needed to stay most sharp, most keen, but his body felt weighted, his thoughts slipping away in fragments of nonsense.

He slowly became aware that the show was over. Camille was now at the centre of the stage, the children standing around her, facing outward, holding hands.

'If you would like to meet one of the performers, Mr. Hawksworth, I suggest you act swiftly. These are the most popular and tend to be snatched up quickly,' the voice beside him whispered smoothly.

Hawksworth responded but was unsure of what he said. The room seemed to be revolving like a wheel.

Then the stage went dark, the only lights in the room now coming from the dim red lanterns. Camille Sodavalle materialised out of the puce light and smoke, wrapped in a black silk kimono. She was perspiring from the exertions on stage. 'Hello again, Chief Detective Inspector. My brother told me that you would be in attendance tonight. Did you enjoy the show?' she leaned in close, her body heat strong against him.

He tried to speak but could not form the words. The muscles around his mouth were going slack.

'Camille, Mr. Hawksworth seems to have had a little too much to drink. Some fresh air would be in order. Can you escort him to the back garden?'

'It would be my pleasure.'

Next he knew, his tall frame was supported against her supple body, his sword cane grasped in his other hand. Her heady odour, the smell of sex and sweat, overpowered his other senses. Instead of seeing the narrow hallway, he seemed to inhale Camille Sodavalle, so that she expanded to fill his mind. He stumbled and nearly retched at the backdoor.

Then they were in the garden, seated on a stone bench under

the gnarled frangipani tree, the night air heavy with fragrant plumeria blossoms, which mingled with her smell. Was his head on her lap? Was she caressing his hair? He felt himself drifting off into a peaceful darkness when a sudden pain jabbed at his neck, ripping him back into consciousness. Fingers were tightly gripping his throat. As he jerked and flailed, a fist landed in his face and he reeled backward. His feet went out from underneath him and then he was on his hands and knees. A kick to his head sent him over, knocking him back to wakefulness. He spun on the dew-wet grass to entangle the legs of his attacker, slipping his ankles between the standing man's, then scissoring his legs outward. The attacker went down.

Hawksworth pushed himself unsteadily upward and aimed a swift kick at the rib cage of the man on the ground, nearly stumbling over himself in the process.

His attacker rolled over to face upward. It was Dawnaday. Hawksworth groped for his sword cane, but it was nowhere to be found.

Arms suddenly grabbed him from behind – feminine arms wrapped in black silk. Camille Sodavalle shouted for help, trying to hold the struggling man as Dawnaday closed in on him. In two swift moves, Hawksworth jabbed an elbow into Sodavalle's breasts and landed a hard knee kick into Dawnaday's groin. Both fell away, groaning.

Free for the moment, the world spinning around him, he spotted a garden shed beside the high wall and clumsily made for it. Struggling, bolts of pain shooting through his bad foot, he managed to pull himself atop just as Ahmed and another of the club's guards dashed into the garden. From the top of the shed he quickly scaled the compound wall, flinging himself over the side.

He landed with a sickening thud in the wet mud of a fetid

drainage ditch and lay still for a moment, breathing deeply, hovering on consciousness. His mind filled with the image of a burning pagoda completely encased in yellow flame that rose and curved to a point high in the sky.

A sharp pain in his hip jolted him back to full consciousness. He realised he only had seconds before they came for him. He lurched upward and started to run toward Beach Road, where even if he could not find transport at this late hour, he could hide himself in the mass of ropes and boxes and carts that were found by the godowns on the wharf where native craft were repaired.

As it turned out, he was able to rouse a sleeping hackney coach driver and convince him to take a bleeding drunken man home. His last thought before collapsing into the darkness of the carriage was that they would come for him at home, and he would be unconscious and unable to defend Ni.

But no one came.

CHAPTER XIII

Sticking Pigs

SUPERINTENDENT FAIRER WAS inside Hawksworth's office before the detective had his topee off.

'With me. Now,' the older man snarled.

As they walked the hallway, Hawksworth felt as though the floor were slipping beneath his feet, as though it were slick with oil.

'The Inspector General is here,' Fairer said angrily. 'I warned you, David, I tried to warn you. Now there is nothing I can do.' He added sharply, 'You look terrible. Sozzled and bruised and unkempt. Your drinking habit is getting out of hand. You would do well to stay sober for a few days, assuming of course that you are not in gaol before the day is out.'

'Sir, before we go in, at least let me tell you that last night I was drugged and attacked. Allow me to tell you what I witnessed at The Golden Chersonese.'

Fairer stopped in front of Hawksworth to block his way, peering into his eyes. He spoke quickly, 'What you *witnessed*? Allow me to give you one more piece of advice – whatever good it will do, I do not know. Last night you witnessed *nothing*. Do you hear me? You saw *nothing*. Admit to your own guilt, nothing more. From here forward, implicating others will only make it worse for yourself.'

'Sir, I …'

'David,' Fairer's tone softened, 'I am giving you one last chance to save yourself. You were warned. Now you are deep in the soup. Whether you sink or swim will very much depend on what you admit to doing and seeing last night. Do not underestimate the forces arrayed against you.'

Carroll Evans, the Inspector General of Police, was roughly the size and shape of an unpolished block of granite. He was waiting in the Superintendent's small office, a far cry from his own luxurious space in the municipal building near the Cricket Club, one floor below the Legislative Chamber where the political business of all of Malaya was decided.

The block of granite rotated smoothly to face them when the two men entered: he was wearing an impeccably clean suit of fine white linen that shone in the morning light. 'Superintendent Fairer, please wait outside. I would like to be alone with Chief Detective Inspector Hawksworth.' Fairer saluted, then made his exit, gently pulling the door shut behind him.

Hawksworth spoke, 'Good morning, Inspector General …'

'Shut up.'

'Yes, sir.'

'I said shut up!' he shouted. 'I suppose you know what this is about?'

Hawksworth felt his stomach rise in his throat. Bile was choking him.

'I received a call from my friend Estève Sodavalle this morning. Apparently you went to the social club he owns – and of which I am a member – and assaulted his sister last night.'

'Sir, I …'

'I said shut your fecking mouth hole. One more word, and I will have your shield.' He came around the desk to stand close

229

to Hawksworth. 'My understanding is that you have some incoherent theory about the place ... That you have been nosing around making wild accusations. Mr. Sodavalle said that despite a previous incident with his sister, he generously allowed you into the club last night to make peace. You then got disgustingly drunk and attacked his sister in a back garden. Quite fortunately, Detective Inspector Dawnaday was there and saw you assaulting Miss Sodavalle. When he attempted to restrain you, he claims that you beat him then fled.'

He paused, his eyes searching Hawksworth's own. The Chief Detective Inspector knew he was being crucified, so he remained quiet.

'I will take your silence as an admission of guilt,' Evans barked, then running his fingers along the seam of his lapel, continued. 'Normally I would have you suspended and placed under investigation, but you are valuable because of your unparalleled access to the native communities. I suspect that my best course of action will be to have you transferred out of Singapore immediately. One of the Malay states, or Borneo, perhaps.'

'Borneo, sir?' Hawksworth's voice cracked.

'My good friend Charles Brooke, the Rajah of Sarawak, is building a new town upriver of Kuching and is in need of an expert to train his native police. I think that would suit a man of your capacity perfectly. However, I have not made a final decision, so for the time being you are to remain in Singapore, preferably in that bungalow you choose to inhabit with that Siamese ... concubine.' He spat this last word with unmasked disdain, as if in his common-law marriage to Ni, Hawksworth had defiled himself.

Jutting out his chin, Evans continued in a low voice, 'I

understand that you have been in a similar spot before with a European woman, something about misconduct in Madras that also involved a young lady. Perhaps your being raised in Malaya has made you unused to the company of women of your own race. You should learn to control yourself. It is rare indeed that a man in your position is given the opportunity to commit the same folly twice. It is my duty to ensure that it will not happen a third time.'

'Yes, sir,' he said quietly. The hot words from the only book he had owned as an orphan echoed in his head: 'Measureless liar, thou hast made my heart too great for what contains it.'

'Consider yourself under administrative leave until further notice. You are to surrender your shield and shackles to Superintendent Fairer at once. From now, you are no longer part of the police force in this Settlement.'

He stared again into Hawksworth's eyes, daring the taller man to speak, to condemn himself. When his stare was met with silence, he barked hoarsely in a voice that rumbled through the room, 'Dismissed.'

* * *

'I have been suspended from duty, pending a transfer to some blazing black-hole in Borneo,' Hawksworth announced to Rizby after returning to his office. 'For all intents and purposes I am under house arrest until the Inspector General decides my fate.'

Rizby was on his feet, his narrow fox-like face wrinkled in consternation. 'Good god, man, why?'

'I have overstepped my bounds. Put my foot in The Golden Chersonese one time too many. They trapped me last night like a dumb coney.'

'Who?'

'The Sodavalles,' he grunted. 'Estève let me in then drugged me. Camille then lured me into the back garden where Detective Inspector Dawnaday attacked me. I managed an escape, but this morning I was called before the Inspector General. Sodavalle claims that I drunkenly attempted to assault his sister and that Dawnaday, by lucky coincidence, was there to intervene on the girl's behalf. Rizby, I tell you, they intend to ship me as far away from here as possible, where hopefully I will meet an untimely end. In the meantime, they are wisely leaving me to my own recognisance, most likely hoping I will attempt to escape. Or indeed will escape. So long as I disappear.'

'Dawnaday is part of this?'

'The rot goes straight to the top. And we, Detective Inspector Rizby, being at one remove from the powers-on-high, are supposed to kneel helplessly before it.' He then described the show at The Golden Chersonese. Rizby listened in numb silence.

'What do you intend to do?' Rizby said in a small voice.

'Do?' he rapped his knuckles hollowly on the desktop. 'Sergeant Major Walker has returned from Malacca, has he not?'

'He has indeed. In fact he stopped by here hoping to catch you yesterday but you were out.'

'Find him and tell him what I told you about The Golden Chersonese Club, and be specific about the children,' he said, remembering what Walker had told him of his own sad past in Shanghai. 'We may yet be able to take action, though it will put us all at great risk.'

'What action can we take?'

Arching one eyebrow, Hawksworth said abstractly, 'We will force Dawnaday to confess.'

The fox-like face cocked to one side quizzically. 'And how can we get him to do that?' Rizby wondered, his thumb and forefinger rubbing his earlobe like a prayer bead.

'We will need to isolate and interrogate him. The mechanics of this operation I leave to the Sergeant Major and yourself,' he said archly. 'Dawnaday will not be expecting any further interference, so use that to your advantage. When you speak with the Sergeant Major, impress upon him the need for expeditious action. I fear that if we do not act tonight, it will be too late for all of us. After what I witnessed, I can tell you that we are dealing with people who lack any conscience at all, so we must move quickly.'

Rizby smiled grimly, 'I understand, sir. You can expect word from me once we have Dawnaday in ...' he nearly said 'custody' then realised that what they would truly be doing is kidnapping a fellow officer. 'Once we have him securely in hand,' he finished.

'I will interrogate the bastard myself,' Hawksworth added coldly, then with a wink. 'As of now, of course, I am on administrative leave and should not be seen in public. When the need arises for my presence, you will be able to find me at home in Geylang. Good day, Detective Inspector.'

'Good day, sir.'

'And Rizby?'

The alert fox-face turned to his, eyes sharpening. 'Yes?'

'Good luck.'

*   *   *

That night he sat on his veranda with Ni, listening to the breeze rolling about in the palm trees of the plantation surrounding them. He was wearing his house sarong, sipping arrack with ice. Ni was beside him, peeling an orange with great deliberation. She popped each wedge into her mouth before biting down so that the juicy pulp exploded in her mouth. It was something she did when she was nervous.

He had done his best to explain the situation to her, but the complexities eluded their shared mish-mash of English, Siamese and Malay. She understood that all his years of loyal service suddenly meant nothing. Despite his reassurances, she could intuit that he was under threat and that their home might be taken from them, that they were potentially faced with forceful and permanent separation.

Detective Inspector Rizby pulled up in a hackney carriage a little before ten o'clock. 'Good evening, Chief Detective Inspector! And to you, Ni,' he called out cheerfully. 'Sergeant Major Walker is expecting you in town.'

Detective Faheem Zalani, one of the men on Hawksworth's squad whose loyalty was beyond question, stepped from behind the carriage. He had a carbine rifle with him.

'I have asked Detective Zalani to stay here to keep watch in your absence,' Rizby said.

Seeing the man with the rifle made Ni jump. As Hawksworth explained why the man with the gun would stay with her, she studied his face intently then popped another orange wedge in her mouth. Sudden late night departures were part of his routine, but she grasped the extra weight of this situation. 'Very *teun ten*,' she explained in her mix of English and Siamese, her brow wrinkled as she embraced him, softly whispering a prayer. Despite her nervousness, she had the stove stoked for tea for Detective Zalani before the carriage had departed.

Hawksworth and Rizby rode together in silence through the countryside, the darkness giving way to light as they entered the city streets. It was serenely quiet, though the silhouettes behind the shutters of the buildings betrayed the presence of nocturnal activity.

Once they crossed Coleman Bridge, Hawksworth knew where they were headed. It was Pulau Saigon, the largest island on the Singapore River, covered with warehouses and godowns, an industrial area that was usually vacant at night. The detective branch kept a warehouse there for storing equipment – and unofficially as a place to question recalcitrant suspects.

The carriage pulled up before the dark building, Rizby leaping out to knock three times on the rough wooden plank of the front door. It swung open, and Hawksworth recognised the stern face of another of his loyal men, Detective Anaiz Majid.

'The Sergeant Major is expecting you in the back room.'

'And you?'

'We will keep watch so you can be alone,' Rizby flashed a wicked smile.

He could see the yellow light shining around the outline of the far door in the otherwise pitch-black space. The back room was lit by a single paraffin lamp. Sergeant Major Walker was seated at the table, eating a bowl of porridge. Beside him was a man shackled to a chair, a burlap sack over his head. The Sergeant Major nodded at Hawksworth, then slurped the last of his porridge, the spoon scraping the bottom of the clay bowl. He stood and pulled away the sack to uncover the bruised face of Detective Inspector Dawnaday. A rag was stuffed into his mouth, and his eyes bulged with fierce indignation. He started jerking against the restraints, emitting guttural yelps around the rag when he saw Hawksworth.

Without preamble, Walker said, 'I plucked him from his carriage on his way home from the Central Station. The mouth gag was necessary because of the amount of noise he was making.'

Hawksworth smiled warmly at the Sergeant Major, 'Plucked him, did you?'

He leaned down and pulled the gag from Dawnaday's mouth.

The man spat then yelled, the veins in his neck bulging, 'Who in the blues blazes do you think you are, Hawksworth? Release me at once!'

Walker backhanded the shackled man so hard the chair tipped back.

'Detective Inspector Dawnaday, you are in very serious trouble,' Hawksworth said calmly.

'You will pay very dearly for this, Hawksworth. You too, Walker. Both of you!'

The Sergeant Major backhanded him again, then stepped behind him, resting his thick hands menacingly on the man's shoulders, close to the neck. 'I would be very quiet now if I were you, Detective Inspector Dawnaday.'

'We have some questions concerning The Golden Chersonese Club, and we would appreciate your cooperation.'

'Rack off! I do not have to answer anything to you! You have been stripped of your position, you worm.'

'Allow me to make you aware of what would seem to be obvious, Detective Inspector,' Hawksworth said placidly. 'We are now operating outside of the normal parameters of police procedure.'

'Do not threaten me!' Dawnaday yelled, but a tremor in his voice revealed his fear.

Walker jammed his elbow into the trapezium muscles near the base of his neck, and Dawnaday yelled in pain. Walker kept the sharp point of his elbow pressed down until he began to shake.

'Are you willing to cooperate now?'

'Sod off.'

Walker smacked him hard against the side of the head, causing his teeth to cut into the flesh of his lip and tongue. Blood filled his mouth, and he spat.

Hawksworth sat down opposite the man, studying him while thrumming his fingertips on the table top. After a short while, he asked politely, 'Have you ever watched the Chinese slaughter a swine?'

Dawnaday merely stared at him, a steady stream of blood running down his chin.

'They jab a sharp stick here,' Hawksworth poked an erect thumb into his neck, under his chin, against the carotid artery. 'The pig is trussed and hanging, you see, so that the head is down and it only takes one strong poke for it to bleed out.'

Walker's meaty fingers were gripping Dawnaday's neck tightly, holding him immobile.

'The beast squeals a little but not for long, twitching and kicking as the blood drains from the hole in its neck. I imagine that it is an incredibly painful experience until death finally comes. Of course it is hard to understand how a pig would appreciate the coming of its own demise,' Hawksworth leaned on the table, gazing directly into the frightened eyes across from him, 'but I can well imagine what a man would experience. I can imagine the pain and panic as the blood empties out, the veins collapsing, the pointless impulse to grab hold of the life that is ebbing away ever more quickly, yet your hands and feet are bound so you merely convulse in terror and agony. The men standing around you are laughing at your convulsions, watching impassively as you realise that you will never again quench your thirst or hold a woman or see your children grow. Yet these men standing around you, the men who killed you and now joke and laugh while you convulse and die, they will keep on going. They will drink and love and lay in the grass ... And you will not, not ever again. You will be aware that in another moment you will blink out, like a candle, and in that final moment you can picture your corpse dangling from the tree, smeared in your own shit and blood, while the men laugh.'

Tears were now rolling down Dawnaday's cheeks, mixing with the blood flowing from his cut lip. A sound like air escaping a balloon came from his mouth. His head slumped forward. Walker pulled it back upright by his thinning hair.

'I am going to ask you a series of questions, and much, very much indeed, will depend on your responses. Question one: were you aware that the children in The Golden Chersonese Club were kidnapped from Malaya?'

Dawnaday nodded affirmatively.

'I am sorry, Detective Inspector, but I will require vocal responses to my questions. I ask again, were you aware that the children in The Golden Chersonese Club were kidnapped from Malaya?'

'Yes.'

'Explain the kidnapping and smuggling operation to us, and kindly do not leave out any names.'

Dawnaday sighed. 'Raiding parties are organised by Suliman Alsagoff in Malacca under the guise of surveying expeditions. Ayer Panas is used as the transhipment base because the Chinese mining activities in the area offer cover. The children are smuggled down to Muar on the river and then they are taken on Alsagoff's ship into Singapore.'

'What did the unfortunate Resident of Negeri Sembilan have to do with it?'

'He had uncovered part of the operation and was investigating of his own accord. We arranged to have him come to Ayer Panas, and ...'

'And there the dirty deed was done. Whose idea was it?'

'Suliman Alsagoff. He arranged for the Chinese killers.'

'Were you aware that once the kidnapped children were brought into Singapore they were forced into prostitution?'

'Yes.'

'And on occasion the kidnapped children were provided to high profile clientele for private purposes in their homes, correct?'

'Yes.'

'And sometimes these special arrangements resulted in the death of the child, correct?'

Dawnaday was silent.

'Answer the question,' Walker said, squeezing tightly so that his knuckles went white.

His face bunched in fear and pain, Dawnaday whispered, 'Yes.'

'And were you aware who was committing these murders?'

Dawnaday whimpered.

'Louder, please, Detective Inspector.'

'Yes,' he said, then started to sob.

'And you helped to cover them up, by burying the little bodies and then by controlling and directing police investigations.'

'Yes.'

'You did so at the direction of officials higher than yourself?'

'Yes.'

'Ah. We will get to their names in a moment. The attack on me in Sailor Town, was that also at their direction?'

At this Dawnaday looked confused. 'I do not know about that. I had heard that you were assaulted but that was not our doing ... At least not as far as I know.'

'And the half-sovereign coin?'

Again he shrugged, hoarsely mumbling, 'I do not know ...'

Hawksworth sat very erect in his seat and squared his shoulders. 'Now, Detective Inspector, I want to ask you to give me the names of all the private citizens and high officials you are aware participated in these depraved orgies.'

Dawnaday sobbed loudly, clear green snot running out of his nose.

'I do apologise, but I cannot hear you clearly,' Hawksworth said. Walker slammed an elbow once more into the raw trapezium muscles.

'I cannot tell you. It would be better for me to die than to tell you. Kill me if you must, but I cannot say.'

'Detective Inspector Dawnaday, you seem to labour under a misconception,' Hawksworth spoke in a measured tone. 'I am not an executioner. I am only here to question you. The Sergeant Major and I have merely provided a portal for the truth so as to help you contribute your share to the proper course of justice.'

Walker took the heavy ceramic noodle bowl he had been eating from and swung it into the back of Dawnaday's head, hard enough to hurt but not to shatter. The terrified man broke into screams.

'Please understand,' Hawksworth continued evenly, 'that the only hope you have left for clemency is to tell me all you know about the public officials involved with The Golden Chersonese Club, the murder of children, and the attempt to pervert the law. Then perhaps I can arrange to have you sent to a prison far beyond the reach of the powerful men of whom you are about to make mortal enemies. We will start with the deceased Colonial Secretary then proceed to the living.'

Dawnaday stiffened in his chair, then sighed, relaxing his muscles. He told all he knew.

Suliman Alsagoff was the mastermind of the entire operation. The Sodavalles were the operators in Singapore. Because of certain youthful indiscretions, the brother in Malacca was a pariah of the family, and the Marseille siblings were seen by the Singapore branch of the family as nothing more than undeserving bastards.

As for the other Europeans, not all officials who were members of The Golden Chersonese Club were participants in the child orgies. In fact, Dawnaday explained, it was only a minority, and those were carefully vetted and invited by the Sodavalles before being granted entry. The Inspector General of Police, Hawksworth, noted, was often involved in the pressing of flesh, and it was he who protected club members by blocking investigations. Dawnaday admitted he was largely his tool in these efforts but insisted that he never himself had touched one of the children.

The murder of the Colonial Secretary was organised and executed entirely by this inner cabal. After the body of the *orang asli* girl was discovered, it was decided that the Colonial Secretary needed to be dispatched; the others feared he would be caught for her murder and would then expose the entire operation. The order came down from Alsagoff, but trying to make it look as if the Hai San were behind the attack was Estève Sodavalle's idea – a move born of desperation, they were aware even at the time.

They looked at Dawnaday as he slouched down, his hands folded on the table. He was finished. They called Rizby in to watch the prisoner while Hawksworth and Walker stepped out to speak.

'Now that we have gone as far as kidnapping Dawnaday we can delay no more. We must act tonight.'

'Act how?' Walker barked. 'Arrest the entire ruling class of the Settlement?'

'We shall raid The Golden Chersonese Club, find and free the enslaved children, arrest the Sodavalles, and acquire evidence. We will present our findings in the morning, along with Dawnaday, to the Chief Justice. He at least seems to be utterly unconnected with this sordid business.'

'I see. So we will conduct a rogue raid and then hope we can accumulate enough evidence to exonerate ourselves while condemning the malefactors?'

'Yes.'

'And if we encounter resistance at the club?'

'Then it will be met with the full force of the police. I may be suspended, Sergeant Major, but you can still act will full authority.'

'And if the resistance is formidable?'

'I understand what you are driving at. All men should be fully armed. Bring all the men in my squad that can be trusted – Rizby will tell you who. While you are gathering them, I will pay a visit to the Mother-Flower *kongsi* house.'

Walker's face curled in disgust. 'Those savages? What in god's name do you need them for?'

'Estève Sodavalle owes the Mother-Flowers a great deal of money. I am sure they would be interested to know that he will soon be in a position to repay them in full.'

*   *   *

It was dead quiet when Hawksworth reached the Mother-Flowers' house on Neil Road, though a light was shining in the front window. Hawksworth rapped on the windowpane. A squeak and a creak then the front door opened and a Chinese head popped out from behind the *pintu pagar*. Dark eyes looked into Hawksworth's own then the head wordlessly disappeared and the door softly shut. All was quiet again. He was about to rap on the glass once more when the door swung open, and a groggy Yong Seng greeted Hawksworth. His queue was undone, the inky black hair slipping around his neck and shoulders like a velvet hood. The smell of stale rice wine was strong on his breath. He stood swaying, waiting for Hawksworth to speak.

'I do not have much time,' he said. 'Are you interested in collecting your money from Estève Sodavalle?'

'I told you before, he is a protected man,' Yong Seng belched. 'We cannot touch him.'

'Tonight his protection is revoked,' Hawksworth snapped. 'He will try to escape from Singapore no later than dawn. You are to be sure he does not. Capture him and exact whatever payment you deem fit, but Yong Seng, understand that I will need him alive to testify.'

The purplish lips curled back into a smile. 'He must be alive, and capable of testifying in court, but otherwise, he is ours?' he asked, clarifying.

'*Dui.*' Hawksworth returned the smile.

Yong Seng spoke rapidly in Hokkien to a man standing behind him. When he finished, they both laughed. Turning back to Hawksworth, he explained, 'I have sent men to watch him. We will take him when he tries to flee. He will not escape.'

'You might also alert your friends on the docks, just to be certain.'

Yong Seng shrugged the Chinese shrug that meant, 'I have already considered that and taken care of it'.

Softening, Hawksworth added, 'Please inform my darling Shu En that once again her desires will be met. She will have her own puppet show very soon.'

Yong Seng scrutinized him through narrowed eyes, 'What are you going to do tonight?'

'Tonight,' Hawksworth spoke calmly, 'I am going to close The Golden Chersonese Club forever.'

CHAPTER XIV

Night Raid!

HAWKSWORTH'S RICKSHAW WALLAH deposited him on the corner of Jalan Sultan and Java Road just before 3 o'clock in the morning. He and Walker had agreed to conduct the raid at this hour to make sure that its patrons had left the club's premises; most were ignorant of the activities in the back room, and the two policemen did not want them caught in the crossfire. Rizby had stayed back at the warehouse with Dawnaday, not only to keep the man under guard but to bring him to the Chief Justice in the morning should the Chief Detective Inspector and Sergeant Major fail to return from their raid.

In the police waggon with Walker, Detectives Anaiz, Rajan Nair, Iqbal and young Joseph Jeremiah were waiting for him. The streets were dark and silent as a grave, but he could smell the sweet odour of baking, the scent of fresh *prata* bread wafting on the air. Even if the houses were shuttered, someone was awake.

He climbed into the back of the packed waggon. 'Good morning, gentlemen,' he said in a stage whisper. 'As you know, we are conducting a raid on The Golden Chersonese Club. And as you are aware, we are operating beyond the parameters of official authority. If any of you do not want to participate, now is the time to step away. You will not be judged by the rest of us.'

No one moved.

'Then I will outline our objectives. I believe that within the compound of the club there is a group of about a dozen children being held captive, both boys and girls. We are to find them and bring them out. They will be extremely frightened and may try to run from us. We are to hold them.'

'Language?' Rajan asked.

'Most will speak Malay,' Hawksworth said. 'As for defence, we expect there will be four to five men, all lightly armed. There will also be an *ang-moh* woman named Sodavalle and possibly her brother. They are to be taken into custody.'

'If they resist?' asked Iqbal.

'They are to be taken alive,' he snapped his fingers. 'Finally, if there is enough time, we will confiscate as much documentary evidence as possible, especially membership rolls and payment ledgers.'

'What do you mean by "enough time"?'

'It should be assumed that an alarm will be raised and we will have only a brief period before uniformed officers arrive. As we are conducting an illicit operation, it is imperative that we free the children, arrest the Sodavalles, and collect evidence before the uniforms arrive on the scene. Perhaps thirty minutes, most likely less. Once away, we will present our evidence, our suspects, and the children to the Chief Justice ... and hope that he sees fits to exonerate our conduct based on the magnitude of the criminal allegations. Is all this clear?'

'How are we going to get into the place?' Walker spoke in a gruff voice. 'We would need a battering ram to get through the front door. All we have is a jack bar.'

'There is a garden. We will go over the wall and through the back door. The wall is high, so be careful as you come down.'

They crept off the waggon and along the drainage ditch in

the narrow street. Rings of light from the gas lamps cast broken shadows over the road. They moved in silence, sliding along the garden wall. Hawksworth could vaguely recognise where he had fallen over it the previous night, where the shed stood on the other side in the garden.

The Chief Detective Inspector, being the tallest, would give each man a leg up then climb over the wall himself with the help of Jeremiah, who would stay outside with the waggon. Walker, along with his two Webley pistols, would be the first over the top, it was agreed. Hawksworth braced his back against the wall, his arms straight, fingers laced. When Walker placed his boot in his hands, he asked softly, 'What was the name of your boy in Shanghai, the one you told me about in the Ophir camp?'

'I called him Robert,' Walker replied with a grim smile, then he was boosted upward. In a single swift movement he grasped the top of the wall and swung himself over. Rajan and Anaiz silently followed. As Iqbal was being helped up, the shouting began on the other side of the wall.

By the time Hawksworth had painfully hoisted himself over the top, the shooting had started.

As he scrambled across the roof of the shed, he heard Walker's Webley roar twice. He landed badly because of his foot, tumbling forward and hitting his knee on something hard. Cursing, he stumbled upward to take in the chaotic scene before him.

In the half-light of the garden, he could see one body lying face down in the grass, its head a shredded mess. Walker had put two rounds in quick succession into the man's face at point blank range, nearly decapitating him.

A shadow shifted in his peripheral and he crouched swiftly, the blade of a shovel whistling just over his head. Standing, he brought his fist upward with his body's momentum, landing it squarely in the solar plexus of the attacker, who doubled over. The shovel dropped, and Hawksworth kicked hard, the toe of his boot landing squarely in the attacker's face. The man, he saw now it was a young Malay, instinctively mashed his hands into his face, his head bent forward as he tried to regain his breath.

Aware of the commotion happening all around, of more gunshots and shouts, he snatched the shovel up and with a single elegant stroke, brought the flat end of it down hard on the back of the young man's head. The attacker collapsed and did not stir.

A shot rang out, a round whizzing past his ear. He leapt forward toward the side of the shed, seeking cover. Another young man, this one in a waiter's tunic, ran past him, just out of grasp, and made for the wall. Iqbal was in pursuit and grabbed the younger man around the waist, tugging him back down as he writhed, struggling to get free. Hawksworth spotted the gleam of the knife in the man's hands and stepped forward to grip his wrist before he could turn the blade on Iqbal. A harsh twist, and the fist released the weapon, while Hawksworth punched the man's face once, then twice, giving Iqbal time to shift his grasp into a rear chokehold, which he held until the man's body went limp.

A series of three quick shots caught their attention. Hawksworth sprinted on his bad leg toward the back entrance of the club. Walker and Anaiz were crouching on either side of the back door that now lay crumpled inward. He heard a shout and turned to see Rajan struggling with a slim adolescent – probably a serving boy. The thin arms lashed around the bigger man like eels until the younger man slipped free, then dashed away to the frangipani tree, quickly pulling himself into the thin branches and leaping off them to get himself over the wall.

'The alarm will be raised quickly now,' Hawksworth yelled. 'We must hurry.'

A loud blast focused his attention on the back door. It was not one of Walker's Webleys – someone inside was pinning them down with fire from a big firearm. Hawksworth and the others dashed to take up positions behind Walker and Anaiz. 'The guard inside has a fowling gun,' Anaiz spoke quickly as another blast smashed into the doorframe, shredding the wood.

Iqbal stuck his head around the corner of the door and caught a load of shot full in the face. He fell back onto the lawn, clutching his head and gurgling. Rajan tugged him into shelter, covering his face with his jacket, trying to stanch the flow of blood. The body jerked once then lay still.

Hawksworth saw none of this – the second shot meant that the shooter had to reload, so both he and Walker had their necks craned around the doorjamb. Walker held his Webley steady against the shattered wood and neatly put one bullet through the breastbone of the man fumbling with the gun at the other end of the hallway. The next bullet went squarely between his eyes, punching a hole out the back of his skull. Walker pulled back to reload.

Hawksworth watched the heavy body crumple then collapse. Standing directly behind it was Camille Sodavalle, her face twisted demonically in rage and fear. She was dressed in a black silk kimono and nothing else, her long legs planted akimbo. Pulp and brain matter from the dead bodyguard was splattered all over her, bright red blood streaming down her fair skin. She had a small silver revolver in her hand that she levelled at Hawksworth's face. He was able to catch a glimpse of the flaming red pubic hair before he had to duck back around the corner to avoid the two shots she sent toward him.

From his cover, he yelled, 'Drop the revolver, Camille! You are hopelessly surrounded.'

'Not a chance!' she screamed, snapping off two more rounds.

Walker looked at him, mouthing the words 'four shots'.

'Surrender!' Hawksworth shouted.

She fired again.

'Give up the children, Sodavalle! Nothing can save you now!'

Her reply was to send another round down the hallway.

'Her gun is empty!' Walker shouted, charging forward. He did not reach her in time. In the echoing of the last shot, Hawksworth heard the loud slam of the office door. She had locked herself inside the impregnable room. He ran down the hallway to find Walker pounding on the door, cursing.

'We will not get through that door, Sergeant Major. Take Anaiz and inspect the rest of the building. Arrest anyone you find,' Hawksworth rasped, 'I will begin looking for the children.'

Walker nodded then called to Anaiz, who came running up the hallway. 'Sir, Iqbal ...'

'Yes?'

'He is dead. In the garden.'

'Damn!' Hawksworth bellowed. The three men cast their gaze toward the back door.

They exchanged glances, then Walker motioned for Anaiz to follow him, and the two began to move cautiously through the darkened club.

Hobbling from the pain in his knee, Hawksworth made his way back to garden where Rajan was crouched over the body of Iqbal. 'You must find a way out of the garden,' he said quietly. 'Look under that mass of devil's ivy at the back.' He helped the inconsolable detective to his feet, 'Leave him for now, Rajan. We will mourn him soon, but now we must find a way out faster than the one that brought us in.'

In the moonlight of the garden he could see Rajan's brown

eyes glazing with sadness. 'Steady, man. Now we must think of the living,' Hawksworth said to him. 'Go and see if there is a way out.' Rajan nodded then stooped to collect the jack bar from the grass. 'Good lad,' Hawksworth said before trotting back into the hallway. All was quiet inside the house.

He realised that he was standing outside the Ophir Room – the door was closed but not locked. He shoved it open to find the room deserted, nearly pitch black. But the smell that hit him was immediately recognisable from the previous night, the repulsive mixture of paraffin and sweat and flesh. As the ringing in his ears from the gunshots faded, he became aware of the sound of crying coming faintly from the room behind the arched doorway across the hall.

The door was sturdy. There was a skeleton key lock on one side but no handle. He called 'Hello!' loudly in English, and the crying turned to shouting behind the door. He yelled for the Sergeant Major and Anaiz, who swiftly came running. 'The rest of the building is empty,' Walker said, catching his breath. 'Any remaining staff must have slipped out through a side window which we found smashed open.'

'The children are behind this door,' Hawksworth said.

Walker listened to the muffled sounds of their crying then nodded. They knocked against it and the pleading shouts from inside increased in volume. Anaiz yelled in Malay – and a chorus of children's voices came out in response.

The response was unintelligible. Anaiz tried again, this time asking only one child to reply. A boy's voice came back. The door was bolted from the inside, but there was a second door the keepers used to enter and exit the room.

'Where is that door?'

The boy said he was not sure.

'It must lead to the office where Sodavalle is taking refuge, I am certain. We must act now doubly quick. Batter it down. Now!' Hawksworth yelled. In a coordinated effort, the three threw their full weight against the wood, but it did not budge. Hawksworth ran to the back door, calling out into the garden, 'Rajan, bring the jack bar, quick.'

They jammed the metal bar against the hinge, pulling hard. The wood splintered, the hinge giving way, but still the door held fast. The children inside were screaming hysterically. Hawksworth began kicking the splintered hinge with the flat of his boot, once, twice, three times, then smashed his full weight into the door, bellowing with each effort. Walker joined him, ramming himself against the wood, like a rhino. They managed to split the door all the way down the middle, then the seam burst into splinters. A dozen children came pouring out, screaming and crying, running helter-skelter.

'Stop them from getting out!' Hawksworth yelled.

With some effort they corralled the children into the front room. Most simply thudded against the walls then fell to the floor, weeping fearfully. After several moments Anaiz was able to explain that they were police detectives and were here to take them home.

Hawksworth dashed into the dark room. Along both walls were flat wooden bunk beds with thin sheets; a bucket filled with stinking waste served as the only chamber pot. At the far end he found that the inner office door was almost as massive as the outer door, and it had no external lock.

He banged on it, shouting, 'Come out, Camille. We have the children. There is no use in holing up now.' He pounded again on the door, calling for her to surrender, but again there was no reply.

Then he noticed the acrid smoke seeping out from beneath

the door.

He ran back to the others. 'She is burning the building! We must get out quickly.'

'Children hold hands, we must leave now,' Anaiz said. He took the hand of the child closest to him and led the chain of shivering bodies out of the building.

The smoke inside was becoming thicker. Hawksworth called to Sodavalle one last time – but there was no response. He could do no more for her. He rushed with the others down the hall and out into the garden.

Rajan Nair called out to them from the darkness. Beneath the mound of devil's ivy was a gate, long since rusted shut. Walker yelled to Jeremiah over the wall and together, after much noisy exertion, they were able to force a section open. As they shepherded the trembling children out into the alley, Hawksworth saw flames rising from the roof: the fire had burned through the office.

By the time the last of the children were safely beyond the gate, bright orange tongues of flame were flapping from the back windows. The last one out was Rajan, with Iqbal's body draped over his shoulders, escaping just as the smoke began filling the back garden.

They circled around to the front where Jeremiah waited with the waggon. As the flames leaped higher, it brightened their faces freakishly so that they appeared ghostly in the darkened street. Hawksworth noted that the massive front door of the building remained closed. Hopefully the compound walls would contain the fire before it spread.

The uniformed officers arrived at the same time as the fire brigade, but there was little they could do. The conflagration had grown massive, engulfing the entire building. A bucket line was quickly set up to water down the adjacent property. A palm tree in the compound burst into flames, the fronds splitting off and flying away in burning shards that the uniformed officers and fire brigade tried to chase one by one. The remainder of the uniforms were busy keeping the crowd back, for by now most of the neighbourhood had turned out to watch the mysterious fortress-like structure burn to the ground.

As they were being distracted, Hawksworth's men loaded the children into the waggon, their horse stamping the ground uneasily in the smoke and heat. Hawksworth was about to swing himself onto the open seat when suddenly the front door of the burning building exploded open in a shower of sparks.

Camille Sodavalle burst out of the inferno, screaming, a human torch. Hawksworth stood momentarily frozen in shock. She ran straight toward him, arms flung out to grip him in a fiery embrace. The flames created the illusion of flight, as though she were streaming through the air at him, a flying apparition of death. She got close enough to shriek into his face, searing his skin, singeing his hair, before collapsing at his feet, a pyre of stinking burning flesh.

He pedalled backward in horror. The burning Camille had come flying at him just like the *pontianak* that had haunted his dreams.

CHAPTER XV

Return to Malacca

IT WAS NARAKA CHATURDASHI, the second day of the celebration of Deepavali. It was on this day that Narakasura, demon of filth, overlord of the heavens and earth, enslaver of sixteen-thousand women, torturer and consumer of men and gods, was beheaded by Lord Krishna, thus freeing the world, albeit temporarily, from darkness.

On his trip to the quay, he saw Tamil women kneeling by the light of dim lamps, creating elaborate *kolams* with chalk and rice powder, the brightly coloured rosette patterns spread before their homes to ward off evil. He had been told by his Hindu detectives that on this day taking a bath before sunrise, when the stars are still visible in the sky, is equivalent to washing oneself in the holy river Ganges, and thus cleansing away a lifetime of sin.

He was standing on the quayside at Tanjong Pagar Dock, waiting to board the steamer, when the news arrived. It was brought to him by a pigtailed Chinese boy – a messenger from the Mother-Flowers.

Estève Sodavalle had been discovered slouched against the front door of the Central Police Station, like a puppet with cut strings. Once they had cleaned the blood away they discovered that he had been given what the Chinese gangs called the 'lazy monkey' treatment. The tendons and muscles of each of his joints, the bits of wire that keep the body taut at ankles, knees, elbows, wrists, the frenulum of the tongue, and the muscles in the perineum between penis and anus, had been precisely severed, with the result that he flopped around like an indolent ape, splattering blood everywhere.

When it later came time for him to testify, he was only able to communicate clearly with a small slate and a stick of chalk held in his teeth, but it was enough. He testified that the operation at The Golden Chersonese Club had begun in an attempt to implicate businessmen involved with the Blue Funnel Line so that the half-brother in Malacca could blackmail them into throwing their support behind the Solomon Company's schemes and help him develop a shipping company that would outshine his brother's. Alsagoff had contacted his bastard half-siblings in Marseille to invite them to Singapore to run the operations for him, to be his eyes and ears in the European community. The brothel operation was a greater success than they had anticipated, and once they were able to use the club as a honey trap for high colonial officials, the die was cast.

Sodavalle was convicted to life in prison. The judge had been a friend of the Colonial Secretary and believed that death, which would simply have taken the man out of his misery, was far too gentle a sentence. He was instead returned to his cell, where, reduced to a ragged cripple, he had for the rest of his cramped life to depend on his fellow inmates to feed and bathe him once a week, when they could be troubled.

During the trial, the high and mighty fell one after the next. As all the hard evidence was lost in the fire at the club, most of them escaped prison terms, though each stepped down in disgrace and made quick exits from Singapore. One or two went back to England, though most made their way to far-flung regions of the empire where their connections offered a menial job with the safety of anonymity.

Dawnaday squealed liberally in a bid to save his own skin. After the trial, it was deemed unsafe to lock him up in Singapore, where convicts he had put in prison would be walking the yard with him and where friends of his now powerful enemies could reach him. For his own safety, it was decided to send him far from the colony. Eventually, he was chucked into the Hole of Ceylon, the notorious Welikada Prison, to be kept chained in a block of cells reserved for native criminals. Lacking any support from friends, he was eventually reduced to rags and forgotten by the outside world entirely.

The Inspector General of Police stepped down before the hearing and fled the Settlement. It was rumoured that he used his relationship with the retired police from the Sikh community to secure himself a post in a remote outpost in Punjab, though no one seemed to know for certain. Promoted in his place was Superintendent of Police Martin Fairer, who received the honorary benefits of a larger bungalow and increased salary befitting the position.

Consequently, into Fairer's place was promoted David Hawksworth, who found himself elevated to Superintendent of the Detective Branch, with special oversight of a newly formed Native Crimes Squad, of which Detective Inspector Dunu Vidi Hevage Rizby would have direct command. The offer of an officer's bungalow was declined as he would rather stay in his home in Geylang, though he accepted the increased pay. It would be especially useful as Ni announced that she was with child and they would need the additional income to hire an extra hand to help with the newborn.

After the fire, Hawksworth had helped to bring the liberated children to the Convent of the Holy Infant Jesus, where they were sheltered and cared for by the sisters until they could be returned to their native villages. Sergeant Major Walker had volunteered to put together the expedition that would take the children home, one by one, through the treacherous jungle.

And in the end, Shu En's wish had come true: she got her puppet show. About six months after The Golden Chersonese Club burned down – about the same time the Alsagoff family broke ground on the cleared site for an orphanage and school for Malay children – a new nightspot opened on the crown of Duxton Hill. Set in an ornate shophouse in the residential quiet near Craig Road, away from the squalor of a nearby slum, the After Eight Club quickly established itself as a place where high colonial officials and business elites of all races could have their most intimate needs cared for in a setting of simple luxury and assured discretion. The former *mui tsai* girl made certain that the participants were all of acceptable age and worked of their own volition. Her spies, she knew, must be treated with total respect.

But all that lay in the future. On Naraka Chaturdashi, Hawksworth was boarding an East India Ocean Company steam ship to Malacca. He was going to take Suliman Alsagoff into custody and return with him to Singapore for trial. A telegram had been sent the morning after the raid, on the instructions of the Chief Justice, informing the Malacca police to detain and hold the accused until Hawksworth's arrival.

* * *

That afternoon on the rolling ship, he was gladdened to find a familiar black-clad figure in the aft parlour. Hunched over a bottle of gin was Mr. Bosworth, whose red face flushed a deeper shade of scarlet when the two men greeted one another.

'We seem to constantly move in one another's orbit, Mr. Bosworth.'

'Ha! Indeed, Chief Detective Inspector. If I may be so bold, you look quite exhausted.'

'It has been a difficult investigation.'

'Care for a gin bitters?' he said, motioning toward the bottle.

Hawksworth thought a moment before answering. He had vowed to reduce his alcohol intake. 'Only one. Thank you.'

'If I may ask, why are you returning to Malacca?' Bosworth cocked an eyebrow in curiosity.

'I am going there to take custody of our mutual acquaintance, Suliman Alsagoff.'

The fat man roared with laughter. 'So the obnoxious little man in the black velvet hat is a crook! I knew it from the moment I first set eyes on him. This is something to do with the crate I saw loaded at Muar?'

'It does. We suspect him to have been involved in extremely nefarious activities that go far beyond mere impropriety in business. His partner in crime, Estève Sodavalle, has already been apprehended in Singapore, and I expect that his testimony will prove Alsagoff to be guilty beyond all doubt.'

'Gaol for the swine?'

'If our suspicions are correct, then yes, assuredly. Perhaps even the noose.'

Raising his glass to catch the sunlight through the porthole, Bosworth said calmly, 'I suppose removing the competition is something one should celebrate.'

'The removal has come at a terrible cost.'

Ignoring him, Bosworth stared absently into space. 'I wonder what will become of the Solomon Company land holdings?' He poured himself another gin then leaned back in his chair. 'It might interest you to learn that the company of Bosworth and Hatras has completed its purchase of its inaugural patch of land, just to the west of Mount Ophir.'

'Congratulations. Is it gold you are after?'

'No, no, something far less uncertain. We are clearing land for rubber trees. Way of the future is rubber.'

'So I have been told.'

'We wanted more land, further east toward Gading, but we were bested by a Singapore outfit, a consortium owned by the Low family.'

'It certainly seems like the Lows keep themselves busy in the region.'

'I would say so. They, or one of their companies, now own every piece of land surrounding our own in Malacca. With Alsagoff out of the way, they will become the new masters of the territory. What is more, at the rate they are buying land up and down the peninsula, they will soon be the *de facto* rulers of Malaya.'

'The Union Jack will fly over Malaya for many years more, Mr. Bosworth, of that I can assure you.'

'I have no doubt that we will continue to administer the territory for a long while yet, Chief Detective Inspector. But administration is one thing, ownership is another. We do not rule like the Dutch. They act brutally because they act like the owners of the land. We merely levy duties and administer laws.'

'You miss the old ways, do you? The more direct ways of the East India Company?'

'It ruled most of India effectively. Why question its methods?'

'We must change with the age if we are to survive.'

'I thought *we* were the age,' Bosworth snorted, slurping his gin in the bright amber light of the liquid afternoon.

* * *

They reached Malacca in late evening, after the sun had set, though the sky remained bright. As before, he walked with Bosworth along the length of the jetty, the fat man huffing and puffing through a litany of complaints about the town.

Acting Resident Councillor Shaw was there to greet him at the foot of the jetty, as before. Instead of the man's usually cheerful face, however, he wore a mask of despair.

'Whatever is the matter, Mr. Shaw?' Hawksworth asked in genuine concern.

'I have some bad news about your prisoner, Chief Detective Inspector.'

'Oh?' a slight panic set in: had the bird flown the coop, disappeared forever into the jungle?

'Unfortunately, he managed to hang himself in his cell last night. You were already en route and unreachable when the body was discovered.'

'Alsagoff is dead?' Hawksworth inhaled sharply.

'It is strange, because he adamantly maintained his innocence until we informed him that you were coming to take him back to Singapore. That was yesterday afternoon. Now he is gone, never to return.'

A smile twitched on Hawksworth's lips. 'Why the long face then, Mr. Shaw?'

The younger man looked up into the Chief Detective Inspector's eyes. 'Now justice will not be served.'

'I believe that the local populace would say *Tuan Allah suka*, that the Lord's will is done. As for us, we are now spared the expense of a trial and execution.'

Shaw stood quietly in the gathering gloom, then nodded and

led the way to the old gaol house near the Stadthuys. 'The body is in there.'

As they walked in the soft air, the coarse gravel crunching pleasantly beneath their boots, Hawksworth asked, 'Has the family in Singapore been notified?'

'By telegram.'

'The body is to be sent?'

'No. Their reply was simple: do as you wish with the body.'

'They have disowned him,' Hawksworth muttered ruminatively.

Laid out in his prison garb, Alsagoff looked shorter and less substantial. The *songkok* was gone and for the first time Hawksworth realised that the man was as bald as a cue ball. The face denoted death by strangulation, the eyes popping, the blue tongue protruding, turning black. He noted the bruising around the neck from a rope made of sheets. Then he saw the deep scratches on the back of the head, as though someone had forced his head into the noose.

'Are you certain he committed suicide?'

'What are you suggesting?'

'Alsagoff had made powerful enemies.'

'No one at the gaol reported anything amiss. The body was discovered during routine inspection of the cells. He was alone and his cell still locked when they found him.'

'Then we shall leave it be,' Hawksworth shrugged. Some deaths are better left unexamined, he knew.

'Your trip will have been a waste. My apologies. At least allow me to treat you to a repast tonight,' he said, turning away from the body.

'Thank you. My trip is not an entire waste. I would like to see Mrs. Lim Suan Imm again. She was not in town on my last visit.'

'I shall send a messenger to arrange a meeting for tomorrow afternoon, if she is available.'

They walked out of the gaol house and strolled quietly, the small breaking waves of the surf the only sound. The darkness had come on suddenly, so that the men could only glimpse one another in purple shadow, bats swooping low overhead. They paused for a moment before the square clock tower that stood sentinel over the forecourt of the Stadthuys, then turned toward the colonnaded portico. The door was opened into a brightly light foyer by a smiling Aloysius, and Hawksworth felt a sensation he had not expected: a welcome homecoming to this somnolent town.

*   *   *

The next afternoon was uncannily like the last afternoon he had spent in Malacca, all those weeks before. It was as if time had simply stopped, holding in suspension the same bright hot moment. Streets lay abandoned as if the town were suffering a plague. Massive monitor lizards drowsed in the sun, barely raising their heads to acknowledge him as he walked past. If news of Alsagoff's passing had any effect on the denizens of this place, they were keeping it to themselves.

He found the ornate house on Heeren Street easily enough. The door swung open before he knocked, and the same servant stood smiling at him. It was like returning to a moment in a dream, walking into this ageless space: he felt the disorienting tug of déjà vu and leaned out to grasp the edge of a mahogany sideboard to steady himself.

'Chief Detective Inspector Lightheart, how good it is to see you again,' he heard Suan Imm say. Then with concern, she added, 'You look as though you have had too much sun. Come sit down and join me.'

He looked up to see her standing in the centre of the indoor garden, dressed in a brilliant red *baju kebaya*. Her hair was pulled in an immaculate chignon held fast with a gold pin from which dangled a small ruby. In the bright light, he realised (as he had not before) that she was wore a wig. She motioned for him to join her. The cool air inside was refreshing and he quickly forgot the eerie sensation he had felt when he entered.

A tea service was brought and set on a folding table beside a bird's nest fern sprouting wilding from a glazed earthen pot. The service was enamelled in vibrant pinks, yellows, and greens; delicate branches with fantastic blossoms intertwined along the glossy surface; a polychrome phoenix motif emblazoned on the side of the pot was repeated at the base of tea cups.

'You are admiring my tea service, I see. It is new, ordered from Jingdezhen. We usually use it only for special occasions, but those seem so few and far between these days that I use it almost daily merely to enjoy it. Of course, your return visit is an occasion worth celebrating.'

'It is exquisite.'

'The tea itself is special, from Ceylon. *Hongcha*, black tea. I like to take mine unsweetened.'

'Then so shall I,' he said. The air was fragrant with unseen jasmine blossoms, the light from above warm without being hot. He sipped the tea, which was deliciously complex in both taste and fragrance.

'I understand that you travelled to Gading.'

'I did.'

'Did you find Isabella Lightheart?'

'What I found was the burned-out remains of an orphanage, and a grave, several years old, which contained her mortal remains.'

'Dear lord, I am sorry to hear that. I truly did not know.'

They both sipped their tea in quiet while she absorbed the sad news.

'I did meet a woman there who worked for Madam Lightheart,' Hawksworth said gently.

'Was it Fatima?'

'Yes. You know her?'

'I have not seen her in many years. Is she well?'

'She has cataracts, though she is still of strong body and mind. She lives alone in the house that belonged to her mistress, and I am afraid that it is not in a very good state of repair.'

Suan Imm pressed her lips together, looking pensive. 'That will not do. I will invite her to live with me here. I have ample room, and the company would be welcome. She is a dear woman and should not spend her last years in solitude.'

He was unsure if she was speaking of Fatima or herself.

Leaning close, she asked, 'And what did you learn of your mother?'

'Mother ... Yes, perhaps Lightheart was my mother. Fatima presented me with a locket with her photograph – as you say, the resemblance between us cannot be denied.'

'You have the locket?'

He produced it from his jacket pocket. She took the bluish silver from him, snapped it open to study the dark photograph inside. 'That is the likeness of Isabella Lightheart.'

'I was also given a diary that Fatima claimed was kept by Lightheart. It is a slim volume, leather-bound vellum, very old. It appears that she stopped writing in it long ago.'

'Do you believe that the woman in the grave at Gading was your mother?'

'I am willing to believe it so long as I am able to find proof. The locket is compelling, but one needs more than resemblance to establish parentage.'

'The diary?'

'It is written in a book cipher that I have not been able to decode.'

'Isabella Lightheart was a deeply spiritual person. It was the fervency of her belief that kept her going all those years. Perhaps you should consider the New Testament as a source for the book code?' she suggested sagely.

He nodded in agreement. 'I had not thought of that. I shall look into it carefully once I return to Singapore.' He sipped more tea, gazing abstractly at the carving of a rooster on the cornice of the second story of the light well. 'I am to be a father soon myself. It offers me some comfort to think that I may have made a connection, unexpected and perplexing as it may be, with the person who gave me life. Or perhaps I am merely growing sentimental.'

Suan Imm shrugged daintily. 'I congratulate you. You have found your past and made your future.'

Still lost in his abstraction, he said quietly, 'I wonder what she thought was so important that she needed to write it in code? She hid herself away in the jungle all my life. Whatever it was, she must have been very afraid, indeed.'

'She was not a woman to be easily frightened.'

They fell silent, sipping tea, lost in thought. Suddenly Hawksworth sat erect.

'Something strange happened during the course of my investigation, and perhaps there is a chance that you could shed light on it. I was assaulted but not badly hurt. The attackers' purpose seemed to be to send a message, but it is not one I can fathom. After beating me, they pressed a gold half-sovereign coin into my hand. What do you make of that?'

'A gold coin?' Her eyes went wide in surprise. 'The attackers were Chinese?'

'They were Teochew, I believe.'

She reclined, her face crinkling slyly. 'I can tell you that the Chinese pirates in the Straits used to place a gold coin in the hand of people whom they wished to watch. It was a curse, like the "evil eye". But that is an old custom. I doubt it is still used in our modern electric age.'

'Pirates?'

'Yes.' She sipped tea, watching him over the rim.

'But why use such a precious metal?'

Her smile widened to reveal a denture of false enamel teeth, yellowed and capped with tarnished silver. 'Because they had to be sure that the victim would always carry the item on his person.'

He felt the weight of the coin in his trouser pocket.

'You can tell me no more about the man whom Lightheart claimed was my father?'

She sighed, gazing at him intently before speaking. 'You say that you are to be a father soon. Take my advice: give your attention now to your own family, your wife and child. Let the past go. Lock the coded diary away and forget about it.'

'I am not sure that I will be able to do that.'

Setting her cup down, she rose from her seat to indicate cordially that the meeting was over. A servant promptly came in to clear away the empty tea service. 'Thank you for coming to see me again, Chief Detective Inspector Lightheart. It has been a pleasure.'

'Thank you.'

The foyer was lit by sun through green glass, so that red appeared black and white turned aquamarine. Before the door, she grasped his arm with surprising strength, pulling him nearer so she could whisper in his ear. 'Be wary. Frequently we want to know something only because it needs to be kept secret.'

Then she released him.

* * *

He spent the day walking the town and when he arrived back at the Stadthuys, across the small bridge over the muddy river, he felt the need to keep moving. The shadows of evening were long when he reached the ruined chapel at the top of the hill, but he pushed inside all the same. He wanted again to inspect the intricate gravestone of the three Dutch boys. Having run his fingers over the delicate relief of the stone ship, he turned to go but sought another grave: *Here lies Domingas Franco, Daughter of Luiz Franco and Antonia de Faria, who died April 1581.* Day of birth, unrecorded. Day of death, forever illegible. His own life ran along a parallel if opposite track. His date of death would be recorded, he assumed, but the date of his birth remained shrouded, as illegible as the stone before him.

Outside the church, standing on the hill above the town, his thoughts drifted to Ni and the baby in her belly, of the life he would be responsible for protecting and sustaining in a world indifferent to its suffering.

From below he could hear the beginning of *maghrib*, the sunset call to prayer. First one, then another, and another, then one more voice was raised, until the sound became a rich, full wail resonating across the town. He looked east. The granite ridges of Mount Ophir rose above the lavender hills. Catching the final rays of the day's sun, they glowed brightly in the violet evening, shining like a distant lantern of gold.

Historical Note

In this book, as in *Singapore Black*, I have done my best to maintain historical accuracy while writing fiction for entertainment, and surely a few anachronisms have slipped through. All characters are fictional except for historical figures.

In 1892, the country now known as Malaysia was highly fragmented. The Straits Settlements of Singapore, Malacca and Penang (along with Province Wellesley and the Dinding Islands) were administered as Crown Colonies from 1867 (Labuan, in Borneo, joined the Settlements in 1907). This meant that they came under the direct control of the Colonial Office in London instead of the India Office in Calcutta. In theory, from 1867 the Settlements were administered by professional civil servants as opposed to the entrenched mercantile-military elite of the British East India Company. The seat of power was Singapore.

The government operated under the auspices of a Governor of the Settlements, an Executive of eight members appointed by the Crown, and a body of seven Members of Council, two of whom were elected by the Chambers of Commerce in Penang and Singapore, the rest nominated by the Governor. The Executive consisted of the General in charge of troops, the Colonial Secretary, Colonial Treasurer, Attorney General, Auditor General, Colonial Engineer, and two Resident Councillors, one for Penang and another for Malacca. Together with the seven Members of

Council, they formed the Legislative Council of the Colony, who generally voted as directed by the Colonial Office.

From March 1892, the Colonial Secretary of Singapore was Sir William Edward Maxwell, who would become Acting Governor of the Straits Settlements from 1893 to 1894. His younger brother Robert Walter Maxwell was the Inspector General of Police in Singapore between 1891 and 1894. His youngest brother, Francis R.O. Maxwell, was later the Resident of Sarawak. His father, Sir Peter Benson Maxwell (1817–1893) was Chief Justice of the Straits Settlements from 1867 to 1871. Maxwell Road in Singapore and the famed Maxwell food court on South Bridge Road are both named for the family. A.P. Talbot was a real person and in 1892 was indeed Assistant Colonial Secretary and Clerk of Council as well as President of the Cricket Club.

In 1892, many of the provinces and states on the Malay Peninsula were administered under a British Resident system, which was pioneered in India. The British Residents were in effect proconsuls of the Crown, though their direct power varied depending on the size and economic clout of the territory. The Residents were nominated by the Governor of the Straits Settlements and approved by the Secretary of State. Most of the Resident states were consolidated into the Federated Malay States of Selangor, Perak, Negeri Sembilan and Pahang in 1895.

The Resident of Negeri Sembilan in this book is fictional. The real Resident of Negeri Sembilan in 1892 was the Honourable Martin Lister, who assumed the post in 1889 when the Negeri Sembilan Confederation was first formed by Tuanku Muhammad Shah (Negeri Sembilan means 'nine states' in Malay). According to the *The Straits Times* of March 29, 1897, Martin Lister died from beriberi on a steam ship near Suez while in transit home. His remains were interred in Port Said. It was said that he contracted the disease while on an expedition in the Ulu Bendul hills to quell fighting between Chinese secret society gangs who had infiltrated migrant camps there. There still stands a Memorial Gateway and Pleasure Garden built in his honour in the town of Kuala Pilah in 1905 by a Chinese business community grateful for his efforts in suppressing crime.

Of the other territories on the peninsula, the northern states of Kedah, Kelantan, Perlis and Terengganu were under Thai control until the Anglo-Siamese treaty of 1909 placed them under a British protectorate system. The southern state of Johor remained independent until 1914, though due to its proximity to the economic powerhouse of Singapore, it was essentially part of British Malaya before that time.

Sarawak territory on the island of Borneo had been ruled by the Brooke family, the so called 'white Rajahs', since 1841. The Brookes were English and maintained close ties with both the Straits Settlements and the Crown. They ruled Sarawak like a British colony, albeit one that they had personal control over, with the seat of power in the town of Kuching. To this day, the countryside of Sarawak is dotted with quaint Protestant churches, a legacy of their long rule.

The Alsagoff family is real, though the character of Suliman Alsagoff in this book is pure fiction, as are the Sodavalles. The Alsagoffs were a prominent family in Singapore and were involved with shipping and passage for Hajj pilgrims – indeed, it was an Alsagoff ship, the *Patna*, that served as the model for the story Joseph Conrad tells in *Lord Jim* (1899). The Hajjah Fatimah mosque still stands, though it is now embedded in a government housing (HDB) complex on Beach Road. The onion-shaped dome above the prayer hall was added in 1933 by the architecture firm of Chung and Wong.

As in *Singapore Black*, I have used the words *kongsi* and 'clan' to refer to the Chinese secret societies simply for the sake of narrative expediency. Depending on the activity of the group, different words may have applied; however to keep from bogging the reader down in arcane sociological details, I have simply used the two words above. The history of the Chinese secret societies of Southeast Asia is rich and has been documented in numerous academic sources.

More by William L. Gibson

Singapore Black (Vol. I)

Singapore/Malaya, 1892: When a dead American is found floating in Rochor Canal, Chief Detective Inspector David Hawksworth begins an investigation that quickly leads into a labyrinth of deceit and violence in the polyglot steam-cooker of turn-of-the-century Singapore. As Chinese gangs verge on open turf war and powerful commercial enterprises vie for control of the economy, a stolen statue that houses an ancient Hindu goddess becomes the object of a pursuit with a mounting body count, and its seems that everyone is suffering from maniacal erotic nightmares. Will Hawksworth be able to restore order before the colony is tipped into a bloodbath?

Singapore Red (Vol. III)

Singapore/Malaya, 1890s: A cholera epidemic breaks out in Singapore's congested Chinatown, and Chief Detective Inspector Hawksworth finds himself embroiled in a case that threatens to spill over into regional warfare. While the immigrant population threatens to riot, someone is smuggling powerful new American weapons into the colony, and rumours of Chinese undead wandering the night-time streets puts even the powerful Chinese clans on edge. When a son of the Low family is murdered, an ongoing confrontation between the Low and the Mother-Flower clans explodes, and Hawksworth finally learns the shocking truth about his father's life ... and death. Continuing on from *Singapore Black* and *Singapore Yellow*, the battle for the future of Singapore's underworld is decided in this exciting finale to the series.